SUMMER IN *Sydney*

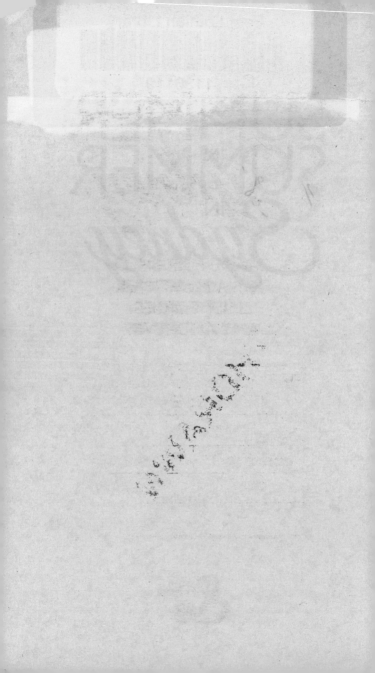

SUMMER
IN
Sydney

CAROL MARINELLI
FIONA McARTHUR
EMILY FORBES
AMY ANDREWS

MILLS & BOON

Published in Great Britain 2015
by Mills & Boon, an imprint of Harlequin (UK) Limited,
Eton House, 18-24 Paradise Road, Richmond, Surrey, TW9 1SR

SUMMER IN SYDNEY © 2015 Harlequin Books S.A.

Cort Mason – Dr Delectable © 2011 Carol Marinelli
Survival Guide to Dating Your Boss © 2011 Fiona McArthur
Breaking Her No-Dates Rule © 2011 Emily Forbes
Waking Up With Dr Off-Limits © 2011 Amy Andrews

ISBN: 978-0-263-25381-8

011-0815

Printed and bound by
CPI Group (UK) Ltd, Croydon, CR0 4YY

CORT MASON – DR DELECTABLE

CAROL MARINELLI

Carol Marinelli recently filled in a form where she was asked for her job title and was thrilled, after all these years, to be able to put down her answer as 'writer'.

Then it asked what Carol did for relaxation and, after chewing on her pen for a moment, Carol put down the truth—'writing'. The third question asked, 'What are your hobbies?' Well, not wanting to look obsessed or, worse still, boring, she crossed the fingers on her free hand and answered 'swimming and tennis'. But, given that the chlorine in the pool does terrible things to her highlights and the closest she's got to a tennis racket in the last couple of years is watching the Australian Open, I'm sure you can guess the real answer!

PROLOGUE

'You need to get back out there, Cort.'

'Leave it, Elise.'

'I won't leave it,' his sister said.

'Beth's only been dead for a month—do you really think it appropriate that I start getting "back out there"?'

And on anyone else his argument would have worked, but his sister was too matter-of-fact, and had been there through it all, and would not be swayed.

'You've been grieving for her for years,' Elise said. 'You mourned Beth long, long, long before she died.'

'So now I should suddenly start partying?'

'You've never partied in your life.' Elise grinned at her rather serious older brother. 'So, no, I don't expect you to start at thirty-two.' Elise had come here not just to see how her brother was doing since Beth's death but with intention too, and she was determined to see this conversation through. 'But there is more to life than work. You need to start going out a bit, do something you haven't done before, try new things…'

Cort knew she was right—had it been Elise in his position he'd have said exactly the same, except he just didn't know how to start. Cort had moved back to

Sydney three years ago and had chosen not to tell his colleagues about his *other* life in Melbourne. He had moved back to Sydney to get away from the endless questions from colleagues, and pointless platitudes that did nothing to help.

The last years had been spent working in Sydney and then travelling back to Melbourne on his days off to sit in a nursing home and watch a woman who had once been so educated, so dignified, dribble her food and strip naked at whim. He had watched endless seizures erode what had been left of her brain and, yes, Elise was right—bit by bit, over these past years he had mourned.

'Say yes.' Elise drained her glass and bade her brother goodnight.

'Say yes to what?' Cort asked.

'Just say yes next time someone suggests something.'

'Sure,' Cort said with absolutely no intention of doing so.

'For Beth,' Elise said as she headed to his apartment door. 'She'd hate both your lives to have been cut short that night.'

She was right.

Cort knew that. He crossed his apartment and could hear the ocean from the open French doors, but he closed them to shut out the roar and the noise, and the room fell silent. Not just from the sound of the ocean but from the roar and the noise in his head.

Beth was gone.

CHAPTER ONE

'ARE you free to give me a hand in the suture room?' Cort Mason, the senior emergency registrar, asked, and Ruby swung around. 'It might take a while, though.'

Ruby jumped down from the footstool she was perched on while restocking the cupboard and turned to the voice that was aimed in her direction. She decided that she'd be delighted to give him a hand.

It had nothing to do with the fact he was gorgeous.

Really, it had completely nothing to do with it.

She just wanted an empty Resus before it filled again, which it inevitably would. Sheila, the NUM, had told her to stay in there today, that this was her area, but with a senior registrar asking for her to assist with a patient, well, surely she had no choice in the matter?

None.

'I'd be happy to.' Ruby beamed, except her smile wasn't returned. In fact, he wasn't even waiting for her response. Already Cort had walked off and was heading into the suture room, rightly perhaps assuming that a student nurse wasn't likely to say no to his request for assistance.

'Mr Mason has asked if I can give him a hand.' Ruby

let Connor, the RN in charge of Resus, know where she was going. 'Is that okay?'

'Sure,' Connor said. 'It's not as if we're doing anything.' He frowned at her. 'Ruby, why have you got a crepe bandage in your hair?'

'Sheila!' Ruby rolled her eyes, because the NUM was surely out to get her. Not only had she insisted that Ruby be allocated the most grisly part of Emergency, she also had a thing about Ruby's long auburn hair, which was so thick it often defied the hair ties and clips she attempted to hold it back with. This afternoon Sheila had handed her a bandage and told her to sort it once and for all.

'She's really got it in for you.'

'I remind her of her daughter apparently—I've no idea why. Anyway, Mr Mason will be wondering where I've got to. He said it might take a while.'

'You might as well go to coffee afterwards, then,' Connor said. 'And we're on first-name terms here—it's Cort.'

She'd stick with 'Mr Mason'—her dad was Chief of Surgery at another hospital and had drilled it into her over the years just how important titles were so Ruby had decided it was better to play safe than offend anyone.

She had a quick look around for Sheila and seeing she was busy up the other end darted off, more relieved than Connor could know. Sheila had been very specific in her allocation, ensuring that Ruby was working in Resus, but apart from a febrile convulsion and couple of patients who had been brought over briefly while awaiting blood results it had been delightfully quiet.

'Put some gloves on,' Cort said as she entered the suture room. 'I just need someone to hold Ted's arm while I suture it. He keeps forgetting to stay still, don't you, Ted?'

The elderly man grunted and Ruby could smell the brandy fumes that filled the small room.

'How are you, Ted?' Ruby asked, pulling on some gloves and looking at the wound, happy, though not for the patient, to see it was a huge cut that *would* hopefully take ages, and then it would be time for her coffee break and with her assessment and everything, well, she might just not have to go back out there.

She loathed Accident and Emergency, not that anyone could tell. She was always light, breezy and happy and had chosen not to tell even her closest friends just how hard this final unit of her training had been, knowing there was nothing they could do to fix it and choosing just to soldier on.

She had never expected to like it, but the loathing was so acute Ruby was seriously wondering if she would even make it through these last weeks of her training. There was no tangible reason for hating it, nothing Ruby could point to as the reason she hated it so, but walking to her shift, every ambulance that passed, every glimpse of Eastern Beaches Hospital made her want to turn tail and run for home.

Looking back, there had been a few wobbles that might have given warning that Emergency might be un-settling for her—a young man suddenly collapsing after a routine appendectomy and the crash team being called while she was on the surgical ward had stunned Ruby

and made her question her decision to study nursing—
but she had, for the most part, liked her training. Only
liked, though—her real aim was to work as a mental
health nurse, but general training was a prerequisite if
she wanted to get anywhere in her future career.

'Okay?' Cort said. 'We might be here a while, so I'd
make yourself comfortable.'

He took off his jacket and tied on a plastic gown,
then washed his hands, dragged a stool over with his
foot and settled in for the long haul.

'He's asleep,' Ruby said, stating the obvious, because
Ted was snoring loudly now, and even Ruby could see
that she might be better utilised elsewhere.

'I don't want to wrestle with him if he wakes up.' He
gave a tight smile. 'Sorry if it's boring.'

'Oh, I'm not bored. I'm *delighted* to be here,' Ruby
said, hearing a noise from outside, a relative arguing
with a security guard close to the suture-room door.
She gave Cort a wide smile, a smile so bright that he
hesitated for a moment before returning it with a slightly
bemused one, then he turned his attention back to his
patient. He cleaned the wound and injected anaesthetic
as Ruby watched and only then did he offer a response,
not looking at her, just concentrating on the wound as
he spoke.

'It's not often you hear that in this place.'

'What?' Ruby asked, her mind elsewhere.

'People saying that they're delighted to be here.'

'I'm a happy apple,' Ruby said, and watched as his
hands stopped, the first knot of the stitch neatly tied.
He seemed to be waiting for her to do something.

'Are you going to cut?'

'Oh!' She picked up the scissors with her free hand. 'I feel like a real nurse. Where do I cut?' She held the scissors over the thread.

'A bit shorter.'

There was something lovely and soothing about sitting here and actually doing something, rather than just holding the patient's hand. And contrary to what she'd heard, Cort Mason was far from grumpy. One on one with him, he was really rather nice.

She'd heard his name mentioned a lot of times. He'd been on annual leave for the first four weeks of her time here and had only been back a week, but he was nothing like the man she'd imagined, the staid man her colleagues had led her to believe he was.

Nothing.

From the way she'd heard people speaking about him Ruby had expected a dour serious man in his fifties.

Instead he'd be in his thirties, with brown hair and hazel eyes, a long straight nose and, not so much dour, or sharp, just… She couldn't really sum him up in word, and she tried for a moment.

Outside the suture room, she'd never been privy to small talk with him, had never really seen him smile. He was formal with the patients, distant with the staff, and any hint of ineptness or bureaucracy seemed to irritate him.

Crabby was the best she could come up with.

Except he wasn't being crabby now.

Ruby looked at his white thick cotton shirt and lilac tie, which was an odd sort of match for his brown suit, yet it went really well and she wondered, just for a second, how it was really possible to find someone who wore a brown suit attractive—except he was.

Up close he really, really was.

There was a lovely fresh scent to him and she thought it came from his hair, which was very close to her face as he bent over to work. She looked at it, and it was lovely and glossy and very straight and neat but there was a jagged edge to the cut that she liked too.

'Cut,' Cort reminded her when her eyes wandered, and she snipped the neat stitch he'd tied. 'I need some more 4/0.'

'You're really making me earn my keep!' Ruby jumped off the stool and tried to locate what he wanted amongst box upon box of different sutures.

'Left,' Cort said, to her hand that hovered. 'Up one,' he said.

'Got it.' She opened the material and tipped it on his tray then washed her hands and again pulled on some gloves before rejoining him. Cort was having another good look at the wound so there was nothing much for her to do and her eyes roamed the room again, landing on his jacket hanging on the door.

'It's not really brown,' she said out loud, and then she blushed, because she did this far too often. Ruby had zero attention span and her mind was constantly chatting and occasionally words just slipped out.

He glanced up and saw her cheeks were bright pink.

'Your jacket,' Ruby croaked. 'It's not really brown.'

He said nothing, just carried on checking the wound,

but his lips twitched for a moment, because he'd had a similar discussion with the shop assistant.

Sick to the back teeth of dour greys and navy suits, he'd bought a couple of new ones, and some shirts and ties. He wasn't a great shopper, hated it, in fact, and had decided to put his faith in the judgement of the eager shop assistant. But when she'd held up the suit he'd baulked and said there was no way he was wearing brown.

Brown was the sort of thing his father wore, Cort had said to her.

'It's not brown,' the shop assistant had said. 'It's taupe.'

'It's taupe.' After a few minutes' silence, he glanced up to the rather surprised eyes of Ruby. 'Apparently.'

'Well, it's very nice.'

And he didn't *quite* smile, but there was just a hint as he got back to his stitches and he saw her hands were just a little bit shaky when she snipped, though he was sure they had been steady before.

He didn't look up, but he could see her in his mind's eye for a moment. She was quite a stunning little thing—tiny, with very dark brown eyes and a thick curtain of hair that he'd heard Sheila pull her up about a few times. It was held back today with a ridiculous bandage, but defiantly kept escaping. It was lovely hair, red but not…

'It's not really ginger…' Cort said, and still didn't look up.

'Absolutely not,' was Ruby's response.

'Auburn?'

'Close,' came her voice. 'But I prefer titian.'

And he gave a very brief nod and then worked on quietly. It was actually a lovely silence, just nice to sit and watch him work, especially as she could hear things starting to pick up outside. She could hear Connor calling out for assistance and feet running and though it was par for the course here, she screwed her eyes closed for just a second, but he must have looked up and noticed.

'You okay?'

'I'm fine.'

'You don't need to cut if it's making you feel sick—just hold his hand.'

'Really, I'm fine,' Ruby said, because a nasty cut and tendons and muscle and all of that didn't bother her a jot.

It was out there that did.

It wasn't a fear of seeing people sick, Ruby thought as she snipped Cort's stitches, and it wasn't a fear of death because she'd actually enjoyed some agency shifts on the palliative care ward.

It was *this*, Ruby thought as a buzzer sounded and Cort looked up.

This moment, which arrived at any given time, the intense drama that was constantly played out here, and it actually made her feel physically ill.

'Do you need me?' She heard Cort shout in the direction of Resus, ready to drop everything at a moment's notice, and Ruby sat, staring at the hand she was holding, sweat beading on her forehead. She would hold this hand all night if only it meant that she didn't have to go out there.

'Jamelia's here,' came Sheila's voice, and because apparently Cort liked to be kept up to date with everything, her voice came closer to the open suture-room door.

'We've got a head and facial injuries. He arrested at the approach to the hospital and they're having trouble intubating.'

'I'll come.'

'There's no need,' Sheila called. 'Jamelia's got it and the anaesthetist is on his way.' But he wasn't listening. Already he'd peeled off his gloves and was pulling off his plastic apron. 'Wait here,' he called over his shoulder. Given he was halfway through stitching, and the patient couldn't be left, Ruby had no choice but to sit and wait, which she did for a full ten or fifteen minutes before Cort returned, and if she'd seen him crabby this past week, he was really angry now.

She could feel it as he tied on a new gown and washed his hands.

'What the hell was that?' Sheila was less than impressed as she swung into the room. 'I told you we had it under control.'

'No. You told me they were having trouble intubating. Jamelia gets nervous…'

'Well, she's never going to get any confidence if you keep coming in and taking over.'

'So, what?' Cort said. 'Do we just let her stumble through and kill off a few more brain cells?'

'Give her a go, would you?' Sheila responded.

'No,' Cort said, and didn't qualify further, even as

Sheila waited, but when Cort remained silent, Sheila turned her frustration back to its regular recipient.

'What are you doing here, Ruby? I told you! I specifically told you not to leave Resus.'

'Mr Mason asked me to come and hold an arm.' Ruby gulped.

'Someone else could have done that. Now you've missed watching an emergency tracheotomy…'

'Oh.' Ruby wondered how she could even attempt to sound disappointed at having missed out on seeing that! 'That's a shame.'

'A shame?' Sheila replied. 'Are you being sarcastic?'

'I asked her to come in here.' Cort intervened as Ruby struggled for a better response. 'She was sorting out a cupboard, so I thought I'd give her—'

'I'll deal with my nurses, thanks, Cort.' She turned back to Ruby. 'I'm sick of this, Ruby…' She shook her head in frustration. 'I haven't got time for this right now. I'll speak to you at your assessment this evening. Bring a coffee,' she added. 'We might be there for a while.'

Sheila stormed off, and Cort carried on stitching as Ruby sat there with cheeks flaming. Cort knew that if he didn't deal with this situation now, he'd forget about it or miss out on seeing Sheila later, and with a small hiss born of frustration and anger he stood again, peeled off another pair of gloves and waded out into the department, leaving Ruby sitting there.

'It's not her fault.' Cort walked into Resus and straight up to Sheila, who was coming off the phone to ICU. 'What is a student supposed to say when a senior registrar asks her to come and do something for him? She checked with Connor...'

'Ruby finds excuses all the time, Cort,' Sheila said. 'She'd do anything to avoid work and you just gave her the perfect excuse. She searches for them...'

'She didn't, though,' Cort said. 'I approached her.'

'Fine,' Sheila said. 'I'll bear it in mind. Right now I've got more important things to deal with.' Cort looked over to the screened area where Sheila was heading, where the team was working solidly. He caught Jamelia's eye and she came over.

'Thanks, Cort.' Jamelia meant it. The hellish intubation had turned into a nightmare just as Cort had arrived and she was incredibly grateful that Cort had taken over when he had.

'Call for help,' Cort said, 'preferably before you really need it.'

Jamelia nodded.

'So,' Ruby said when he returned to the suture room. 'It looks like we're both in trouble.'

'I'm not in trouble,' Cort said. 'I'm just running out of size 9 gloves.'

He sat down and blew up his hair, because it really was warm in the suture room and he was still so angry he could spit. 'There's a big difference,' he said, 'between hero and ego. If you take anything from this place—take that.'

Ruby nodded.

'I told Sheila it wasn't your fault,' he added as she snipped the last of the stitches.

'Thanks,' Ruby said. 'Though I doubt it will help.'

He wanted to ask more, wanted to find out why she was in trouble, but he didn't want to wonder more about her as well. She stayed quiet as he finished the neat row of sutures then he asked her to put on a dressing, thanked her for her help, peeled off the plastic gloves and washed his hands.

'Cort.' Jamelia came to the door and it sounded an awful lot as if she'd been crying. 'Would you mind…?' She gave a small swallow. 'Would you mind talking to the relatives for me?'

'I'll come and take a look at him first.' Cort nodded and picked up his jacket just as Sheila bustled in.

'Jamelia, the relatives really do need to be spoken to ASAP.'

'I'm going to do it,' Cort said.

'You go with Cort.' Sheila glanced over at Ruby. 'I'll finish up in here.'

Ruby would have preferred an emergency tracheotomy, even ten of them, rather than the prospect of sitting with relatives as bad news was delivered, and she fumbled for yet another excuse. 'Connor said I was to go straight to coffee after doing this.'

'You couldn't say no to the senior reg when he asked you to do something for him, I can understand that.' Sheila fixed her with a stare. 'So don't say no to the NUM.'

Ruby nodded and swallowed and glanced up to Cort.

'Come on,' he said. 'I just want to see for myself how he is first.'

They walked into Resus and the anaesthetist gave Cort a full briefing. Ruby stood quietly and looked at the young man for a moment then looked away as Cort examined his eyes and his ears and checked his reflexes for himself. She could hear all the anaesthetist was saying and it sounded a lot less than hopeful.

'Let's do this, then.'

They walked down the corridor to the little interview room and just as they got there, Ruby was quite sure that she couldn't go in.

'I don't know what to say,' she admitted, and Cort turned round briefly.

'You don't have to say anything,' Cort said. 'Come on.'

And she wanted to turn, wanted to run. For a full three seconds she seriously considered it, except he'd knocked and opened the door and there was a whole family whose eyes turned anxiously towards them. A nurse running off would only terrify them more than they were already.

It was the only reason she forced herself to go in.

CHAPTER TWO

COULD he not give them a little more hope?

Ruby sat in with the family and listened as Cort gave the grim diagnosis.

'The paramedics were unable to intubate him,' Cort reiterated.

'But he was bagged…' The young man's sister was a nurse and she was absolutely not having it, refusing to accept the grim diagnosis. 'He would have got some oxygen. And it was just a couple of minutes from the hospital when he went into respiratory arrest.'

'Yes,' Cort said. 'However, his airway was severely obstructed, so we're not sure how effective that was. His head injuries are extensive too,' he added, and the ping-pong match went on as Ruby sat there, the family demanding more hope than Cort would permit.

'We're going to move him up to ICU within the next half hour—they're just preparing for him.'

'Can we see him first?'

'Briefly,' Cort said, then he warned them all what to expect and Ruby just sat there. He told them it would be a little while till they were able to go in, but someone would be along just as soon as they could to fetch them.

And as Ruby stared at her knees, she tried not to cry as Cort finished the interview.

'I really am very sorry.'

'Don't be sorry,' the sister answered tartly. 'Just save him.'

'I see from his notes that he's Catholic,' Cort said. 'Would you like us to arrange the priest to visit him?'

Ruby thought she might stand and run out of there as the family started really sobbing, but at that point Cort stood.

'Someone will be in shortly.'

'Could you not have been a bit gentler with them?' Ruby asked when they were outside.

'Why?' Cort asked. 'Soon they're going to be approached to consider organ donation…'

'Excuse me.'

He watched as she walked quickly to the patient toilet and he thought of waiting till she came out, but it wasn't his problem. Instead he went and spoke to Connor then gave ICU a ring. He then found Jamelia in tears in his office and dealt with her as kindly as he could. Vomiting nurses and emergency doctors who couldn't deal with emergencies really weren't his problem.

He actually felt sorry for Jamelia.

A temporary locum, she had worked mainly in the country and simply wasn't used to the volume of patients that came through Eastern Beaches' doors. She was filling big shoes too—Nick, a popular locum, was on his honeymoon, and though their paths had never crossed, Cort knew the energy and fun he had brought to this difficult place. Jamelia told him that after Nick, and with Cort now back, she felt as though she was a disappointment to everyone. So after a long chat with Jamelia he headed to the kitchen, where someone had made a pot of tea. He poured himself a cup, then frowned at the watery fluid and opened the lid of the pot, only to see a pile of leaves and herbs. He made a mug of coffee instead and headed for the staffroom.

'Why is there a garden growing in the teapot?' he asked, and sat down.

'Ruby's herbs!' Siobhan, another nurse on duty, rolled her eyes. 'Just in case your immune system needs boosting.'

'I'll stick with caffeine, thanks.'

He glanced over to where Ruby sat, reading a book on her coffee break, her complexion a touch whiter than it had been in the suture room.

'Where's Jamelia?' Doug, the consultant, popped his head in. 'Hiding in the office again?'

'Go easy,' Cort sighed.

'Someone has to say something,' Doug said.

'I just have.'

'Okay.' Doug nodded. 'I'll leave her for now.'

'You know what they say…' Siobhan yawned and stretched out her legs. 'If you can't stand the heat…'

And Ruby couldn't stand this place.

They just spoke about everything and anyone wherever they wanted, just bitched and dissected people, and didn't care who heard. She couldn't stand Siobhan and her snide comments, and she really thought she might say something, just might stand up and tell her what an absolute bitch she was, that any normal person would be sitting in an office sobbing when a twenty-three-year-old was going to die. That laughing and joking and eating chocolate and watching television as the priest walked past the staffroom was bizarre behaviour.

'Ruby.' It was Sheila who popped her head round the door now. 'Are you finished your break?'

'Yes.' She closed the book she had seemed so focused on, except she had never turned a page, Cort realised as she stood up.

'Come into my office then—bring a drink if you want to.'

'Sure.'

He could see two spots of red on the apple of her cheeks, could see the effort behind her bright smile as a couple of staff offered their best wishes as she headed out of the room, then Siobhan called out to her as she reached the door.

'Ruby, can you empty out the teapot when you use it?' Siobhan said.

'Sure.'

'Only it's annoying,' Siobhan said. 'Perhaps you could bring in your own teapot?'

Cort watched the set of her shoulders, saw her turn and look over at Siobhan, and for a second she looked as if she was about to say something less than pleasant, but instead she gave that wide smile. 'Fine,' Ruby said, and headed off for her assessment.

'Love to be a fly on the wall!' Siobhan smirked. 'Sheila's going to rip her in two.'

Someone else sniggered and Cort just sat there.

'What is it with her bloody herbs?' Siobhan just

would not let up and Cort was about to tell her to do just that, but he knew what would happen if he did— there'd be rumours then that he was sticking up for a certain nurse, that he fancied her.

But Siobhan was still banging on and his mood was less than pleasant.

'Her immune system probably needs all the help it can get in this place,' Cort said as he stood up and headed out of the staffroom. 'Given how toxic this place can be at times.'

CHAPTER THREE

THEY could fail her.

Ruby tried not to think about it as she stalled the car coming out of the staff car park. There were new boom gates and the car was so low that, as she leant out of the window to swipe her ID card, it stalled and, grinding the gears in the shiny silver sports car all the way home she wished, not for the first time, that her brother had bought an automatic.

Normally she walked or took the bus to work, but it was Saturday and she'd promised her housemates to get home as soon as she could and meet them at the Stat Bar, so had taken the car. But as she pulled into Hill Street, the temptation to change her mind and forgo the rapid change of clothes and mad dash out was almost overwhelming—a noisy bar was the last place she wanted to be tonight.

Far preferable would it be to curl up on the sofa and just hide, but she'd had two excited texts from Tilly already, urging her to get there ASAP because she had some wonderful news.

Ruby let herself into the house and could smell the perfume her housemates had left behind on their way out. There was a bottle of wine opened on the kitchen table and a box of chocolates too. How much nicer it would be to pour a glass of wine and sit in the darkness alone with chocolate than head out there, but then they'd ring her, Ruby realised, and as if to prove the point her mobile shrilled.

'Where are you?' Tilly demanded.

She was about to say that she was going to give it a miss, but could not face the barrage of questions. 'I'm just getting changed.'

'Well, hurry. I'll look out for you.'

Ruby trudged up the stairs, had a rapid shower then tried to work out what to wear—nothing in her wardrobe, or over the chair, or on the floor, matched her mood.

And it wasn't just what Sheila had said that was upsetting her. As she'd headed away from her hellish shift and a very prolonged assessment, she'd passed the young man's family, comforting each other outside the hospital—and worse, far worse, the daughter had come over and thanked her.

For what? Ruby had wanted to ask, because she'd done absolutely nothing.

'You were lovely with Mum,' the daughter had said, and only then had Ruby recalled that when Cort had asked them about the priest she'd found herself holding the woman's hand.

Their grief was so palpable, so thick and real that it seemed to have followed her home, and despite the shower it felt as if it had seeped into her skin.

'Come on, Ruby,' she told herself. She turned on

some music and danced around the room for a moment, doing all she could to raise her spirits.

And it worked a bit because she selected a nice cream skirt and a backless halter-neck top, pulled on all her silver bangles and put big silver earrings on. Looking in the mirror, Ruby decided that with a nice dash of lipstick she could pass as happy.

She didn't feel quite so brave, though, as she walked down Hill Street, turned the corner and walked past the New-Age shop she had worked in for two years after finishing school. She'd been happy then, if a little restless. Her desk had been stuffed with nursing brochures and forms and she had tried to pluck up the courage to apply to study nursing, telling herself she could do it, that even if didn't appeal, she could get through her general training and then go on to work in mental health.

It would seem she'd been wrong.

She could hear the noise and laughter from the beer garden, knew her friends were wondering where she had got to, and she stood outside for a moment and pretended to read a text on her phone. She looked out at Coogee Beach and longed to walk there in the darkness and gather her thoughts.

'Ruby!' Tilly, her housemate, caught her just as her decision to wander was made. 'Finally you're here!' Tilly said, and then frowned. 'Are you okay?' Tilly always looked out for her, for all the girls really. Ruby wondered whether she should just come out and say that Sheila had warned her that unless things improved she was going to have to repeat her Emergency rotation, except Ruby remembered that Tilly had news of her own and was desperate to tell her friend.

'I'm fine. So what's your news?'

Tilly's face spread into a smile. She was a redhead too, but there the similarities ended. Her hair was lighter and much curlier than Ruby's and Tilly was taller and a calmer, more centred person. Also unlike Ruby, she was totally in love with her work. 'I delivered an unexpected breech today. Ruby, it was brilliant, the best feeling ever.' Tilly was a newly qualified midwife and babies, mothers, bonding, skin to skin were absolutely her passion. Even if Ruby could think of nothing more terrifying than delivering a breech baby, she knew this was food for Tilly's soul.

'That's brilliant.' Ruby didn't force her smile and hug. She was genuinely thrilled for Tilly.

'I just saw this little bottom…' Tilly gushed. 'I called for help but as quickly as that he just unfolded, his little legs and hips came out and he just hung there. Mum was amazing. I mean just amazing…'

Ruby stood and listened as Tilly gave her the first of no doubt many detailed accounts of how the senior midwife had let her finish the job, how the doctor had arrived just as the delivery was complete.

'I'm talking too much,' Tilly said.

'You're not!'

'Come on,' Tilly said. 'Your mob are here too.'

'My mob?' Ruby asked as they walked in. 'You're my mob!'

'There are loads from Emergency here.'

God, that was all she needed. Half of Ruby's problem

with Emergency was that she didn't like the staff. Okay, it was probably an eighth of her problem, but they were just so confident, so cliquey, and so bloody bitchy as well, and close proximity to them was so not needed tonight.

Ruby walked in and straight over to her friends, deliberately pretending not to even see the rowdy Emergency crowd and hoping that they wouldn't see her. Not that there was much chance of that. With her long auburn hair she always stood out, but they'd hardly be wanting a student nurse to join them, she consoled herself.

'Here she is!' Jess, another housemate, had already bought her a beer and Ruby took a sip as Jess asked how her shift had gone.

'Long,' Ruby said, and she did what she always did and smiled, because she was a happy person, a positive, outgoing, slightly flaky person—it was just Emergency that affected her so much. 'Where's Ellie?'

'Chatting up "the one".' Jess grinned and nodded over to the bar, where Ellie was sitting on some guy's lap, the pair earnestly talking, utterly engrossed and oblivious to everyone around them. Ruby laughed, because for the next few weeks he would be all they heard about. Ellie, determined to find her life partner and get the family she craved, drifted happily from boyfriend to boyfriend in her quest for 'the one', but as Ruby turned back to Jess and Tilly, her eyes drifted to the emergency table, and inadvertently she caught Connor's eye.

'Ruby!' Connor waved for her to come over and she was about to pretend she hadn't noticed but knew it would be rude, so she beamed in his direction and gave a wave. 'I'll just be two minutes,' she said to her friends. 'Any longer and you *have* to come and rescue me.'

'Where did you get to at work?' Connor asked as she came over. 'I never saw you after supper. I thought you were down to work with me in Resus?'

'My assessment took a bit longer than expected,' Ruby answered.

'Yeah,' Connor joked, 'you've always got an excuse.' He was just chatting and joking, he certainly wasn't there to talk about work, or tell her off, except inadvertently he had echoed Sheila's words. It seemed to have been noticed that any patient that needed to be taken to the ward, Ruby put her hand up. Any stores or laundry that needed to be put away, Ruby was already onto it and, yes, people had noticed.

'So?' Connor asked. 'How was it?'

'How was what?' Ruby said, biting into her lemon.

'Your assessment?'

'Oh, you know…' She forced a smile and rolled her eyes. 'Must try harder.'

Her face was burning, but she certainly wasn't going to share with Connor all that had been said and stupidly she felt as if she was going to start crying. God, Ruby thought, she should have had that walk on the beach before she'd come in. Her eyes darted for escape, for a reason to excuse herself, and suddenly there he was. Cort Mason was back in her line of vision. This time, though, his tie was loosened and he was sitting next to a doctor she vaguely recognised. He gave her a very brief nod, or did he? Ruby couldn't be sure, and then he turned back to his conversation but, not that she could have known it, his mind was on her.

It had been since she'd walked into the bar and perhaps, Cort admitted to himself, for a while before that.

'Hey, Ruby!' He pretended not to be looking, except his eyes roamed the bar and his ears were certainly not on Geoff's conversation as Ruby's friend came over. 'We're supposed to be celebrating with Tilly…'

'Sorry, Jess!' Ruby smiled, glad they'd remembered to rescue her! 'Just coming… See you, Connor.' She glanced over to the table but everyone was busy with conversations of their own, but she did, Cort noticed, make an effort. 'Catch you guys.' She gave a brief unreturned wave that had the light reflecting off all her silver bracelets and then as she drifted off he saw her back and there was a lot of back because she was wearing a halter neck that showed her white shoulders and way down her spine. She was also wearing a small skirt and flat sandals and for the fist time in a very long time Cort noticed everything. Then he glanced across the table and saw Siobhan's eyes on him, watching him watching Ruby, and Cort knew to be more careful than that. So very deliberately he didn't look out for her again after that. Instead, he chatted to Geoff and the rest of the table, yet she was there in the background, laughing and happy, a blaze of colour in the middle of the bar. Though he tried not to notice, he still did, so much so that he was aware the minute she left.

'Leaving?' Siobhan asked as he drained his drink.

'No,' Cort said, even though it had been his intention. 'Just getting another.'

And he headed for the bar rather than for home, but though still packed, the Stat Bar felt empty now. Well, not empty, Cort thought as he squeezed his way back to the table, it just felt pointless, he decided as he sat down to wait it out.

'We're going to Adam's,' Geoff said a little while later, when Cort really was about to head for home. 'Are you coming?'

'Adam?' Cort asked.

'Adam Carmichael.'

'Oh!' He'd worked with Adam in the past and even if they kept only loosely in touch as Cort commuted between Melbourne and Sydney and Adam roamed the globe, working for Operation New Faces, Cort considered him a friend. 'Is he back?'

Geoff didn't answer. Everyone was drifting off and Cort was about to do the same, but that morning, before he'd pulled on the brown suit and chosen a lighter tie, he'd walked along a beach just a couple of suburbs from here and he'd made a promise, not to his sister, but to Beth, to say yes.

To live this life.

Except, now that he was starting to, Cort so did not want to be doing this.

One drink and he'd be out of there, Cort decided as they turned into Hill Street.

It was a nice house, Cort thought as Geoff opened the creaking gate. Sure, it needed a bit of work, but it was a lovely older building and just a two-minute walk from the beach. Who cared if it was in need of a little TLC?

There was a small decked area and the front door was open. Suddenly the music was turned on and wafted out to greet them, and as he walked in through the hall Cort wanted to turn around and walk back out, because there was a dangerous vision walking towards him.

She looked the same from the waist up as she had in the pub, though instead of a beer she was holding a glass of milk and a bag of pistachio nuts and her auburn, or rather *titian*, hair was now loosely clipped up.

He noticed, he really noticed, because if he didn't then his eyes would flick down and he really didn't want to notice that her sandals and skirt were off, that she was wearing lilac boy pants and that there was a gap between the top of them and her top, which showed a soft, pale stomach.

She'd been crying—her eyes were red and the tip of her nose was too.

'Are you okay?' her friend asked.

'I'm fine, Tilly, just watching a sad movie. I didn't realise there'd be a home invasion tonight—I'll go and get dressed.'

She slipped past him and up the stairs and Cort headed through to the lounge—a large area with lots of sofas and magazines and a little pile of tissues. Emergency registrars sometimes made good detectives, because for reasons that shouldn't matter to him, as someone handed him a beer, Cort put his hand on the turned-off television and confirmed what he suspected—it was cold.

And why should it even matter to him that Ruby was sitting at home crying Cort would rather not explore, he had more than enough troubles of his own to be dealing with.

No, he didn't, Cort told himself, at least, not any more.

'Where's Adam?' Cort asked Ruby's friend.

'He's away.' She smiled. 'He's hardly ever here…' She must have seen him frown, and she took a moment to explain. 'I'm Tilly, there's Jess.' She pointed to a blonde and then to another one. 'And that's Ellie.'

'And…' Cort started and then stopped, because what business of his was it if there had been a redhead in her underwear in their lounge just a few moments ago?

'Oh.' Tilly smiled. 'There's also Ruby—she's the one who's just gone to get changed. We rent the house from Adam.'

He was at a student nurses' party.

He so did not need this.

Okay, they weren't all students. Tilly was telling him now that she was a graduate midwife and that she'd had her first breech today, and as he tried to stop his eyes from glazing over as she went into detail, Cort decided to excuse himself and leave just the second that he could—he'd done enough 'must get out more' for one night.

He was just about to slip away unnoticed when Ruby came downstairs.

Whatever had been upsetting her had clearly been taken care of because there was no evidence of tears and she was back to happy now. She turned up the music and started dancing, and Cort was determined to leave, except she really was lovely to watch, all sort of loose limbed and free, and what's more she was dancing her way over to him.

'You look how I feel,' Ruby said, because if ever someone didn't want to be there it was Cort Mason. He belonged in that suit, Ruby had decided before their encounter today. He belonged behind a stethoscope, or peering down his nose at minions, except he hadn't been like that today and she'd revised her judgement. Though she loathed Emergency and most of the staff that came with it, Cort wasn't like the others, he was just aloof.

'You look like I never would,' Cort said in return, and he wasn't sure if that made sense, but even without the hellish last five years, even a decade ago, when he had belonged at student parties, he'd been the boring one. He would never stand in a room and dance alone with others watching, had never been as free as she appeared tonight. She must have caught his words because she smiled up at him.

'Takes practice,' Ruby said, and she picked up one of the many little bowls that Tilly was dotting about the place and offered it to him. He should have just said no, should have made no comment, or just taken a handful, but he screwed his nose up at the Bombay mix, and maybe her attitude was somehow catching because a teeny, tiny corner of it seemed to have worked its way over to him.

'I'd rather have some pistachios,' Cort said, which told her he'd noticed her when he'd walked in.

'Ah, no.' Ruby shook her head. 'They're not to be

put out for the general public, you get the Bombay mix. I've hidden *my* pistachios.'

'Sensible girl,' Cort said, and he wanted to pause time for a moment, have a little conversation with himself to ask himself if he was flirting. But he wasn't, he quickly told himself, because, well, he just didn't do that and certainly not with student nurses.

'Not generally.'

'Sorry?' He was too busy thinking to keep track of the conversation.

'I'm not generally considered sensible.'

'So why?' Cort asked, when really he shouldn't, when really he should just leave. 'Do you feel how I look?'

'You first,' Ruby said. 'Why do you look like you're about to head off?'

Cort didn't answer.

'Why should I tell you what's upsetting me, only to have you leave five minutes later?'

'Fair enough,' Cort said, because what right did he have to ask her what was on her mind when soon he'd be out of there? Anyway, he knew she was in trouble with work, but would that really matter to a flighty little thing like her?

'How was your holiday?' It was Ruby's turn to probe, but she'd been in Emergency for four weeks now and he'd just been there for only one of them.

'It wasn't really a holiday,' Cort said.

'Oh.'

'Family.' Cort certainly wasn't about to tell her the truth. Hardly anyone at work knew, just his direct boss and a couple of people in Admin, but he had always been private and in this he was intensely so, not just for his sake but for Beth's.

There really wasn't that much to talk about anyway. It didn't feel quite right that he was even here, except he was and he asked her something now about her family, if she was local, but didn't quite catch her answer and had to lower his head a bit to hear.

'At Whale Beach,' Ruby said. 'About an hour or so from here.'

And he could have lifted his head then—after all, he'd heard now what she had said—except he was terribly aware of the sensation of her face close to his, just as he had been in the suture room.

Something tightened inside Ruby as she inhaled the scent of his hair again, and she was sure, quite, quite sure that if she just stayed still, if she did not move, if she could somehow now not breathe, whatever was in the air between them would turn his mouth those few inches to hers—and she wanted it to.

'I think I should go.' Strange that he didn't lift his head, strange that still he lingered.

'Hey, Cort…' He heard his name and turned to see that another mob from Emergency was arriving and he couldn't believe how close he'd come, how very careless he had almost been, especially as there was motormouth Siobhan too, so for Ruby's sake he was relieved when she quickly excused herself and slipped away.

Ruby, too, had seen them arriving and a busman's holiday she did not need, so as they blocked the stairs, talking, Ruby stepped out onto the veranda, her heart hammering just a little bit harder than normal, her lips regretting the absence of Cort's, and her problems, which she'd momentarily escaped from, caught up with her all over again. She could hear the noise and the throb of the party and decided she would pop over next door tomorrow morning just to check that Mrs. Bennett wasn't upset about the party. The old lady insisted she didn't mind a bit, but it was always nice to have a reason to pop over.

Maybe she could talk to her a little, Ruby mused. Mrs. Bennett was so lovely and wise, except…Ruby closed her eyes…nothing any one might say could actually change things. Quite simply, she was terrified to go back to work and terrified of failing too. Sheila's ominous warning replayed in her mind for perhaps the two hundred and fifty-second time that night.

'It's a pass or fail unit, Ruby.' Sheila was immutable. 'If you don't pass, you'll have to repeat.'

Six more weeks of Emergency was something she could not do. Six more shifts, six more hours, six more minutes was bad enough, but six more weeks was nigh on impossible.

She thought about telling her friends, but she was so embarrassed. They all seemed to be breezing through. Tilly just loved midwifery and Ellie and Jess were loving their studies and placements too. How could she explain that she could very easily chuck it in this minute rather than face going back there tomorrow, let alone having to repeat?

She glanced down towards the beach and thought of the little shop she had worked in for a couple of years, selling jewellery and crystals and candles, and how much safer that had been, yet it hadn't been quite enough.

She wanted so desperately to do mental health, wanted just to scrape through her emergency rotation so she could go on and study what she truly loved.

And then she saw it.

Hope hung in the sky in the shape of a new moon and Ruby smiled in relief.

'Please.' She made her wish. 'Please get me through A and E. Please find a way for me to get through it.'

Cort walked out and found her standing talking to the sky and not remotely embarrassed at being caught.

'I was just making my new-moon wishes.'

'As you do,' was Cort's rather dry response, because it would never even have entered his head that as he'd walked along his own beach, just that very morning, he'd made, if not a wish, a promise. ''Night, then. I'm off.'

He walked down the path and opened a squeaking gate and had every intention of heading down Hill Street and seeing if there was a taxi—it was his absolute intention, but he found himself turning around. 'What did you wish for?'

'You're not supposed to tell anyone,' Ruby explained, 'or it won't happen...' She saw his brief nod, knew he would turn to go again, but she also knew that she didn't want him to. 'It was a sensible wish, though.'

'Glad to hear it.'

Keep walking, he told himself, and his legs obeyed,

just not in the direction he had intended because he was walking towards her.

'Why were you crying when we came in?'

'I wasn't.' Instantly she was defensive.

'Ruby?'

'Okay—why wouldn't I be crying? A twenty-three-year-old is almost certainly going to lose his life…he's my age.'

Cort nodded, because he knew how confronting that could be. Ruby was right, she had every reason to be sitting alone in tears over a patient. 'Talk to people at work,' Cort suggested. 'We've got a good team—let them know…' He saw her eyes shutter, saw her close off, so he decided there was nothing further to be said. She had given him a reason, he'd in turn given advice, except something told him there was more to it than just that.

'What about Sheila?' He saw her shrug. 'Your assessment?'

All he got was silence and he was determined not to break it, just stood till after perhaps a full minute finally she responded.

'She wants to see an improvement.'

'In what area?' Cort asked, and this time he gave in and broke the ensuing silence. 'How much longer have you got in A and E?'

'Two weeks. Well, just tomorrow and Monday, then I'm off for a while and back for three nights the following Monday.'

'And then?'

'Then I'm finished,' Ruby said. 'Then I start, I

suppose— I want to be a mental health nurse.' As he opened his mouth, she got in first. 'I know, I know, the staff are as mad as the patients—' she smiled as she said it '—so I'll fit right in. Really, I'm just biding my time…'

'Biding your time doesn't work in A and E,' Cort said. 'And Sheila's tough, but she's good—listen to her.'

'I will.'

'Are you going back in?' He didn't like leaving her, didn't understand why she would rather stand alone in the dark than join her friends.

'I might just stay out here for a while.' She thought of Siobhan and Connor and thought of going back in and doing the happy-clappy but she really couldn't face it. 'I might just go to bed.'

'You're not going to get much sleep with that noise.'

'It's not the noise that'll disturb me. I'll have Tilly coming up to find out what's wrong, then Ellie then Jess. It's just easier to…' She gave another shrug. 'I might go for a walk on the beach.'

'Now, that really would be stupid—walking alone…'

'Come with me, then.' He could see the white of her teeth as she spoke, could hear the waves in the background, and for a moment he actually considered it, a bizarre moment because Cort didn't do midnight walks. Well, he did, but not with company, except he did like talking to her.

'I don't think that's a very good idea.'

'I think it's a very good idea,' Ruby said, because he'd stepped a little bit closer and she didn't want him to go. Cort had been the only solace in a day that had

been horrible, and even if a while ago she had wanted
to be alone, it was far, far nicer being here with him. 'I
like walking on the beach.'

'I meant…' Cort hesitated, 'I meant you and me…'
He tried to change what he'd said, but only made mat-
ters worse. 'Us,' he attempted, and Ruby smiled.

'As I said…' She looked at his tie which was grey in
the darkness, but which she knew was really a lovely
lilac, and she did what she had wanted to do in the
suture room—she put her hand up and felt the cool silk.
She wanted him to go with her, wanted a little more of
the peace she had found with him today. 'I think it's a
very good idea.'

Cort wanted to go with her too, though not neces-
sarily to the beach.

He didn't do this type of thing.

He didn't find himself at student nurse parties, neither did he find himself in situations such as this one
because he didn't put himself there.

He liked it now that he was, though.

Liked it a lot because the next thing he knew he was
kissing her.

It was the nicest thing. It really was a lovely kiss.
He sort of bent down and caught her, not completely by
surprise because she'd felt his presence all night, or had
it been before that? Ruby thought as his mouth roamed
hers.

She'd never kissed anyone in a suit.

Never kissed anyone as lovely before, come to think
of it.

She couldn't hear the music from the house now,

wasn't aware of anything except the lovely circle his arms created around them and what was happening in the centre. He had a hand on the wall and one in her hair over her neck, and his kiss was measured and deep like its owner, but as his tongue met hers, as she tasted his breath, there was more passion in his kiss than she'd ever anticipated, more passion than she'd ever tasted, and that it came from Cort made it all the more wild, like a secret only she was privy to. He pulled her head closer just a fraction and his mouth welcomed her a whole lot more and Ruby wanted to climb up his chest to wrap herself around him. She wanted his tie off, she wanted his shirt off, she wanted the party to disappear... she wanted more.

He pulled back just a fraction, and if their mouths weren't touching any more, they still thrummed. He looked down, not at a student nurse and a whole set of problems but into velvet-brown eyes and felt rare intimacy. It wasn't just lust or a sudden urge. It was, quite simply, just nice to *feel*, and he hadn't felt anything for so very long now—yet he was able to with her.

'Do you want a nut?' He could taste her words, could feel them because as she spoke her lips dusted his.

And in turn Ruby felt rather than saw him smile, felt his lips spread, and, yes, she would kiss them again in a moment, just not here. He was like her beloved pistachios, she decided, all brittle and hard but so readily cracked and such a reward to get to the delicious centre.

Cort was used to making rapid decisions—it was what he did for a living after all—but always his de-

cisions were measured, tempered by outcomes and responsibilities. They just weren't tonight.

'I want you,' Cort said.

Which he did.

It was as simple as that.

CHAPTER FOUR

SHE went in first and checked that the coast was clear. It was, well, sort of. There was a couple necking in the hall, but the rest were all gathered in the lounge room, so she waved him in and up the stairs and they bolted along the hall.

'Won't they all come up?' Cort asked as they stepped into her bedroom. 'To see how you are?'

'No,' Ruby said, and grabbed a scarf and tied it onto the handle. 'That means don't disturb…'

He wanted to kiss her again, wanted to see her, but as his hand groped for the light switch she stopped him.

'Don't,' Ruby said. 'Don't break it.'

'Break what?'

'Just…whatever it is that we've got.'

He stood a touch unsure as she lit a candle in the corner and then another and another till the room was bathed in dancing fingers of orange and white. Then she hauled over a chair and, just to be sure, wedged it against the door handle.

It was a room called Ruby. There were drapes, curtains, cushions, candles and crystals, all things that usually did not interest him.

There was the beat of the music and noises from downstairs and he was too old, too jaded, too bitter for someone so light and so lovely, but she'd been crying, he reminded himself as she turned to him.

He was going to leave, Ruby knew that. He was going to change his mind, but he could change it in the morning, because she wanted him tonight.

She wanted him in a way she had never wanted someone before. It was an imperative, a knowledge that this was their only chance, and she was incredibly bold in a way she wasn't usually. She took him by the hand and to a bed that was really rather small. She felt his hesitation and tension and she wanted it gone so she kissed him, and in that moment she welcomed him back in an instant, because out went trouble as he kissed her onto the bed and they tumbled into paradise.

Tongues and taste and the lovely wedge of his body blew cares away as he lay sort of over and beside her— backed into a corner in possibly the nicest of ways. She could feel the belt of his suit against her stomach, feel the roaming of his hands over her waist then sliding to her bottom then almost apologetically heading back to her waist. She could feel him holding back when he didn't want to.

When she didn't want him to.

She kissed his chin and up his cheek, moved his hand back to her bottom and heard the sigh of his breath, and she pressed just a little into him and kissed his eyes and his ears, and it was like tripping a switch, because suddenly he was on top of her, his mouth hungry and urgent. He kissed her throat and then up to her mouth and her body pressed into him some more, and then she could climb up and wrap herself around him as she had wanted to before, but she pulled back his head, wanted to see him again, to hear him again, before she kissed him again.

'Why,' she whispered, 'are you always so crabby?'

'Because I'm miserable?' He stopped and smiled down at her.

'But you're not.'

'I am,' he insisted. 'I really am.'

'You're not tonight,' Ruby said, and he had to agree with her.

'No. I'm not tonight.'

He wanted her skirt off, wanted to see her as she had been when he'd walked into the house, but it would seem Ruby had rules.

'I'm not making love to a man in a suit—in a brown suit.'

'Taupe.' Cort smiled, not even a little smile but a full, wide smile that she had never before seen, and Ruby caught her breath because it completely changed him. She went for his tie, then changed her mind.

'You do it,' she said.

She wriggled from under him and climbed off the bed and left him lying there. She looked down at him and he undid his tie, but that was as far as he went.

'You want it off…' Cort said. 'Come and get it.' So she did, pulling it off before she went for his jacket next.

'Shoes,' he said, and she took off one. 'Both of them.'

'You've got more clothes than me.'

Wasn't he supposed to be riddled with guilt, or

aching with regret? Not sitting up just to get her to remove another sandal, which she did.

'Shirt,' Ruby said, and he obliged.

'Skirt,' Cort said, and so too did she.

She wanted to go over to the bed and climb onto him, she couldn't have ever guessed just how wanton she could be, but he rewarded her not with this game but with his smile, with a Cort Mason she would never have guessed was there beneath the austere exterior. She liked standing before him, drunk on lust and shivering with want, teasing each other and making each other wait.

'Belt,' said Ruby.

'Hardly fair on you,' Cort said, because she was down to her halter and panties and he still had socks and shoes and trousers and belt, but Ruby didn't seem to mind. In fact, she stopped him when he magnanimously went to undo his zipper.

'Just the belt will do,' Ruby said, and as with his tie he merely loosened it.

'Take it off, then.'

Which meant she got to touch him. Slowly, very slowly she pulled loose the belt and she wanted to dive onto him then, but Cort reminded her it was her turn. She slid her top up slowly and she had to close her eyes at one point because, so close to him, she wanted to bend towards his mouth, wanted to climb into bed and be with him, but instead she took off her top and it was bizarre but she didn't feel shy or stupid. Instead, with Cort she felt free.

She stared down and saw the lust and approval in

the eyes that caressed her skin. Then she stared down at herself and saw two very small breasts that she now rather liked, because how could she not when Cort craved them so much that he reached out his hand and stroked one slowly, till she blew out a held breath and thought she'd sink to her knees.

'I'll help with your shoes.'

She bent over him and as he stroked her breast she took off his shoes and socks, and then she kissed his toes.

And he lay there about to pull away because how could he let her? Except her tongue was so sure.

Would he regret this?

He asked himself once as she stood again and then he answered, never, because this wasn't sad or guilt ridden. There was no one else in his head but Ruby, nothing else but him and her.

He could never have thought it would be so magical.

That it could ever be so pure and good again.

That they would have their own rules and their own ways.

He watched her kneel and rummage in a drawer and come out with pistachios.

'Trousers,' Ruby said.

'It's your turn.'

'Only if you catch this with your mouth.'

She was mad, he decided as he lay in the bed, trying to catch a pistachio. Then he didn't want to play that game, so he stood and Ruby stood maybe just a little bit embarrassed because she had never been so free before, never felt so able to be herself with another person. He was so, so slow and tender as he knelt down and slid down her pants. She squirmed just a little, but then he stroked the little hairs and he blew onto her and then she felt his lips press there and she thought her knees might give way.

She held onto his head, her thighs closed tight and shaking as his tongue slid in. His hands pushed at her bottom and his mouth worked to part her some more and she could hear a moan and it came from her.

He laid her down and parted her knees and it was so close to heaven that she felt like crying. All the tears that weren't ever allowed to fall seemed to whoosh up as his mouth found her.

It was as if he'd found her.

The real Ruby, who she couldn't be, who he mustn't see, because then he'd leave. She stopped him, rolled a little way and found a condom, which was just as well, Cort thought, because it had been a long time since he'd carried any on him.

He slid the condom on even though he didn't want it.

Didn't want a one-night stand, though this surely was what it was.

And he wanted to get back what he'd had a moment ago. He had felt her collapse beneath his mouth, had felt her about to give in, but then she'd regrouped and held back. He would have it, Cort decided, he would find her again.

She wanted him. She wanted him as he kissed her, she wanted all of him, and as his thick thigh parted her legs there was nothing more she wanted than him inside her.

Nothing else surrounded them now, no one else present, no chance of interruption, and he was so deep inside her now, and she wanted him to come so that she could too.

Just a little bit.

She didn't want the tears that had been close, and perhaps still were, to impinge on this moment; she didn't want to give in completely.

She pushed up a little, her clitoris swollen from his attention, and pressed in harder, and she felt the pulse of her body that would signal him to join her.

'Cort.' She said his name, and lifted her body to his, because she wanted him with her, but still he pushed on.

'Cort.' She heard the demand in her voice, because she was coming and now so could he and it would be done, but still his arms were not beneath her, he was on his elbows and looking down at her.

'Come on,' he said as if he knew there was more. 'It's okay,' he said as if he knew that this scared her.

Not him.

This.

Because sex was okay and all that had gone on beforehand too.

But this, lying naked beneath him, eyes open and watching, and him knowing there was more to give.

She wanted a one-night stand, not for him to know her. She wanted him to climb off and get dressed and be out of there.

She wanted chocolate or pizza, not to expose her soul.

She didn't want to cry, but all evening it had been building.

She could feel her tears and then his tongue, feel the sob in her mouth and then his over hers, and he didn't stifle it, he took it, kissed it, accepted it, and he was so deep inside her, not just her body but her mind.

'Help me.' She didn't know what she was saying, but he seemed to get it. He smothered her with his body, just scooped her right in and she pressed her face to his lovely hot chest and screamed into it, like a pillow. She clutched at his back and wrapped her legs around him, feeling the jolt of her body, and it was more than she could deal with so she let him absorb all the tension as it shot through her, let his body smother her as he released too.

Oh, God, she was crying, she really was crying, but he didn't seem to mind.

She was spent and it was over, but she didn't want it to be. She could feel the last throes of him and inside her still flickered a tiny, magical beat.

They could hear the party and the music and the voices coming back into their consciousness, could feel control seeping in where there had just been none, and she felt as if she'd been on holiday and had now returned, her world the same as when she had left it but richer for the experience, for the glimpse into another world. One she could surely never belong in.

'You're going to hate yourself in the morning,' Ruby said, but he just smiled.

'Probably,' Cort said. 'But not you.' It seemed imperative that she know that and she nodded.

'No regrets, then,' Ruby said, because they both knew it was impossible for it to be anything more than this.

'None,' Cort said. All the candles had died now and the room was in darkness as he lay on his back with her curled up beside him and tried to find a hint of regret, but right now there was none.

They slept with the window open, because Ruby loved to fall asleep to the sound of the ocean, but the slam of the front door and the sound of the last revellers leaving woke her in the small hours and for a moment she struggled to orientate herself. She looked at a sky that was all stars and hardly any moon and remembered she had to go back into work tomorrow, panicked more than a little as she recalled all that Sheila had said, and then Cort pulled her more into him. He mumbled something, that it would all be okay, and she closed her eyes and let her mind agree.

It had to be okay, Ruby told herself.

It had to be.

CHAPTER FIVE

IT WAS Ruby who woke with regret.

Well, not regret so much, she thought as she wrapped herself in a green and gold sarong and headed downstairs. More embarrassment. She'd never let herself go like that—never been so free with another. Deciding she needed more than herbal tea this morning, Ruby made two coffees and involuntarily recalled her impromptu striptease and nut-throwing act and she closed her eyes for a moment. She remembered she'd been crying, but closing your eyes while holding a kettle wasn't the most sensible of moves, and she poured scalding water onto the bench.

'Are you okay?' Tilly asked as Ruby yelped and jumped back.

'Of course,' Ruby said, but her face was burning, not because there was a man in her room but because of how she'd been with him last night.

'Is that the A and E registrar you're making coffee for?' Tilly asked as Ruby headed to her own little fridge for milk. 'Maybe he'd like normal milk?' Tilly suggested, and Ruby gave a worried nod and headed to the main fridge because, yes, most people didn't drink rice milk. 'So is it?' Tilly grinned as Ruby added milk to the coffees.

'Can't you just pretend not to have noticed?' Ruby glanced over her shoulder and looked at her friend. 'Did anyone see us?'

'No one said anything. I don't think anyone saw, I was just keeping an eye out because I was worried about you—you seemed a bit off at the pub.'

'Was I drunk?' Ruby asked hopefully, because then she'd have an excuse for her tears and her stupidity. She closed her eyes in horror as she remembered flinging nuts and swore never to eat another pistachio again.

'Were you?' Tilly asked. 'You seemed fine to me. Did you have a lot?'

'Two beers.' Ruby sighed.

'What's the problem?' Tilly asked, because she'd never seen Ruby like this. Ruby was always happy-go-lucky, but the smile seemed a bit more strained these days, and though it was hardly a nunnery they were running, Ruby really wasn't one for hauling guys off to her room.

'What was I thinking?' Ruby muttered. 'I've got to work with him. I'm in enough trouble there as it is.'

'Trouble?' Tilly checked as Jess wandered in.

'Not trouble.' Quickly she tried to backtrack. 'I had my assessment yesterday and Sheila doesn't seem to think I'm pulling my weight.'

'You—not pulling your weight?' Jess asked, her voice more than a little incredulous, because that sounded nothing like Ruby. They'd worked together last year on the children's ward, and Jess knew that couldn't be right. 'What exactly did she say?'

'It's no big deal.' Ruby waved Jess's concerns away. 'I'll be fine. I'll be fine. I've just got to get rid of the registrar in my bed.' And she did as she always did, made herself smile, even made the others laugh as she rolled her eyes and picked up the mugs of coffee. 'Wish me luck.'

Cort wasn't faring too well either.

At twenty past seven he jolted awake and the room that had last night looked so sensual, such a haven, was just a rather chaotic jumble now and a riot of colour that made him want to close his eyes again, except when he did he could smell the musk and the sex and a scent he couldn't quite decipher. He opened his eyes and saw what must be a joint lying on her bedside table and he picked it up and smelt it and wondered if that was what had possessed him, if somehow it had permeated his brain and made him act as he had last night?

'It's a smudge stick.' Ruby walked in, determinedly all smiles but absolutely unable to meet his eyes. 'It's just sage.'

'Sage?'

'You light it…' She put a mug of coffee into his hands. 'It's supposed to clear the room of negative energy…'

Why didn't he think of that?

'And these?' He picked up some tiny little figures, no bigger than her fingernails.

'They're my worry dolls,' Ruby said. 'You tell them

your problems at night and then put them in a little bag under your pillow and they take care of them while you sleep…'

This was so not him.

This hadn't even been him ten years ago when it had been okay to wake up with a student nurse with a joint by her bedside.

He could hear wind chimes outside her window and they grated on his nerves.

'What time do you have to be in?' Ruby asked as he glanced again at his watch.

'I'm off today. You?' Cort asked.

'I'm on a late shift.' She was grateful of the temporary reprieve, that now she wouldn't have to face him at work till tomorrow and then she was off for almost a week before she did her stint of nights.

His phone rang then and he looked at it and grimaced.

'Cort Mason.' He took a drink of coffee, perhaps sensing that would be all he had for a long time. 'What do you mean, she's not coming in?' He shook his head. 'No it's fine to call. What's the problem?' He listened for a moment, taking in more coffee. 'Okay, tell him to leave it. Just put on a saline soak and I'll be in as soon as I can. Make sure he's got analgesia.'

'Okay?' Ruby checked.

'I've got to go in after all. Jamelia…' He didn't elaborate. 'They need me in.' He was cursing himself because he just hadn't been thinking, had not been thinking last night. He just wanted to go home and clear his head, but now he had to go into work.

'I'd better go.' Cort grimaced as his phone rang

again, because now he'd said he was coming in, he was public property. Ruby felt a bit sorry for whoever was on the end of the line because he was more than a bit crabby as he took the call while at the same time retrieving his discarded, crumpled shirt. 'I said I'll be there as soon as I can,' Cort snapped, and then hung up. 'I need to get there, but I can't go in yesterday's suit.'

'You can have a shower here,' she offered. 'Maybe wear some scrubs.'

She didn't get it, but it wasn't her fault. 'I can't look as if I've been out all night,' Cort said, because, well, he couldn't. 'You know what they're like.'

'God, yes.' Because she did—the whole clique of them, with their noses in everybody's business—and she could understand why he wouldn't want them in his, especially if it involved her.

'I can get you something to wear from Adam's room,' Ruby offered, and Cort closed his eyes. God, had it really come to this? But reluctantly he nodded and then headed down the hall to a very cluttered bathroom, brimming with straighteners and make-up and tampons spilling out of a box and beach towels instead of towels. He was too bloody staid and sensible to be doing this.

Ruby had to go back downstairs, because that was where Adam's room was.

'Poor Adam.' Jess grinned as Ruby came out with a black casual shirt that looked the sort of thing a registrar might wear on a Sunday. 'No wonder he's always moaning he can't find his things when he gets back.'

Ruby met Cort in the bedroom, wrapped in a beach

towel, and she averted her eyes as he dropped it and pulled on his clothes.

'Thanks for this,' he said as he pulled on Adam's shirt.

'No problem.'

He picked up his jacket and was obviously wondering what to do with it.

'You can pick it up later,' Ruby said, and because she knew he didn't want that awkward moment where he had to face her later, she added kindly, 'I'm on a late shift so I won't be here. I'll leave it on the porch.'

'It's just…'

'I know.'

She did.

'It's not just for me,' Cort said. 'I don't want it to be difficult for you at work—and, believe me, it would be.'

'It won't be,' Ruby said, 'because no-one will find out.'

He could hear the chatter from the kitchen, the little gaggle he'd have to walk past on the way out, but she must have read his thoughts. 'It's just my housemates, they won't say anything.'

'Ruby…'

She shook her head, because she didn't want the big speech or promises that wouldn't be kept and she really didn't want to examine last night with him.

In fact, confused as to her own part in this, her own behaviour with him, Ruby didn't want to examine last night at all.

'Go on,' she said. 'Get back to being crabby.'

And he'd do that.

He had no choice but to do that, but it would be a hard ask to forget last night.

He went to go, but he couldn't quite yet.

Couldn't just leave it at that, as if it had been nothing.

He walked over and took her into his arms and she let him hold her, and she knew he would soon be back to crabby, knew at work he had to ignore her and that was a blessing because she felt as if he had exposed her last night, but it was nice that it ended with a cuddle.

Okay, a kiss, Ruby thought as he searched for her lips.

Why couldn't he be a bastard? Ruby thought as his lips roamed hers.

Bastards were gone when you woke up, or chatted up your friend on the way out, or 'borrowed' twenty dollars for a taxi. Every girl knew that. There was even a coded list on the fridge downstairs, and now that he was kissing her, and so very nicely too, she couldn't even add him to it.

It really was a lovely kiss that tasted different from last night. It was slow and tender and laced with regret because she'd be back at work this afternoon and so would he and last night wouldn't have happened.

Except, Ruby realised as he let her go and walked out her bedroom door, it had.

CHAPTER SIX

'RUBY...' He did not look up as the nurses did their handover and Sheila did the allocations. He'd deliberately avoided the staffroom as the late staff arrived, but Cort knew there really was no avoiding her. 'You're with me in Resus.'

'Sure,' came her voice and *still* he didn't look up.

Just this awkward first bit to get through, he told himself, but really he knew that for as long as she was there, awkward was how it was going to feel.

Still, no one would notice if he ignored her. He wasn't exactly known for his small talk, or for flirting with the nurses.

'Where did you disappear to last night, Cort?' Siobhan wasted no time in asking. 'One minute you were there...'

'I wasn't aware...' Ruby found she was holding her breath as Cort stood up and ended Siobhan's fishing with a very frosty response '...I needed to hand you a sick note.'

Sheila's eyes widened as Cort stalked off. Siobhan's face reddened and Connor let out a low whistle.

'Someone got out of the wrong side of bed,' Connor explained. 'He's been like that all morning.'

Or just the wrong bed perhaps, Ruby thought. As the afternoon wore on, crabby was actually a very good description that she'd come up with, because he growled at any member of staff who approached, whether on foot or by phone, although he was very nice to the patients, not that they had many in.

Resus, to Sheila's clear annoyance, was quiet. One chest pain came in and Ruby attached him to the monitors and ran off a trace, her hands shaking as Cort came over and she handed over to him.

'ST elevation…' Cort spoke to her just as he would any student, pointed out the abnormalities in the tracing and took bloods as an X-ray was performed, but the cardiologists were quiet too, and the patient was soon taken up to the catherisation lab, leaving Ruby just to clean up and then mooch around, checking and double-checking everything.

'The ward's ready for Justin.' Hannah came off the phone and Ruby saw her chance to escape.

'I'll take him,' Ruby offered, because it wasn't Resus she wanted to avoid now but Cort, who was sitting nearby.

'Hannah can take him,' Sheila said. 'I want you to stay in Resus.'

'There are no patients, though,' Ruby pointed out.

'There will be,' Sheila said. 'For now you can check all the equipment.'

'I just have,' Ruby said.

'Double-check,' Sheila said, 'and then you can re-check the crash drug trolley.'

It was possibly the longest, most excruciating shift of her life. Sheila was determined that Ruby was not going to get caught up, as she so often managed to, in other things, and Cort watched, while trying not to, and simply couldn't make her out.

Ruby was competent and certainly not lazy. If anything, she was looking for jobs to do, and she was smiling and happy with all the patients, more than happy to stand and talk to them. He didn't get why she annoyed Sheila so much.

'God, it's quiet,' Sheila moaned, and Cort looked up, because in Emergency you can *think* it's quiet, you can *know* it's quiet, you just never ever say that it *is*—and in response to Sheila's foolishness the emergency phone shrilled.

'You've jinxed us now.' He gave a half-smile and calmly picked up the phone, before a leaping Sheila could answer it, but he wasn't smiling at all when he hung up.

'House fire. Mum's out—she's coming to us with smoke inhalation, they're going in for the children. Seems that there are two.'

'Okay.' Sheila snapped into action, and so too did Cort, calling down the anaesthetist and paediatric team as Sheila allocated her staff. 'Ruby, come with me and set up for number one, Hannah and Siobhan take number two...'

Mum arrived and though distraught was physically well enough to go to the trolleys, but Ruby could smell smoke as she was rushed past and she could smell it on a firefighter who was brought in too, as well as a paramedic who came and gave them more information as he received it on his radio, before it made it to the emergency phone.

'They're out, both in full arrest.'

Happy now? Ruby wanted to say to Sheila as her stomach churned in dread. Is this *busy* enough for you?

But of course Ruby didn't say anything. Instead, she did everything she was told and everything she possibly could to save the little girl in front of them. And she would have given anything she could if only it might work.

She watched Cort work and work and work on the child and she stood there when she really wanted to run. She saw her hands shaking so much she actually stabbed herself with a needle and had to discard the drug and put a sticky plaster on as Sheila snatched up a new vial and swiftly pulled up the drug.

She could feel her body soaked with adrenaline, every instinct begging her to flee as, when hope had long since left the building, Cort made the decision to stop.

And if that wasn't bad enough, the whole team then moved and helped work on the other little doll that had been brought in behind her sister.

She was bright red from the carbon monoxide, and absolutely and completely perfect, on the outside at least. Again Ruby just stood there as Siobhan and a horde of people moved her up to ICU, with her little sister forever left behind.

'I'll go and speak to the parents,' Cort said.

'Dad's just arrived,' Hannah said. 'He's in with Mum.'

'Okay.' Cort's eyes flicked to Ruby, but he wasn't that cruel. 'Hannah, could you come with me?'

'Ruby,' Sheila said. 'Come and help me get Violet ready.'

'Sorry?'

'Her parents will want to see her.'

She stared at the curtain and what was behind it.

'I can't,' Ruby said.

'You need to.' Sheila was insistent. 'We still need to look after Violet and her family.'

'I can't,' Ruby said, and it was final. She could not be in the department for even a second longer. She could smell the smoke and hear the mother's screams, and she wasn't leaving them short because as a student she was supernumerary anyway and, Ruby realised as she headed to her locker and took her bag, they didn't need a nurse who couldn't cope.

'You can't just walk out mid-shift,' Sheila said as Ruby walked back with her bag.

'I'm sorry, Sheila.' She just had to get out of there. She wasn't being a drama queen, she knew Sheila was far too busy to beg or to follow her, and her warning was brusque and firm when it came. 'Ruby, do you realise what you're doing?' Sheila checked.

'Absolutely,' Ruby answered. Siobhan had just returned from ICU and actually smirked as Ruby walked past. 'I'm getting out of the kitchen.'

CHAPTER SEVEN

'THAT was too much, Sheila.' Cort looked at the NUM as Ruby walked out.

'We can't choose our patients,' Sheila responded. 'I can't hand-pick what comes through the doors so that it doesn't upset Ruby Carmichael.'

Cort hesitated, but just for a moment. Her surname was not the point, or the fact he might have slept with a good friend's little sister last night.

The point was, if he said anything, he'd say way too much, and right now he had a grieving family to deal with.

'Later,' he said. 'I'll talk to you later.'

He did.

Perhaps Sunday afternoon wasn't the best time to do it, especially not with the day that they'd had, but by that time he should have been home hours ago. Cort was seething—not that anyone would really notice, he wasn't the most sunny person at the best of times, but when his office door closed on Sheila there was no doubting his dark mood.

'The students are not your concern, Cort.' Sheila did not want to discuss this.

'The morale in this place is my concern, though,' Cort said. 'I'm a day away from speaking to Doug about it. There's a student nurse running out in the middle of her shift, and a doctor not turning up because she doesn't want to be here on her own because she feels the nurses have no respect for her.'

'It's not my fault Jamelia can't cope.'

He looked at Sheila, whom he liked and respected and was the leader of a good team. Yet, as happened at times, the team was splintering. Emergency was the toughest of places to work and in an effort to survive the things they saw, people hardened. Black humour darkened and sometimes it needed reeling in.

'We're supposed to be a team.'

'Really?' Sheila gave him a wide-eyed look. 'Since when, Cort? You've been hell since you got back from your holidays. You do nothing to be a part of this so-called team. Look at yesterday with Jamelia—you just swanned in and took over...' Her voice trailed off, because it wasn't the best of examples. After all, without him the patient wouldn't have even made it to ICU, so she tried a different tack instead. 'I don't see you at any of the staff functions—you didn't come on the team-building exercise. I've worked with you for years and I don't know anything more about you than I did on the first day we met.'

'I'm talking about work,' Cort said. 'We don't need to be in every aspect of each other's lives to function as a team.'

'Then I'll try to ensure we *function* better.' Sheila spat his chosen word back at him, and Cort knew she was right, knew he was asking more than he was prepared to give.

'Okay,' Cort said. 'Point taken. I am trying to make more of an effort…' He just hated the touchy-feely stuff, and a day shooting paint balls in a team-building exercise simply wasn't him. 'And I'll work the roster and see if I can shadow Jamelia for a couple of weeks—maybe build up her confidence. What about you?' Cort said, demanding compromise.

'Fine,' Sheila snapped. 'I'll have a word, keep an eye open…' She gave a weary nod. 'I was actually going to speak to Siobhan anyway. I know how she can come across at times, but her heart is in the right place. I'll talk to them,' Sheila offered.

'Good,' Cort said, and really he should have left it there, except as he turned, he couldn't.

'What about the student?'

'Ruby.' Sheila didn't play games. 'I think we both know her name.'

Cort chose not to dwell on whatever point Sheila was making. Instead, he tried to act as he always did. 'As you said, the nursing staff are your concern.'

But weren't they supposed to be changing how they did things around here? Cort thought as he went to walk out. Hadn't Sheila demanded that he didn't act as he always had, that instead he get more involved? For the second time he turned. 'Maybe you could give her—'

'I'll think about it,' Sheila said, without Cort having the chance to speak, because despite an exchange of words she respected him far too much to make him ask what he possibly shouldn't. 'I'll ring Ruby later—I just hope she's in the right frame of mind to listen.'

He hoped so too.

He *really* hoped so, as he walked to his car, which had been parked overnight in the hospital. Cort ached, not just for a bed that was a bit bigger than the small one he'd shared last night but space and a shower and clean socks and underwear and some beans on toast and some lovely silence.

He'd done all he could, Cort told himself, turning on the radio, because silence actually sent his mind back to her.

It was up to her now, Cort insisted.

So why on earth was he indicating to turn left?

Ruby had walked along the beach, backwards and forwards, backwards and forwards, looking at the waves that kept rolling in. A little child was gone and there was no point regretting her decision to flee from Emergency because absolutely she could not have gone in to her, could not have laid a little child out.

And if that made her a bad nurse, then she was one.

If this meant she had failed, so be it.

And now she'd head home to her friends who loved her and who would try to talk her out of it, who would do everything they could to encourage her to go back, which they might have succeeded in doing had she told them everything.

'What are you doing here?' Jess looked up as Ruby walked in. 'I thought you were on a late.'

'I had to come home.' Ruby saw them all carefree

and smiling and hated what her work would do to their evening. 'There was a house fire...'

'I heard about it on the radio,' Ellie groaned. 'I never even thought... Did they come in to you? Oh, Ruby...' Ellie stood, but Ruby didn't want to hear it and shrugged off Ellie's words and her waiting hug and just headed to her room.

'Leave her,' Ruby heard Tilly say, and was grateful for it as she went to her room. The scarf was still on her door, but she knew Tilly would ignore it and felt the indentation of the bed a little while later when Tilly came in and sat down.

'I don't want to go back,' Ruby said.

'I know.' Tilly did her best to be understanding. 'Remember when I helped deliver that stillbirth?' Tilly said gently. 'I knew the mum was coming in for induction the next day and I honestly didn't know if I was up to it, but you told me the mum would be better off for having me there.'

'It's not the same,' Ruby said. 'Because you're good at what you do, whereas all I did today was stab myself with a needle when I was pulling up the drugs and yesterday, when I sat with the relatives, I couldn't say even one single word. I'm useless...'

'You'll be a wonderful psych nurse.'

'I'll only be a wonderful psych nurse so long as the patients don't go collapsing or fainting or getting sick.' She closed her eyes. 'And psych patients die too... Just leave me, Tilly,' Ruby said.

'I'm not leaving you.'

'Aren't you all going to the beach for a barbecue?'

'I don't want to leave you—I'm going to stay home.'

'Please don't,' Ruby begged. 'I just want to be on my own.'

She heard her friends leaving and lay there quietly. Her room was warm and she pushed the window wide open then pulled the drape and stripped down to her pants. She turned on the fan and lay on the bed and tried to work out what to do, if there even was something she could do now that she'd burnt all her bridges with Sheila.

She heard the doorbell and ignored it, just not up to speaking to anyone.

She turned on her soothing music and lay there but it didn't soothe. Then there was a knock at her door.

'Tilly, please.' She just wanted to be alone with her thoughts. 'Go out with them…' Her voice trailed off, as standing there was a man who shouldn't be back in her bedroom again. 'What are you doing here?'

'God knows,' Cort said, because she was lying on top of her bed in just her knickers with a fan blowing. She'd been crying, her eyelids were swollen, her nose and lips too, and there was a jumble of used tissues by the bed. But there were two other things he noticed as well and he couldn't have this conversation with them there. 'Don't you cover up when your friends come in?'

'My friends don't come in when there's a scarf on the door,' Ruby said with her eyes closed again. 'And, no, Tilly, probably sees a hundred boobs a day in her job.'

'Please,' he said, and she opened her eyes and with a sigh leant over to a pile of clutter beside the bed and pulled out a very little top, but at least it covered her. She lay back and closed her eyes again and Cort opened the little purple sack on her bedside and tipped out her worry dolls.

'What are you doing?'

'Checking on them,' Cort said. 'And they're looking a lot more frazzled than they did last time I was here.'

She almost smiled.

'I'm a happy person usually,' she said. 'At least I was till I worked there. I'm not going back.'

'Up to you,' he said.

'Anyway—I'm not your responsibility.'

And given twelve hours or so ago they'd been in this bed together, somehow he felt that she was.

'I spoke to Sheila.'

'Oh, that's really going to stop the gossip.'

'Not just about you,' Cort said. 'Emergency is a difficult place to work and sometimes the atmosphere and the people can turn nasty. It's how they deal with it,' Cort explained. 'You see so much, you get hard, you get tough, and sometimes it just gets like that. People forget to support one another and they just need a little bit of nudging. It can be a very nice place. We're a great team usually,' Cort said.

'I don't care if they're all singing and smiling and holding hands,' Ruby said, 'I'm not going back. It's not just the staff, it's the patients and the relatives...' She closed her eyes and tried to explain it. 'It's the violence of the place.'

'It's not exactly a walk in the park on the psych ward,' Cort pointed out. 'If you're talking violence...'

'They're sick, though,' Ruby flared in passionate response. 'In Emergency they're just plain drunk or angry.'

'You're a good nurse.'

'No, I'm not.' She hated being placated. How did he know she was a good nurse? He'd seen her hold one arm. He didn't have much to base it on.

'You're going to be a great psych nurse, but part of that means you need good general training.'

She knew he was right.

'And that also means that you can be appalled and devastated by what happened at work this afternoon. That was a shift from hell.'

Finally she looked at him.

'Are you upset?'

He just sat there, because he tried so hard not to examine it, he really tried to just get on with the job, but she made him do so and finally he answered.

'I'm gutted,' Cort said, realising just how much he was, and he closed his eyes for a moment and blew out a breath. 'I guarantee everyone on that shift today is.' He heard her snort a disbelieving sigh, and even if he didn't go on paint-ball excursions, he always supported his team, everyone, at any time, even here in her bedroom.

'Everyone hurt today—whether or not they show it as you might expect. The thing is, Ruby, you'll be gone from there in a couple of weeks, but they are there, day in, day out, doing their very best not to burn out.'

Her phone rang and Ruby frowned at it.

'It's work.' She swallowed then answered it, and

opened her mouth to speak and then listened, said good-bye and hung up.

'That was Sheila. She wants me back in for my early tomorrow, and she says if I do that she won't say anything about what happened today.' Ruby gave a tight shrug. 'She sounds like my mother.'

To Cort it didn't sound like Sheila, because she always had plenty to say on everything, but he chose to keep quiet, because at least Ruby seemed to be thinking about going back.

'I shouldn't have run out.' She closed her eyes and all she could see was Violet, just a sweet little angel, and she wanted to weep at the horror, to fold up into a ball and sob, but she wouldn't. She couldn't while he was there.

'Just go,' she said.

'No,' he said. 'I'm not leaving you on your own.'

'I'm not your problem. Why would you want to help me?'

'You were very helpful to me last night.' He said it so awkwardly that she actually laughed.

'You make it sound like I cured your erectile dysfunction or something.'

'Er, no.'

'Helpful?' She wouldn't drop it, she really was the strangest person he had ever met. 'What do you mean, I was helpful?'

'Nice, then,' Cort said. 'When I didn't know I even needed someone to be. So now it's my turn to be nice to you. Come on, I'll take you out for dinner.'

'I don't want dinner.'

'Okay, you sit with your tissues and I'll fetch you a bottle of wine, shall I? How about a tragic movie? I'll just sit in the lounge and read a magazine till your friends get home, but I'm not leaving you on your own. Is there anything to eat in this place?'

'Okay, okay!' Ruby said.

He looked at the floor that seemed to be her wardrobe, and after a huff and a puff she stood and went to the real one and selected a skirt that Cort thought a little too short and a top not much bigger than the bra thing she was wearing, then she did something he wasn't expecting.

She turned and gave him a smile, a big, bright, Ruby smile, and he didn't return it because he knew it was false.

'You don't go that fast to happy.'

'I do,' Ruby said. 'Don't worry, I won't mope about.'

'I don't need entertaining,' came Cort's response.

He took her to a place near his flat, which was a suburb further than hers from the hospital, and, yes, he hoped no one from work would see them and, yes, it felt strange to be out with a woman who wasn't his wife.

'Just water for me.' She beamed when the waiter handed him the wine menu. 'You go ahead, though.'

'Just water, thanks,' Cort said, because he needed all his wits about him tonight. As he stared at the menu he told himself he was being stupid. He'd been out with friends, with his sister, with colleagues, but that had been different. Then he looked over his menu to where she sat and knew why. He hadn't been out in a very long time with a woman he'd made love to and he was clearly rubbish at one-night stands because as much as she insisted she wasn't, she felt a whole lot like his problem.

He just couldn't read her.

He knew she was bleeding inside yet those brown eyes smiled up at the waiter.

'Mushroom tortellini, and I'll have some herb bread, please.'

'I'll have a steak.' Cort glanced through the cuts available.

'Actually,' Ruby said, 'I'm a vegetarian.'

'Well, I'm not,' Cort said. He glanced up and was about to select his choice and add 'Rare' to the waiter, but in an entirely one-off gesture, because there would be no more dinners, because this wouldn't happen again, because, after all, she hadn't even wanted to come, he revised his choice. 'I'll have the tortellini, too, thanks.'

He waited for her to interrupt, to say no, go ahead, it didn't bother her, he should have what he wanted, but she didn't, and as he handed back the menu she smiled again.

'Thanks.'

'What do your friends say about it?'

'Well, we don't go out for dinner much, but if they bring home lamb curry or something I just tend to…'

'I meant about today.' He would not let her divert him and he saw the tensing of her jaw, felt her reluctance to talk about it. 'What did they say when you told them about today?'

'That it's understandable—I mean, anyone would be upset about a child…'

'About you running off?' Only then did it dawn on him that she was being deliberately evasive. 'You haven't told them?' Cort frowned as she blushed. 'I thought you were close.'

'We are!' Ruby leapt to the defence of her house-mates. They were together in everything, there for each other through thick and thin… Except Cort was right, she hadn't told anyone how she was feeling. She lifted her eyes and looked at the one person that she had told and couldn't fathom why she'd chosen to reveal it to him.

'I hate it, Cort,' Ruby admitted. 'I feel sick walking to work.' She waited for his reaction, for his eyebrows to rise, for him to frown or dismiss her, but he just sat there, his lack of reaction somehow encouraging. 'I spend the whole time I'm there dreading that buzzer going off or the emergency phone ringing… I was going to run off yesterday before we spoke to the relatives…'

'But you didn't.' Cort tried to lift her up.

'I wish I had.' Ruby was adamant. 'I wish I had, because then I wouldn't have gone back, then I'd never have seen what I did today.'

'What do you think your friends would say?' Cort asked. 'If they knew just how much you're struggling right now?'

'They'd be devastated,' Ruby said, and that was why she felt she couldn't do it to them. 'I don't want to burden them, I don't want…' She didn't want to talk about it and luckily the waiter came with their tortellini and did the cheese and pepper thing, and by the time he'd gone, thankfully for Ruby, Cort had changed the subject.

'Are you Adam's sister?'

Ruby nodded and saw his slight grimace. 'He bought the house and I guess I'm the landlady.' She grinned at the thought. 'I rent it out for him, drive his car now and then, he comes back once in a while and...' Her voice trailed off. She'd been about to make a light-hearted comment about how every time Adam returned and didn't notice Jess he broke her heart all over again, but that would be betraying a confidence, a sort of in-house secret, and she looked over at the man who had taken her out for dinner on the worst of nights, and wondered how he made it so very easy to reveal things she normally never would.

'What's he doing now?'

'He's doing aid work.'

'Still for Operation New Faces?'

Ruby nodded. 'He's in South America, I think. Don't worry, I'm not going to say anything to him about what happened.' She smiled at his shuttered features. 'Anyway, you've treated me very well. We've been out for dinner and everything...' There was almost a smile now on his lips. 'He's hardly an angel himself.'

'Still,' Cort said, and then looked at her lovely red hair and remembered something else. 'I worked once with your dad.'

She winced for him.

'Before I moved to Melbourne I did a surgical rotation. I worked with him in plastics—he was Chief.'

'He's Chief at home too.'

It was a shame he didn't have a steak because he'd have loved to stick his knife into it, because he could suddenly well remember the great Gregory Carmichael, holding court in the theatre, throwing instruments if a nurse was a beat too late in anticipating his needs. He remembered too how he had regaled his audience as he'd worked with the dramas in his home life, the wild teenager who answered back and did everything, it would seem, any normal teenager would, just not a teenager of Gregory's, because, as he told his colleagues, he was once and for all going to sort her out.

'What does he say about you doing nursing?'

'He doesn't like it, especially that I want to go into mental health. I used to work in a little shop on the beach, selling New-Age stuff...'

'He'd have hated that.'

'Not really,' Ruby said. 'They had no problem with me working at the shop, they gave me an allowance as well.'

'It's nice that they can.'

'It's all or nothing with them. I had to follow in his grand footsteps or have a little job while I waited for a suitable Mr Right. A psychiatric nurse isn't something he wants me doing.'

'Are you talking?'

'Of course,' Ruby said. 'We didn't fall out or anything. We talk, just not about what I do.'

'So I'm guessing you can't discuss with him the problems you're having.'

She gave a tight shake of her head.

'What about your mum?'

'She'll just say I should have listened to my father in the first place.'

'What if I keep an eye out for you.'

'How?' Ruby said, because she knew it was impossible. 'Can you imagine Siobhan if she gets so much as a sniff…?'

'Why don't you tell your friends?' Cort suggested. 'And you've got Sheila having a think… Don't give it up, Ruby.'

They didn't talk about it again, not till his car was approaching the turn for Hill Street.

'Drive me down to the beach.'

'It's time to go home, Ruby.'

'It's two hundred metres,' Ruby said, but she knew it wasn't going to happen. He was a senior registrar and didn't park his car by the beach like some newly licensed teenager, so he took her home instead.

'Are you going to come in?'

'No,' Cort said, and his face was the same but had she looked at his hands she would have seen that they were clenched around the wheel.

'Please,' Ruby said, because, well, she wanted him to.

'I'm not going into work in these trousers again,' Cort said, because he knew she wasn't asking him in for coffee. He thought of her room and the little slice of heaven they'd shared there last night, and then he told the truth, because aside from work, aside from the age difference, a relationship between them was the last thing he could consider now. There was so much hurt, so much blackness in his soul, he couldn't darken such a lovely young thing with it. 'We'd never work.' He turned to her.

'I know,' Ruby said, because, well, they couldn't. 'You're going to stop for a burger on the way home, aren't you?'

'Probably.' Still he looked at her. 'Are you going to go in tomorrow?'

'I don't know,' Ruby admitted.

'Try talking to your friends,' Cort said. 'You don't always have to be the happy one.' He saw her rapid blink. 'If they're real friends—'

'They are,' she interrupted.

'Then you can turn to them. Go on in,' he said.

'Don't I get a kiss?'

'Ruby, please…'

'One kiss,' Ruby said. 'Just one…' And she made him smile. Not a big grin, but there was lightness where there had been none. 'Then you can go back to ignoring me.'

'I'm ignoring you now,' Cort said, and went to turn on the engine.

'Just a kiss on the cheek.' Ruby's hand stopped him. 'End it as friends.'

He leant over and went to give her a peck, just to shut her up perhaps, but his lips had less control than he did and they lingered there. He felt her skin and her breath and she felt his, felt the press of his mouth on her cheek and then his lips part and he kissed her skin, traced her cheek with his mouth and traced it again. He held her hair and then removed his mouth and kissed her other cheek till she was trembling inside and her mouth was searching his cheek. If her friends were kneeling up on the sofa, watching, they might wonder why they were licking cheeks like two cats, but it was their kiss and their magic and she wanted his mouth so badly that torture was bliss.

''Night, then,' Ruby breathed, and she turned to go then heard the delicious clunk of four locking car doors. She turned to him, to the reward of his mouth and a proper goodnight kiss.

And as it ended, he did the strangest, nicest thing. He pulled down her top just a little, and kissed the top of her chest, just above her breast but not on it, he really kissed that little area, so hard and so deep that as she pressed into the seat, as her hands buried themselves in his hair, she thought she might come, and then he lifted his head to hers.

'I missed that bit last time,' Cort said, and it would be so easy to accept the invitation in her eyes, to follow every instinct and step inside, except their one night together would turn into two and that was more than Cort was ready for.

'Now, you really had better go.'

'I had,' Ruby said, because getting involved with the senior registrar of the department she was struggling so much in wasn't the most sensible mix.

Sensible.

'It wasn't supposed to be like this,' Ruby mused. 'I mean, it wasn't supposed to be this good.'

Cort gave a very wry smile. 'You make a terrible one-night stand,' he said, and it was very much a compliment, because she was more in his head than she was supposed to be.

'So do you,' Ruby said.

And that was that.

It had to be.

CHAPTER EIGHT

'WHAT time do you call this?'

They were all sitting at the kitchen table, three witches around a cauldron, three mothers to answer to, but Ruby loved them all.

'I just went out for dinner.'

'With?' Jess demanded.

'Cort,' Ruby said, 'but it *was* just dinner.'

'This morning it was supposed to be just one night.' Ellie beamed. 'And now dinner. It sounds like…' Ellie always did this, an eternal Pollyanna. Cort could have simply been giving her a lift home and she'd have them walking down the aisle in a matter of weeks, but Ruby halted her there.

'He's a nice man,' Ruby said. 'But it's not going to turn into anything.'

'Why not?' Ellie asked.

'Because it can't,' Ruby said.

'You look happier,' Tilly said, and Ruby smiled and nodded just as she always did. She really didn't need to trouble them with it, because she'd made her mind up that she was going back to do her shift tomorrow, but Ruby took a deep breath because as much as Cort was on her mind, he wasn't the only thing, and maybe her friends did have a right to know. After all, she'd expect it from them.

'There was a problem at work today. That's why he took me out. I didn't just come home because I was upset. I ran off in the middle of my shift.'

'Because of Cort?' Ellie asked.

'No! I ran off because I hate it there. I mean, I *really* hate it there and they're talking about making me repeat it…' She was close to tears as she said it, more than close to tears because she had to keep sniffing them back. Stupidly she kept saying sorry and trying to smile and apologise for how she felt, but there were arms around her, and the shocked voice of Tilly.

'Ruby, why on earth haven't you said?'

'I just…' Because she was the positive one, the one who told them all over and over that they could lift their mood and change their energy. Yet it wasn't that, it was more that she didn't want to trouble them with this, didn't want to burden them with her problems.

'I couldn't face another day like today, and who's to say it won't happen again? Or worse,' Ruby said, though she couldn't really think of anything that could be worse. 'Sheila's going to fail me if I don't pick up. Then I'll have to repeat the placement and I can't.' Ruby shook her head. 'I cannot repeat it.'

'Then you can't fail.' Jess was firm. 'How long have you got left there?' She went over to the calendar and checked Ruby's shifts. 'You've only got tomorrow left on days, the rest of your shifts are agency on the psych ward…'

'Then I've got nights.' Ruby crumpled. 'It's bad enough during the day.'

'I'm on nights that week,' Tilly said. 'I'll make sure we have our breaks together.'

'I'm on an early tomorrow,' Ellie offered. 'And if I can get away, we can meet in the canteen on your break. If I can't then Jess will. We'll get you through this, Ruby.'

'I know.' Ruby smiled, because that was what they wanted, to cheer her up, to reassure her it would all be okay, but as they said goodnight it was a relief to get to her bedroom and drop the facade because, yes, they'd be there in the mornings and evenings and even there on her breaks, but nobody could do the hard bit for her. No one could take away her very real fear of that place.

Cort had.

She undressed and ran her fingers over the mark his mouth had made, and tonight, with him, for a while she had honestly forgotten.

So too had he.

She didn't know what, but as she climbed into bed and looked at her *frazzled* worry dolls, they reminded her of him, taking all her cares and carrying them for a while, and somehow she did the same for him. He was a different Cort when it was just them together, a lighter, funnier, terribly sexy man that sometimes he allowed her to glimpse.

And despite fighting words, despite telling her friends that it couldn't go further, there was this little question mark burning inside her, a tiny flame of hope that she dared not fan in case she blew it out completely.

Hopefully, in a couple of weeks she'd be finished with Emergency for good—and then it wouldn't be a problem.

Unless she failed.

Unless she had to go back.

It was a very good reason for closing her eyes and willing sleep to come.

She had work to do tomorrow.

And she had to do it well.

CHAPTER NINE

WALKING out had been tough, but walking back was so much harder.

Tilly walked with her to work and even if Ruby felt she couldn't tell her the full extent of how difficult it was, she was grateful for her friend's support.

'Just get through today!' Tilly said, and Ruby nodded, putting on her brightest smile and walking in through the department.

'Morning,' Ruby offered to Hannah in the locker room.

'Morning,' Hannah answered, though her voice was flat. 'Hopefully today will be better.'

Ruby suddenly got a little of what Cort had been saying—that Hannah, even though she was one of the most senior nurses, even though she was so much older and wiser, would have had a rough night processing yesterday's events too.

Ruby had timed it so that she wouldn't have to face the staffroom, so she headed straight to handover, where the early shift were starting to gather.

There was Cort, talking to an intern, but thankfully

he didn't look over as she joined the group and neither did he later when Sheila did the allocations.

'Connor, take Ruby through with you to the obs ward.'

She wasn't sure if she was relieved as she headed round there—the obs ward was the easiest place to be. There were a few patients to be assessed and either discharged or admitted to the main wards, and there was the hand clinic to be held there later. But there was also plenty of time for gossip and chatter and Connor seized on it the second the night nurse had handed over and left.

'What happened?' Connor was the biggest gossip in the world and loathed missing out on anything. 'I heard that you walked out in the middle of your shift.'

'Yes,' Ruby said because she had.

'Was Siobhan giving you a hard time?' Connor rolled his eyes. 'She can be a right bitch.' But Ruby refused to say any more about it, she just wanted it forgotten, and she did her best to just chat and be her usual happy self with the patients. She even managed not to blush, well, maybe just a little bit, when Cort came in to discharge the patients or have them moved to a ward.

He sat writing at the desk as Ruby stripped some beds and, really, they had no need to worry about gossip.For all the attention he paid her, no one could have known that just a couple of nights ago…

'Ruby.' Sheila's voice came over the intercom and Ruby went over, expecting another admission. 'Can you come to my office?'

'She said she wouldn't say anything about it.' She forgot for a moment where they were.

'What's the problem?' Sensing gossip, Connor bounded over.

'Sheila wants to see me. I think it's about my dummy spit yesterday.'

'Then you'd better get there.' Connor grinned. 'I'll have a nice coffee waiting for you afterwards.'

Ruby wanted it forgotten, wanted to get back to happy, not sit in an office and go over things.

'I thought we'd agreed that you wouldn't say anything.' Ruby was shaky as she sat down.

'I meant officially,' Sheila said.

'Oh.'

'I meant if you were back at work this morning then I wasn't going to have to go through all the official channels.' She peered at her student. 'Ruby, you gave no indication you were unhappy, or that the place was distressing you so much. I just thought you were avoiding work.'

'No,' Ruby said, because she'd take a mop now and clean the whole length of the hospital and every toilet in between rather than go through yesterday again.

'You had every opportunity to tell me at your assessment how you were feeling. You coped marvellously with the resuscitation yesterday…'

'I was devastated.'

'We all were,' Sheila said. 'But we all got on with the job—as did you.' Sheila paused for a moment. 'But then suddenly you're running off.'

'I honestly couldn't have gone in there.'

'And I honestly couldn't have known how distressed you were.' Sheila gave an exasperated shrug. 'There has to be communication. How can we help you if we don't even know you're having problems?'

'Well, you know now,' Ruby said.

'Which is why I've given you a gentle day today. You can stay in Obs and run the clinics and I'll bring you out to observe anything interesting…is that what you want?'

'No,' Ruby said. 'Yes.'

'You're supposed to be on nights next week.'

'Is it possible to stay on days?'

'No, Ruby.' Sheila shook her head. She glanced at the roster. 'I don't just give out passes—you chose a busy teaching hospital for your placements, and that means there are certain things that are expected from you. A pass from Eastern Beaches means a lot.' She did, though, relent a touch. 'What if I change your shifts so you're with Connor, Siobhan and I? We're doing nights next week, but we're on over the weekend. It's even crazier then.'

'I don't know,' Ruby said, because night duty with Siobhan wasn't particularly enticing, but Connor was nice and now that Sheila knew… She hesitated too long with her answer.

'Ruby…' Sheila was not going to spoonfeed her. 'We're not going to ask you to deal with things single-handed, we'll be there with you, but you have to fulfil your placement. I'll put you down for Wednesday, Thursday and Friday. I'm on Saturday night as well but I think you might want to miss that one—there's a festival on in the city and the place will be steaming. Do you want me to change you?'

Ruby nodded. 'Thanks, Sheila. I'm sorry to have caused so much trouble, and I really am sorry for walking out yesterday.'

'We've all done it,' Sheila said, and when Ruby shot her a look of disbelief, Sheila smiled. 'Okay, I don't head for home, but I've handed over the keys more than a few times and headed to my office or just out to the car park. And,' Sheila added, 'there is some tentative good news on little Victoria, Violet's sister—it's looking more promising than it did yesterday. They're talking about extubating her later on this afternoon.'

It was good news, far, far better than Ruby had hoped, except it didn't take away the pain—it just didn't.

'How was it?' Cort asked a little later as she took the discharge book through to the main section and asked him to write up some discharge meds. She gave a tight shrug.

'Ruby?'

'I *have* to do nights.'

'You'll be fine.'

'I don't think I can do it, Cort.'

'Did you speak to your housemates?'

She couldn't really talk much more because Siobhan came over, and what could Cort really have to say to a student apart from discussing the patients? He took the folder from her and skimmed through it.

'Is everything quiet around there?' Siobhan asked.

'Fine,' Ruby said. 'One's just waiting for a lift home. I'm just asking Mr Mason to write up some analgesia.'

He didn't get another chance to talk to her.

At about half past three the day staff left, including Ruby, and that was that.

Some one-night stand!

For the rest of the week Cort thought about her. Once when Connor rang Psych to see if they were ready for a patient that was being admitted, Cort almost wanted to rip the phone out of his hand when he realised Connor was talking to Ruby.

'I might just bring the patient up myself!' Connor said, and then laughed at something Ruby had said. 'Well, enjoy it while you can. We'll run you ragged next week.' And then he told her he was on a lunch break soon and then added, 'Two sugars!' Cort felt his jaw tighten, not jealous so much, because Connor would never be interested in Ruby in that way but, yes, jealous, because why did he get to have a drink with Ruby, why did he get to chat to her in his lunch break, why did he get to see her in an environment she loved?

'Because,' Elise said, when, desperate for some female insight, finally Cort cracked and told his sister just a little of what had taken place, 'you're not friends with her.'

'Oh, so just because we've slept together we can't be friends?'

'Cort,' Elise said. 'Do you want to be just friends?'

'No.'

'Friends with benefits?'

'No!' God, no! Cort thought in horror—he really wasn't ready for all this. 'I'm just worried about her. She's got a lot to deal with at the moment. I don't know who, if anyone, she's talking about it with. I guess I just want to be around for her and I don't want to make things more complicated for her either.' He was more confused about a woman than he had ever been in his life.

Ever.

'She's nothing like you'd expect, Elise.'

'You mean she's nothing like Beth.'

And did his sister always have to be so forthright? But she was on to something.

'I thought that was what it would be,' Cort said, because feelings for another woman, if ever they arrived again, were supposed to enter slowly. Another Beth, or close, or similar.

'What do you want, Cort?'

Not this, he thought, but didn't say it.

Not this, Cort thought, because surely he wasn't ready.

'Just leave it,' Cort said, and decided that he would too.

CHAPTER TEN

HE TRIED to leave it.

Cort really did.

But when he was called in late on Monday night, he sensed the second he arrived that Ruby wasn't there.

There was no one he could ask without making things obvious, which was what he was hoping to avoid.

He couldn't even ring her, because they hadn't even swapped phone numbers, which, Cort told himself, was a pretty good indicator as to what they had both wanted from each other that night.

It just felt like something more now.

'I'm going to lie down in the on-call room for a couple of hours.' Cort yawned around seven a.m., because he was officially on duty at nine a.m. and two hours' sleep was too good to pass up.

'No, you're not.' Hannah grinned as she walked over. 'We've got a mum who's not going to make it up to Maternity.'

'Oh, God,' Cort groaned, because this was happening rather too often. The car park for Maternity was currently closed so that new boom gates could be erected, which meant mums-to-be were currently having to walk a considerable distance further, and on more than a couple of occasions they landed in Emergency.

'We've rung Maternity, they're sending someone down.' Hannah smiled 'Come on, Cort—let's go and have a baby!'

'I'm not responsible enough,' Cort said, and Hannah grinned back, but it was Cort who checked himself, because normally he'd have said nothing. Normally, he didn't joke along with the staff, not even a little bit. Usually he just rolled up his sleeves and got on with whatever job presented itself. Ruby had changed him, Cort realised. Ruby really was infectious.

'Hi, there…' Cort smiled at the mother who was groaning in pain but, unlike the last couple of maternity patients who had landed in Emergency, Cort wasn't quite sure if she was at that toe-curling, holding-it-in stage. He put a hand on her stomach and asked a couple of questions, but to save her from two examinations, as Maternity was sending someone down, he decided to hold off for a moment.

'Can you believe it?' Hannah was looking more than a little boot-faced when Cort stepped outside. 'Maternity sent a grad midwife—she's just washing her hands.' Hannah rolled her eyes. 'She looks about twelve!'

Cort said nothing. Hannah was clearly offended that, on her summons, the entire obstetric team wasn't running down the corridors now, but privately he thought it was a little wishful thinking on Hannah's part that an emergency room birth was imminent.

'Hi, there!' Cort deliberately didn't react when it

was Tilly who walked towards them and was also quietly grateful that she introduced herself as if they had never met. 'I'm Matilda. Tilly. We're incredibly busy in Maternity at the moment, so they asked me to dash down and see if I could help.'

'She's through there,' Cort said, and told her a little of his findings, adding, 'Though I haven't done an internal yet.'

'I'll come in with you,' Hannah said.

'I'll be fine,' Tilly politely declined.

She was very calm and unruffled and thanked both Cort and Hannah then disappeared into the cubicle as Hannah sat brooding at the nurses' station, staring at the curtains like a cat put out in a storm. 'If we say we need help,' Hannah said, 'surely they should send—'

'They're busy,' Cort interrupted. 'And I guess they figured the patient can't come to much harm as there are doctors and nurses here.' He would normally have left it there, but Ruby must still be in the air for him, because he looked over and continued the conversation with Hannah. 'Have you thought about doing midwifery?'

'Me?' Hannah scoffed, then rolled her eyes and added a little sheepishly, 'Every day for the last six months or so. I'm just not sure it's worth trying—I'm nearly fifty. I've been in Emergency for ever.'

'Maybe if you're nicer to Tilly you could see if you could spend a few hours up there. It might help you make up your mind.' He looked over as Tilly came towards them.

'She's fine.' Tilly smiled. 'Still a while to go, I

think. I'll take her up to Maternity—how do I arrange a porter?'

'The porters are just having a coffee. I'll take her up with you if you like,' Hannah offered. 'I'll just go and grab my cardigan.'

And there was a moment, just a moment where he could have asked Tilly why Ruby hadn't come in—to check if she was okay or had, in fact, just not shown up. A moment to acknowledge Tilly and to step down from the safe higher ground of Senior Reg and just talk as you would to someone you knew casually, who was a friend of someone you cared about.

He chose not to take it.

Hannah returned with her cardigan and a marked shift in attitude towards the *grad* midwife and Cort pushed through the morning, but it all felt wrong. The busy department felt strangely quiet without that blaze of red to silently ponder, and at lunchtime, unable to face the staffroom, Cort headed up to the canteen.

'It's good to get away from there, even for a little while.' Sheila joined him in the canteen queue and Cort gave her a smile, though his own company was really all that he wanted. It had been a long night, followed by a very long morning.

'I thought you were on nights this week.'

'I'm supposed to be in for a management day,' Sheila said as they shuffled down the queue and rather dispiritedly checked out the food on offer. 'Which is a bit of a joke—I haven't even seen my office.'

The queue slowed down and Cort yawned and asked for another shot to be added to his coffee. Instead of the chicken salad he was half considering, or the cream-cheese bagel that was curling at the edges, he decided to push his luck with the canteen lady.

'Can I have a bacon sandwich?'

'Then they'll all want one,' she said, because most of the meals were wrapped in plastic and pre-made now, except on very rare occasions.

'He's been here eighteen hours straight.' Sheila put in a word for him and as Cort turned to thank her, a normal day, a normal shuffle along the queue in the canteen suddenly somehow brightened.

She was like a butterfly.

Swooping in on a gloomy canteen, which was wall to wall navy and white uniforms and dark green scrubs or sensible suits, Ruby gave it colour.

Her hair was down and she was wearing denim shorts that showed slim, pale legs and a sort of mesh shirt that was reds and golds and swirls of white, and she had on leather strappy sandals and was just so light and breezy that apart from the lanyard round her neck and the anxious-looking woman by her side, you'd never have known she was working.

The queue passed him as he stood waiting for his order and he listened as she stood and helped her patient with her food selection, encouraging her and gently suggesting alternatives, and she made him notice things that he never had before. Like how kind the staff were with the patient, and how other staff behind in the queue didn't huff and puff and moan about how long she was taking, but with a nod from the cashier moved subtly past.

He saw Ruby's calm presence, and he saw something else too—that just as she felt she couldn't do
Emergency, couldn't stand what he did, he realised that
he couldn't readily do her job either. He could not stand
with endless patience as the woman struggled with a
seemingly simple decision, pasta or potato salad, but,
Cort knew, what a vital job it was.

'Maybe rice?' the patient said, and Cort felt his jaw
clench, but Ruby just nodded.

'That sounds good.'

And Ruby waited and waited for her patient's decision, except she didn't seem to be waiting, just paus-
ing, and Cort found himself wanting to know what the
woman would choose, to prod her in the back and say,
'Just have the rice, for God's sake.' Because, yes, there
were some jobs that not everyone could do.

'Here we are, Cort.' The largest bacon sandwich ever
came over the counter and for the first time since he'd
been a teenager, Cort thought he might blush as he took
the plate, headed over to Sheila and sat down.

'I've had a word with some of the staff,' Sheila said,
because it was easier to talk away from the ward. 'As
you know, I'm going to do a stint on nights and see how
it's all going on there.'

Cort took a sip of his coffee and nodded.

'How's Jamelia?'

'She's doing better,' Cort admitted, though his eyes
kept wandering to where Ruby was warming her patient's meal in the microwave. 'She just needs someone
to shadow her and I've spoken with Doug about it—
we'll get there,' he said, because they would.

'I've got a good team, Cort,' Sheila said. 'I know they can go a bit far at times, but they have to deal with a lot.'

'I'm aware of that.' He was *more* than aware of that.

'We just need to remember we are a team,' Sheila said. 'And that sometimes we struggle. All of us do, Cort.' He glanced up at her, because for a moment there he thought she was referring to him. 'It's good to hear you went out last week.'

Cort rolled his eyes and took a large bite of his sandwich.

'It really is,' Sheila said. 'You want teamwork, Cort, well, you have to be a part of it.'

And his eyes roamed the canteen as he went to take another bite and then he saw where she was sitting and Ruby looked over at him and somehow the sandwich didn't taste quite so nice. Part of him wanted to take another bite, a really big one, but instead he put the sandwich down and then he was rewarded with a very private smile, and that did it.

He *would* go there tonight, Cort decided.

He would go over, because he knew that she was struggling and he didn't know if she'd told her friends, and, he admitted to himself, if he was going to be there at any point in the future, then he ought to be there for her now.

'Not hungry?' Sheila frowned at his discarded sandwich.

'Not as much as I thought I was.'

'Is that Ruby?' Sheila asked, knowing full well that it was. 'Doing an agency shift?'

Cort said nothing, just as he usually would.

'She finishes soon,' Sheila said, which she never usually would either. 'I'm having a lot of trouble getting that one through.' She picked up the untouched half of Cort's sandwich and took a bite. 'She's like Lila…'

'Your daughter?'

'Both vegetarians, both live on another planet.'

Cort drained his coffee and still said nothing, but for the second time in fifteen minutes or so he was blushing.

'I still don't know if she'll turn up for her shift. What is it with these girls? My daughter just dropped out of maths—two years of study gone, just like that.'

'Sheila,' Cort asked, 'what if your pager went and they asked you to go and work on Ophthalmology?'

'They wouldn't.' Sheila flushed, because she could not stand eyes—they were her thing, the one thing she ran from—she didn't even like putting in eyedrops.

'If they did, though?' Cort said. 'If they told you that you had to spend six weeks there—and in the ophthalmic theatre too.'

'I'd say no,' Sheila said. 'Because I'm allowed to. Emergency is an essential part of her course. Anyway…' Sheila met him with a firm gaze '…let's hope she turns up and that we can keep things uneventful for her.' And that was all she did say, but he took the warning, because in three years he'd never so much as looked at anyone and, yep, Emergency could be a horrible place to work at times and he didn't want any more of the spotlight falling on Ruby.

'Cort?' Sheila checked, and he nodded. Nothing more was said, but both fully understood.

As he headed back to work, deliberately he avoided Ruby's table, and deliberately he didn't glance back.

It hurt not to be acknowledged, though Ruby did her best not to let it show, just concentrated on her patient, the aim to keep things light and uneventful, because Louise hated eating in public.

'Can we go now?' Louise said, for perhaps the fiftieth time.

'Soon,' Ruby said, gently but firmly, deliberately eating her salad as slowly as she could. 'I want to finish my lunch, I won't get another break.' Though as Sheila walked directly towards them, Ruby was rather tempted to take the easy option and tell Louise they were heading back to the unit.

'Hi, there, Ruby.' She gave a brief smile to Louise too.

'Hi, Sheila.' Ruby wasn't too embarrassed to be seen working. As a third-year student, she was able to practise as a division-two nurse and a lot of the students crammed in as many shifts as they could. Still, it was just a little awkward given she was due to be on night shift tomorrow.

'Are you doing some agency?'

'Hospital bank.' Ruby gave a sweet smile and then pointedly turned her attention back to her patient. When Sheila continued to hover, Ruby extended the conversation a touch. 'It's my last one for this week.'

'Good,' Sheila said, 'because you'll need all your wits about you for night duty. I'll see you tomorrow.'

'Looking forward to it,' Ruby said as Sheila finally left.

'Who was that?' Louise asked.

'The A and E NUM.' Ruby rolled her eyes. 'She's not too bad really, but she runs a tight ship.'

'She reminds me of my mother.' Louise gave a wry smile and Ruby was delighted to see that now the conversation was rather more normal, without thinking, Louise took another mouthful of food.

'Funny you say that!' Ruby grinned. 'I remind her of her daughter apparently.'

It was a slow walk back to the unit, deliberately so, because Louise would have happily run all the way back, just to burn up a few extra calories, but Ruby deliberately ambled, and never in a million years would Sheila, or even Jess, Ellie or Tilly, realise that as she stopped by the guest shop and chatted about some flowers, her mind really was on the patient, that this was, in fact, a deliberate action and part of her job.

Doing this, she was happy, Ruby realised, then tried to push away that thought, although it was occurring all too frequently lately. She could stay a div two if she didn't complete Emergency, or Sheila insisted that she repeat, but Ruby didn't have to—she could still work in her beloved psych. Okay, she might not be able to go as far in her career as she would like, but she could still do the job she loved.

As she swiped her ID card and they entered the unit

that actually felt like home, Ruby had no intention of not showing up tomorrow.

It was just nice to have options, that was all.

CHAPTER ELEVEN

HE SAW her again, walking down the hill towards her home, and, yes, he had guessed at the time she might finish and had taken a different route home, because though he had heeded Sheila's warning he did need to see her—away from the hospital and house—just to check in with her, to find out if she was okay and, Cort admitted, tell her how much he was thinking of her.

'Hey.' He felt like a kerb-crawler as he pulled in beside her, but she gave him a very nice smile. 'Do you want a lift?'

'I'm five minutes away,' Ruby said, but she climbed into the car anyway.

'How come you're not on nights?'

'Sheila swapped them round so that I'd be on with her so I'm doing a couple of shifts on Psych. I can work as a div two,' Ruby explained.

'And you're liking it?'

'Loving it.'

'Not long now till you'll be studying again.' He glanced at her. 'For your mental-health nursing…'

She stayed silent.

'A few nights and you'll be done.'

'Yep.'

He turned and looked at her again and she smiled back at him but he was quite sure it didn't reach her eyes.

'Ruby?'

'It wouldn't be the end of the world if I don't pass,' Ruby said, and instead of looking at him she looked out of the window. 'I can work as a div two—I've loved my shifts.'

'For three nights' work you can be Div One.'

Ruby shrugged. 'If she passes me. If not, maybe I can speak to the uni...'

Cort knew he should just drop her home, should go back to his own and sort out his head instead of her, because he didn't know how he was feeling. Elise was right, as always—if love came again, he'd expected more of the same. With Beth, passion had been a slower-building thing, colleagues first, then friendship, dinner, a steady incline to a higher place, but with Ruby it was like a rapid descent, this jump into the unknown.

'Do you want to come in?' As they sat at the traffic lights he just said it and he saw her frown, because they were two minutes from her home. 'My place,' Cort said.

'Careful,' Ruby warned. 'You'll be giving Ellie ideas.'

'I'm always careful,' Cort said, just not where Ruby was concerned.

It was the most stunning flat she had ever seen—not the interior, more the view.

Cort fetched her a drink and flicked through his post but didn't open it. It was from lawyers who were tying up Beth's estate and one from the nursing home too, no doubt with the final bill. He thought for a moment about telling her, but despite her smile she was dealing with so much already. He knew that, though he longed to share it, it might be better to wait just a little while longer, because this evening was about Ruby and getting her through the next week—his grief, his past, would still be there, waiting. Ruby's future was the only thing that he might be able to change.

'They pay registrars too much.' She looked out at the view and swirled her drink. 'It's gorgeous.'

He couldn't embarrass her or make her feel awkward—couldn't tell her about insurance payouts and the guilt of buying a place that his wife would have loved. So deep was the pain of his past, he just didn't know how to share it.

He knew, though, how to remove it for a while.

And if that sounded selfish, Cort didn't care because he knew he helped her too. Knew that somehow she confided in him.

'You need colour.' She looked at his surroundings. 'This is brown, Cort, not taupe.'

'I've got colour.'

And that made her blush because his eyes were on hers, and her cheeks turned up the colour a little bit more.

'Look,' he said, because he was worried for her, 'about nights—'

'Am I here for a lecture or sex?' Ruby interrupted, 'and if it's both, can we skip the lecture? I'll be fine on nights. I'm just going to…' she gave an impatient shrug '…not think about it.'

'I'm shadowing Jamelia,' Cort said, 'so I'll be around, but…' he hesitated, 'I don't know how she could know anything, but I think Sheila warned me today, about you, about us. I certainly haven't said anything.'

Of that she had no doubt.

'Sheila's a witch,' Ruby said. 'She'd just have to look into her crystal ball.' But Cort just stood there, not impressed with her theory.

'I don't think we've done anything at work that's been obvious, but there were a lot of people at the party and your housemates…'

'They would never say anything.' She had no doubt there either. 'Siobhan was at the party. I don't think she likes me…'

And that made sense to Cort, because Siobhan had made it clear on a number of occasions that she liked him.

'Maybe they just…' Cort tried for the right word and came up with a very simple one. 'Noticed.' Even if he played it down, even if he'd pretended not to notice, from his first day back at work he'd noticed Ruby, had found himself watching her when he hadn't intended to.

And now he told her just how much he had…noticed.

'I didn't need help with that arm,' Cort said, and he watched her blink as his words hit home. 'Ted was completely zonked, I could have done it without local anaesthetic and he wouldn't have felt a thing, wouldn't have moved a muscle.'

Ruby started to laugh. 'So you got me into trouble.'

'You were already in trouble,' Cort pointed out. 'I do feel bad, though.'

'For what?' Ruby asked, and she felt a sort of warmness spread through her that this guarded man, one she'd thought she'd hauled to her room and randomly seduced, had been attracted to her all along.

Had, in fact, instigated it.

She'd never have guessed, not for a moment, not if she looked back and replayed every minute before that night over and over, because all he'd been was crabby.

'I'm glad you told me.'

'And you?' Cort asked, not for ego but he was curious. Had the attraction that had hit been as instant for her?

'I thought you were good looking,' Ruby breathed. 'I guess I didn't think further. You were just...' And she looked at him and told him exactly what he was. 'Gorgeous.'

'We have to be careful,' Cort said, 'till you're done.'

And the warmness that spread through her turned to fire as she realised what he was saying.

'I shouldn't have picked you up today, but I was worried about you,' Cort admitted. 'I thought you hadn't shown up for your nights. You told me you were on nights on Monday.'

'Sheila changed them,' Ruby explained again. 'I have to do three, and she suggested I do them with her. I'm on tomorrow.' He could hear the dread in her voice even though she tried to veil it, and he didn't really understand. There were so many things he loathed. Every step he had walked along the corridor in Beth's nursing home he had dreaded and her funeral hadn't exactly been something he'd looked forward to, but he'd just put one foot in front of the other and got on with it. It had never entered his head to walk away.

'You're going to be fine. I'll be at work, though I'll have to—'

'I know, I know,' Ruby interrupted. 'You'll just ignore me like you ignore everyone.'

'I don't.'

Ruby just shrugged.

'And I won't come to the house…'

'They really wouldn't say anything.'

'It's a few nights, Ruby.' Which sounded easy, except he'd driven around looking for her when he shouldn't have and even a few nights seemed impossible from here. 'Once it's over…' He left the rest to her imagination and, boy, did it soar.

She had been scared to even glimpse at a future, hadn't thought that her blissful night with this incredible man could be anything other than a cherished memory. That a man like Cort might really want to get to know her more.

That, as brilliant as it was, it wasn't just sex.

'You'll get through these nights.' He saw her eyes briefly shutter, knew there was so much more going on behind that smile. 'Ruby…'

'I don't want to talk about it.'

Maybe it was better left, Cort decided. Maybe by talking about it, he would build it up to something bigger than it was for her.

'Can I have a tour?' Quickly she changed the subject.

'I've just got to ring work.'

'You just left there.'

'I said I'd check back.' Which was true, but even though there was no real need to take the call in the bedroom, he did so.

There was only one photo of Beth.

And even that made him feel guilty—that the one he kept was one taken before the accident. He hated the Christmas and birthday photos that the staff had taken of what had been left of his wife afterwards and the guilt that came that he loved the woman she had been.

He chatted to his boss, made sure his messages had been relayed and put the Beth of yesteryear into a drawer for now, because it wasn't the time to share it with Ruby. He wondered how it was even possible that somehow his heart was actually moving on.

Then he turned and he didn't have to wonder how he was moving on because somehow, so easily, Ruby made it possible.

'That is not taupe,' she said of his bedspread when he turned off his phone. 'That's completely brown.'

'We'll go shopping soon,' Cort said, and the thought both thrilled and terrified—not sheets, or whatever, but that she was being asked into his life.Then he gave a slight grimace. 'Actually, I might have to go shopping now...'

'I'm on the Pill,' Ruby said, and she looked at him, 'which is something I've never said to anyone before...'

And he nodded, because he got it, got the enormity

of what they were both saying, the confirmation they were home.

It was different here, in his bedroom, Ruby thought. More special, somehow, to be here in his home. There was no urgency, just purpose in their kiss. And there was no chance of regret tomorrow, because it was still daytime.

She could hear sirens whizzing past and traffic outside as he undressed her, and that it was afternoon mattered, because the world was going on, it was they two that very deliberately chose to stop.

There was no music or booze or party, just each other, and she wasn't scared that the light might break the moment because naked before him the light let this be real.

It was bliss to climb into his bed and watch as he undressed and climbed in beside her. She heard his phone bleep and he checked it.

'I'm going to hate that phone, aren't I?'

'You are,' Cort promised.

'Do you ever get to turn it off?'

'Holidays...' Cort started, and then changed his mind, because he wanted the future to be different, he wanted a part of him to be solely devoted to her. And Doug was there, Cort told himself, and Jamelia was there too, and the world could carry on without him, would just have to carry on without him sometimes. He reached over and turned it off, and it felt like a holiday, felt like freedom, felt like life as he let go of the reins and reached for her.

'What would Sheila say?' Ruby asked as he lay beside her and started kissing her.

'I don't want to think about it.'

'And Siobhan?' Ruby laughed.

And then she wasn't joking any more, she was just next to him and he felt lovely, they felt lovely, in a great big bed with them at the centre and nothing to disturb their kiss except the bleep of her phone. She said a rude word in his mouth and happily chose to ignore it.

'You'd better get it,' Cort said.

'I don't get urgent calls,' Ruby said. 'I'm not important enough.'

'You are to me,' Cort said, and she got back to being kissed, got back to the passionate man that no one but her knew existed. She'd been told that you couldn't faint lying down but that's what his kiss made her feel like. She felt the dizzy sensation of removal as his tongue captured hers, she felt the world slide away as his body met hers, and wondered how she had got so lucky, how the place she hated so much could give her something so sublime.

'You're my new-moon wish,' Ruby said as he kissed her, his hand stroking her slippery warmth. Her mouth moved to his neck and she kissed it, then deeper, as his hand worked on, and she tried to resist her body's demands. She was mindful of him and lifted her head because she didn't want to leave a mark, but his thigh hooked over her and still his fingers worked their magic and still she moved her mouth lower and kissed his taut shoulder and then let herself kiss deeper, sucked on his skin as he brought her so close, and then she worked her head down, kissed him as intimately as he had once kissed her, tasted every lovely inch of him till she breathed and blew on him and kissed him again, and told him her truth. 'You got me through.'

'I haven't finished yet,' Cort said, and then she heard his wry laugh, because if she didn't stop now, he might rue his own words. 'Come here,' he said, and slid her up to face him. There were no sheets now, they had fallen somewhere on the floor, so side by side they kissed and then side by side they watched, no barriers, no protection, because they were already safe, and the moment of merging was overwhelming. Cort slid into her and her body shivered and tightened and wrapped right around him.He pushed deeper into her again then he stilled for a moment but she didn't want that, because he couldn't come soon enough for Ruby, so ready was her body to join his.

'Come with me,' she said.

'Soon,' Cort said, because he wanted to enjoy her longer, he wanted the impossible, because as he drove into her, Ruby's hips moved towards him and then towards him again, and it was Ruby who couldn't wait a moment longer. There was such passion in him, such a rare match of want, that she could let go and feel him, feel the friction they made and the taste of his skin, could drown in their scent and call out his name. She felt the rip of tension run through him, felt the shudder of his release and the lovely spill of him inside her, and the absence of fear and the amazing knowledge that she could do anything if this was her reward at the end of each day.

'You're bad for me.' Cort grinned.

'You're so good for me?' Ruby smiled. 'Can I tell you something?'

'Anything,' Cort said.

'I'm starving,' Ruby admitted. 'I only had a salad at the canteen—I didn't want to freak my patient out.'

'What did she have in the end?' Cort asked, because, amazingly he was curious.

'A jacket potato.'

'I don't know how you do it.'

'That was an easy one,' Ruby said. 'Believe me!'

'I do—and I'm starving too,' Cort admitted. 'A certain someone put me off my sandwich...' He did a quick mental run of what was in the kitchen. 'I can ring out for something. I don't think I've got anything...er... suitable.'

Ruby rolled her eyes. 'We don't just eat vegetables.' She climbed out of bed and headed off to the kitchen. By the time he got there, she was already flinging open his cupboards and raiding his rather pathetic fridge contents. 'It's like when you're on a plane and order vegetarian—we get a stupid apple for dessert and everyone else gets chocolate pudding. Why?' she demanded.

'I have no idea.'

Cort had never considered having anyone back at the flat, let alone the possibility of someone moving in, but now she was here, he wondered how he could stand her to leave.

She was colour.

A lively, vivid colour that was neither blinding nor irritating, but just by her presence she brightened the place. The television was on, not on the news as it normally would be early evening, but she'd commandeered the remote and had flicked to a soap Cort hadn't seen in more than a decade.

'He forgave her!' Ruby was disgusted. 'I can't believe he forgave her.'

'Again!' Cort said, eating beans on toast on the sofa and amazed that even after a decade it was so easy to catch up. 'She was at it last time I watched.'

What was it with Ruby? Cort tried to fathom. It couldn't just be sex, Cort reasoned, even though beneath his towel, things were stirring again—what was it with her that made him want to dive right back into living?

He needed to tell her about Beth.

Cort knew that and sat there wondering what her reaction would be, but she was laughing and she hadn't done that for ages, relaxed for once, which she needed to be.

'Once your nights are finished,' Cort said, 'if it's okay with you, maybe we could go away for a couple of days…' Away from here, he decided. Away from a photo she'd demand instantly to see. To a place that was neither his nor hers—where they could talk properly, and if she was upset, they could work through it. The last thing he wanted was to trouble her now.

Her phone bleeped and, checking her messages, Ruby saw that there had been a couple.

Should I be worried?

'Oh.' Ruby winced. 'It's Tilly. I texted her about…' she glanced at her watch '…oh, a few hours or so ago to tell her to put the kettle on.' She texted back a quick message.

'What did you say?'

'Just that I was fine, and sorry.' She could read his expression. 'They wouldn't say anything. I know you might find it impossible to believe…'

'Not impossible,' Cort said, and realised he'd be wasting his time telling her not to say anything about them. Clearly she trusted them, but reluctantly he stood. 'Come on, I'll take you home.'

'Now?' Ruby grumbled.

'Now,' Cort said, or he'd take her back to bed and then they'd both fall asleep and they'd have all her housemates to answer to. 'Let's just get through the next week—ignoring each other.'

CHAPTER TWELVE

'TELL me again!' Ellie said.

'I've told you four times.' Ruby laughed. Jess and Ellie were home when she tumbled into the house, though Tilly, who was working that night, had left early to help with an antenatal class. 'Once I'm finished in Emergency, once I've got through nights, well, it's not written in stone, but I think we'll be more open, able to show our faces together in public. I don't know…' she admitted, because at the time it had seemed obvious what the other was saying—that once they'd got through this bit, they had a future, but under the scrutiny of her friends, she wondered if she was clutching at straws, and she certainly wasn't about to discuss the absence of condoms.

So she played it down instead, toned it down, tried to calm things down in her heart, and after a good gossip she wished her friends goodnight and headed for bed. Except despite a tired body her mind wouldn't quieten down and Ruby found herself staring out of the window, knowing she had work tomorrow and wishing she could sleep. She eventually did, but only for a little while, she was quite sure of it, when at eight a.m. she staggered into the kitchen.

'What are you doing up?' Tilly was nursing a huge mug of tea. 'I thought you'd have a lie-in.'

'I heard the kettle.' Ruby smiled. 'I'm going back to bed soon.'

'So where did you get to yesterday?' Tilly asked, and Ruby told her, well, some of it, but even though she sounded upbeat and happy she could see the worry in her friend's eyes.

'You haven't known him very long,' Tilly gently pointed out.

'I know.' Ruby ran a hand through her hair and tried to apply logic to a heart that had made up its mind. 'I'm not doing an Ellie—I'm not convincing myself this is "the one". I just can't believe how he makes me feel and I know he feels the same.' She could see Tilly wasn't completely mollified. 'What?' Ruby demanded, because she could do that with her best friend. 'What aren't you telling me?'

'Nothing.' Tilly was honest. 'I don't know a single thing about him. I remember him when I did my emergency rotation and I don't think I said two words to him in the time I was there. He was just "Call Paeds. Organise a social worker..."'

'He's actually not like that at all,' Ruby said, 'once you know him.'

'Good,' Tilly said, and she would never meddle, but she was concerned about Ruby, knew she was struggling at work and knew that her friend didn't give her heart away easily.

'Oh, I got your payslip…you said you were worried…'

Ruby peeled it open and groaned as she scanned the little slip.

'I knew they'd paid me too much. I was hoping it was back pay or something.' But instead they'd put her down as working on a night that her shift had been cancelled. 'I'll ring them later,' Ruby said. 'Right now I'm going back to bed.' But she still couldn't sleep. Tilly's unvoiced concern had her thinking—what did she know about him? She knew that he had family in Melbourne, that he had worked with her brother, there hadn't exactly been time to take a history. Still, as the morning stretched on, and sleep remained elusive, and as a couple of hundred dollars extra in her bank account niggled, a walk into work to clear her conscience seemed like a good idea. Though she'd held little hope of bumping into Cort, as the lift doors opened on the admin floor and she saw him standing there, it was certainly an added bonus.

'Hi.' She smiled and he remembered Sheila's warning.

'Hi.' He stepped aside to let her out, as was the polite thing to do, but Ruby just stood there, temptation beckoning, and he stepped into the lift. 'Shouldn't you be in bed?'

'I wish I was.'

So did Cort. He glanced to the lift panel, wished he knew how to stop the lift, but one push of the button and he'd no doubt get it wrong and they'd come up for air, to find half of security gathered and watching.

'You okay?' Cort checked, and she nodded, but then she changed her mind.

'Cort…' She wanted quiet for her mind, she wanted the assurance only he gave, she wanted supper at his place and the quiet confidence he imbued in her. Maybe if he came for dinner, or she went there… 'Can we…?' But she didn't get to ask. The busy lift was soon in demand and instead she stepped out. But, still, she was all the better for seeing him, because when he was there, there was no doubt in her mind that they would work.

'I think I've been overpaid.' Still high from seeing him, Ruby spoke to one of the girls at the pay office.

'People don't normally complain about that. Let's have a look.' The woman whose name badge said 'Ruth' took Ruby's slip and read through it.

'I didn't work that Saturday,' Ruby explained. 'I was down to work, but my shift got cancelled. You have to take it off me today…' Ruby smiled '…or I'll spend it.'

It was one of those messy problems. Ruby had signed her time sheet apparently, which she hadn't, of course, and Ruby accepted Ruth's offer to take a seat while she located the time sheet to see what had happened.

'Marie?' Ruth called to a colleague. 'Can you take a look at this?'

'One moment,' came the response as Ruby sat reading through a pamphlet on superannuation and not really listening as the women chatted on.

'So what part is annual leave?'

'He had five weeks of annual leave owing,' Ruth said, 'then ten days' paid carer's leave, plus two days paid compassionate from the date his wife died.'

'Do we need to see the death certificate?'

'That's what he just brought in,' Ruth said. 'I've taken a copy.'

They never said his name, and had she not seen him in the lift she would never have known. Even sitting there, Ruby couldn't be absolutely sure.

She just was.

This was the family stuff he had been dealing with.

His wife had just died and he'd been in bed with her.

'I have to go.' Ruby stood.

'I've just found your timesheet,' Ruth said. Ruby wanted to run, but she was trying not to do that any more, so she waited and it was worked out that someone had used her sheet but signed their name and that it would be amended at the next pay cycle. She smiled and thanked them and then she left. Finally free, she didn't take the bus but walked down the hill to her house. There was Mrs Bennett in her garden and she smiled and waved as Ruby went past and Ruby somehow managed to smile and wave back, but she couldn't even force a smile as she saw Tilly on the stairs.

'What on earth's wrong?'

'Nothing.' Ruby brushed past.

'Ruby…' Tilly's feet followed her.

'I've got the worst headache,' Ruby attempted. 'I can't sleep and I have to get to sleep—I'm working tonight.'

'You've got hours till your shift starts,' Tilly soothed, but the hours slipped away and all Ruby could think was that he hadn't told her. She had slept with a man, glimpsed a future with a man she really knew very little about. She was embarrassed too, ashamed to share her problem with her friends. His wife had been dead just over a month after all.

She wasn't sure whether it was nerves, exhaustion or humiliation, but when Tilly heard her retching in the toilet a few hours later, she knew her housemate's plight was genuine.

'I can't go in,' Ruby said. 'I've hardly slept since …' She tried to work it out. 'In ages.' It would, in fact, be irresponsible to go in with no sleep, but how could she not?

'It's okay,' Tilly said. 'You go back to bed. I'll ring in for you.' Ruby lay there and closed her eyes as she heard her friend on the landline.

'Who did you speak to?'

'The ward clerk,' Tilly said. 'She said she'd pass it on.'

'Sheila's going to be furious.'

'You can't help being sick,' Tilly pointed out, and then she looked at her friend, saw the real trouble in her eyes and wasn't sure what was going on. 'Do you want me to go down tonight?' Tilly offered. 'I can explain to Sheila that you really are sick—ask if you can make it up over the weekend…'

'I'll speak to her myself,' Ruby broke in. 'Go on, you get ready for work.'

'Ruby…'

'Please, Tilly…' Ruby said, because that was the good and the bad of sharing a house—there was always someone there when you needed them to be, but there was always someone there too when perhaps you just needed to be alone. 'You've got to get ready for work.'

Cort found himself lingering in the staffroom as the night staff started to drift in.

'We're short tonight,' Siobhan said. 'We've got two from the bank.'

'We don't have a student either,' Sheila said. 'Ruby rang in sick.'

'What a surprise!' Siobhan smirked. 'She must be worn out from all the agency shifts that she's doing.'

Cort kept his face impassive, but he would have loved to tell Siobhan to shut up.

'I've swapped her around so she can come in to do Thursday, Friday and Saturday.'

Which were the worst nights.

He couldn't believe she'd throw it all in—then he thought about Ruby and actually he could. He thought back to the canteen where he'd seen her confident in her own environment, and she *was* like a butterfly, one who'd found herself fluttering around the coals of hell. This place was damaged and wounded.

Cort walked across the ambulance bay towards the car park, unsure what he could do. He could hardly turn up there, and then what? Insist that she go in?

'Hi, there.' It was Tilly who greeted him, walking towards Maternity.

'Hi.' Cort gave a brief nod, which was more than he usually did. 'On nights?' he asked, and she smiled and stopped.

'Yep.'

Normally he'd have nodded and walked on, refused to acknowledge what they both knew.

'How's Ruby?' Cort cleared his throat. 'I heard she'd rung in sick.'

'I don't know how she is,' Tilly said. 'She's not really talking to anyone.'

'If she doesn't do her nights, she's going to have to repeat.'

'I can't see that happening.' He was surprised at the thick sound to her voice, and it dawned on him that Tilly had been crying. 'If she can't do three nights, she's hardly going to do another six weeks. I don't know what to say to her.'

'I'll talk to her.'

'Her phone's off.'

'I'll go round,' Cort said, because if she wasn't going in again, there was nothing to keep things quiet for anyway.

'Door for you,' Ellie called up the stairs to Ruby. As Ellie was on her way out and left it wide open, it gave Ruby no choice but to haul herself out of bed, pull on a sarong and answer it.

'Is everything okay?'

She looked at him.

'Only I wondered…'

She blinked.

'I heard you were sick. I bumped into Tilly. Is everything okay?' Cort checked.

'You tell me?'

'I'm here to find out about you. Ruby, you know you have to do these nights.'

'I don't have to do anything.'

'I know you're having a difficult time. I know this week—'

'How's your week been, Cort?' she interrupted.

'I thought it was going well.'

'How's your month been? Anything happen that you might want to talk about?'

And then he got it—she knew.

She wanted to hop she was so angry. She wanted to shake him as she gave him every opportunity to explain things, to tell her, but he just stood there.

'You bang on about support, about backing each other, helping each other through...being open.'

'How do you know?' Cort said, because to him it mattered. 'Adam?'

'Adam?' Ruby's voice was incredulous. 'Of course it wasn't Adam. Adam doesn't talk about things that matter. I can see now why the two of you are friends.'

'Then how do you know?'

'It doesn't matter how I know,' Ruby said. 'Actually, it does. Do you not think it should have been you who told me? Do you not think...?' She was close to crying, just disgusted with herself and angry with him. 'Six weeks?' Ruby croaked. 'She's been dead six weeks.'

'You don't understand.'

'I'll never understand.' She wouldn't. 'If it had been just that night...' Ruby said. 'But you came back, you took me out, we sat in the car...' She jabbed her finger at the pavement behind. 'And you took me to your home and you still didn't tell me.'

'I don't talk about it with anyone,' Cort said. 'She suffered a brain injury, and for years she was in a home…'

'So you were embarrassed by her?' Ruby said. Sometimes she said things; the thoughts in her head popped out and this was one of those times.

That he didn't deny it really did make her want to cry. 'Maybe you're right, maybe there is no point talking about it. As you said, we can never work.'

'We might.'

'No.' Ruby shook her head. 'We're at different stages.' There was so much against them. 'You're too closed off.'

'That's rich, coming from you.' He looked at her and did the most bizarre thing—stood on her doorstep in his suit, threw his arms in the air and did a brief dance that looked a lot like the one Ruby had done the night of the party. 'The life and soul…' Cort said. 'Happy Ruby…' He turned away. 'You're the one closed off, Ruby, you can't even tell your best friends how you're really feeling.' He walked down to the gate. 'You do your happy-clappy dance rather than admit your true feelings. You just avoid everything—like you're avoiding tonight, like you're refusing to listen about Beth…'

'You want true feelings…' She could not stand that she had a name, that Beth was real and he hadn't told her. 'You're too boring for me, Cort, too old and too staid…' She pushed him away with words, because he was getting too close, not physically, just too close to the real her, and she didn't want anyone to see that.

'Well, at least I see things through,' Cort said. 'Just don't blame me for not showing up.' He tossed the comment over his shoulder. 'To anything.'

CHAPTER THIRTEEN

IT WAS a row. Her first row in more than a decade. It was the one thing she tried to avoid and there was no one home so she fled to her room because that was what she did, Ruby realised.

Avoided.

Hid like a wounded cat and licked her wounds till she was ready to come out.

Except she didn't want to come out to the wreckage she was surely creating.

To repeating A and E or to have thrown it in.

But how could she go back there now, after the way she had spoken to Cort?

He wasn't or ever had been boring.

'Men!' Ellie stood at the door, already back from her date. Clearly the latest love of her life had been relegated to history, but unlike Ruby she wasn't curled up on the bed because Ellie just moved on, determined to find the true love of her life.

Ruby had just lost it.

'What happened with Cort?'

'I said the most awful things…' She told her friend some but not all of them.

'It's called a row,' Ellie said, but it was far more than that.

'I found out…' But she couldn't tell her, couldn't reveal the part of Cort that he clearly didn't want anyone to know, and round and round things went in her head, even after Ellie had gone to bed. When Jess came home, she tried talking to her too, but it was hard when she couldn't tell her Cort's truth.

'I'm going to ring Adam.' Giddy from way too little sleep, Ruby stood up.

Jess, of course, should have suggested she check the time difference, but Jess had an agenda of her own and gave a nod of encouragement, even went and got her the phone. Ruby dialled her brother's number but, of course, got a recorded message.

'You didn't leave a message.'

'What's the point?' Ruby said. 'Adam won't tell me anything. I'm going to bed.'

But ten minutes later she heard the phone ring and Jess laughing and talking, and because it was the land-line that had rung she knew who it was.

'It's Adam,' Jess said as she knocked on her door. 'And he's not best pleased—it's four a.m. in South America apparently!'

'Thanks,' Ruby said when Jess hovered and rather reluctantly handed the phone then dragged herself out the door.

'Do you ever look at the clock, Ruby?' Adam asked, because she did this all the time.

'No. Anyway, I never know where you are to work out the time difference.'

'What's wrong?' Adam asked, because he could tell by her voice that something was.

'Nothing,' Ruby said. 'I just need to ask you something. It's just a friend of mine, well, she's got mixed up with Cort Mason. Apparently you know him.'

'And this friend wants to know more?' Adam asked.

'Yes.'

'Nice guy,' Adam said.

'That's it?' Ruby said, and when Adam was less than forthcoming she pushed a little harder. 'My friend knows about his wife.'

'Really?' Adam said. 'I'm surprised he told her.'

'He didn't,' Ruby said. 'She found out.'

There was a long pause.

'Adam, please.'

'Is this for you, Ruby, or your friend?'

She paused, because Adam didn't gossip, even to his sister. 'Me,' she finally said, and waited through the longest pause.

'You and Cort?' She heard the incredulity in his voice.

'Please,' Ruby said.

'Okay, but there's not much to tell. He took a job in Melbourne some years back. I think he worked at the Children's Hospital and she was a paediatrician. I don't know much, we just emailed now and then, just that there was an accident in Queensland on their honeymoon. Beth got a nasty head injury, it would be four or more years ago now. She ended up in a nursing home.'

'And he moved to Sydney?' She couldn't believe he'd just leave her.

'After a year or so—he's always back there, visiting. Like I said, we don't go out when I'm back, because if Cort's on days off then he's down in Melbourne. I offered to go once when I was down in Melbourne, but he didn't want me to see her like that.'

'And?'

'And what?'

'What he did he say? About her, I mean?'

'I don't know…' Adam wasn't the type to replay conversations in his head, let alone to anyone else. 'We just play golf… Look, Ruby, there's no hope with Beth. I mean, I'm glad Cort's trying to move on, because I do know there's completely no hope…'

'Beth died,' Ruby said, and closed her eyes as Adam went quiet. 'Didn't he tell you?'

'Ruby, I'm in the middle of the jungle. Like I said, we're not that close—I don't think anyone is with Cort.'

She put down the phone and padded out to put it back in its charger, and there, of course, waiting, was Jess.

'How's Adam?' She didn't await Ruby's response. 'Did he say when he was coming home?'

'When does Adam ever really say anything about anything? Honestly…' She looked up at her friend, who carried a torch for her brother, and even if Ruby loved him, she felt it only fair to warn her, properly this time. 'I can see why Caroline broke up with him.'

'Caroline?'

'His fiancée,' Ruby said, and saw Jess's jaw tighten. 'She really thought she'd change him, that somehow Adam would open up. She just didn't get that he's…' She closed her eyes, because Adam was a whole lot like

Cort. 'He's an emotional desert. He is!' Ruby said, when Jess refused to buy it. 'He was in bed with the next one a week after Caroline…and the next and the next… There is no deeper Adam,' Ruby reiterated, because there wasn't. Nice clothes, nice car, lots of women—they were all there waiting for him whenever he returned. It really was just as simple as that with her brother, and she didn't want him breaking her best friend's heart. Except Jess refused to hear it.

'Just because someone doesn't spill out their heart, Ruby, it doesn't mean they don't still have feelings.' Jess would not be swayed. 'We all hurt, Ruby.' Jess huffed off to bed, no doubt to stick pins in a little doll she'd name Caroline. 'We just all have different ways of showing it.'

CHAPTER FOURTEEN

RUBY leapt on the phone when it rang the next evening. Dressed for her shift, her heart leapt in hope that it might be Cort, that he might want to clear the air before she commenced her shifts, but the voice on the other end brought no relief. 'I just wanted to check that you're coming to church on Sunday.' Ruby closed her eyes at the sound of her mother's voice on the phone.

'I'm on nights,' Ruby said, because even if it killed her, she'd at least have died trying.

'You just said you were working Thursday, Friday, Saturday.'

'Which means I'll be home in bed on Sunday,' Ruby explained as patiently as she could.

'Your dad does whole weekends without sleep, and he's doing a reading this Sunday. It would be nice if his family was there,' her mum said. 'It's the nine a.m. service. If you take Adam's car to work, you'll get there in time. I'll do a nice lamb roast.'

And that was it.

There was just no point arguing.

'How's your mum?' Tilly asked when she hung up the phone.

'Still keeping the peace,' Ruby said. She was in her navy shorts and white shirt and her hair was tied tight. If you didn't know how much she was shaking inside, she could almost have passed for a nurse. 'Still keeping the chief happy!'

'Come on,' Tilly said. 'I'll walk with you.'

They walked up the hill under the lovely moon that had once held so much promise and Ruby was so glad to have her friend beside her.

'Cort was widowed recently,' Ruby said. Was it breaking a confidence to confide in her best friend when her heart was breaking? Probably, but she knew it would never be repeated by Tilly, not even to the others, and she was very grateful when Tilly said nothing for a little while and just walked on.

'How recently?' Tilly asked.

'A month,' Ruby said. 'Well, it was a month when we…' It still made her stomach churn to think of it. 'She was in a car accident a few years ago—she had a head injury.'

'It sounds like he lost her a long time ago,' Tilly said gently.

'Still…'

'We had a couple the other week,' Tilly said, 'they were just so happy, so excited to be having this baby, and I found out halfway through labour that the baby wasn't actually his—she'd lost her partner right at the start of the pregnancy.' And they walked up the hill and Ruby listened. 'It's none of my business,' Tilly said, 'but I couldn't get it at first, how she could move on so quickly. And then I saw the love, and I saw how happy they were and how he was with the baby…' Tilly was the kindest person Ruby knew. 'Don't judge him, Ruby.'

'He should have told me.'

'When?' Tilly asked. 'You wanted him out the next morning…'

'He hasn't told anyone about her,' Ruby said. 'Even his colleagues don't know or most of his friends.' Tilly turned then and looked at her.

'Hurts, doesn't it? When someone you care about can't confide in you?' But Tilly didn't hold grudges and she gave her friend a hug as the lights of Emergency came into view. 'Maybe he had his reasons.'

'I think I was supposed to be his get back out there fling.'

'And what was he supposed to be?'

'I don't know,' Ruby admitted. 'If I'd even thought about it for a moment it would never have happened. I've just made things a whole lot more complicated— not only do I have to face Emergency, I have to work alongside him, after all the terrible things that I said.'

'Then say sorry.'

'What if he won't accept it?'

'Then at least you'll have said it.' Which wasn't the answer Ruby wanted, but it was, she knew, the right one.

'You'll be fine,' Tilly said. 'No running away.'

'I won't.'

At night the side door wasn't open so she had to walk through the waiting room and already it was steaming, two people asking her on her way through how much longer they would have to wait. Already her temples were pounding, but she went to the staffroom, took out a little white teapot she had painted her name on in red nail varnish, made a big pot of herbal tea and told herself she could do this.

'Evening, Ruby!' Sheila gave a tight smile as she walked into the staffroom and Cort deliberately didn't turn his head from the television. 'Ready for some action?'

'Bring it on!' Ruby smiled.

Cort had been unable to comprehend that she, that anyone, could throw so much away for the sake of three nights, but as the weekend progressed, he started to see it.

See what he never really had before.

It was like finding out about sex when he had been younger. Suddenly it was there glaring at him at every turn—how on earth had he not noticed? Now, though, it was the dark side of A and E that was illuminated. All the stuff he usually just ignored or shrugged off or put up with was blazingly obvious, and there was this part of him that wanted to shield her from it. There were fights breaking out in the waiting room, angry relatives, abusive patients and the drama of sudden illness. He watched her face become pinched, even though she smiled; he saw her eyes shutter regularly as if another knife had been stabbed in her back; and he started to see that for some, the emergency room was damaging.

Not that he could do anything about it.

Once she tried to talk to him, but Cort was still too churned up, and he blanked her, then regretted it all through the next day when he couldn't sleep, wondering if she'd be back.

She was.

To a place that was twice as busy and twice as angry as before, and he noticed it—all of it—even the little things he would never have seen before.

'I'll eat my supper here.' Siobhan peeled off the lid of her container. Ruby had made it through Thursday and was back for round two—a busy Friday night and the patients were particularly feral.

Siobhan was in the grumpiest of moods because she'd been brought back from the staffroom as the numbers were too low for her to take a proper break. They had a young overdose in cubicle six and they couldn't identify the tablets she'd taken, despite poring through books and the internet, and Sheila had asked Siobhan to make a phone call. Now Siobhan sat, stuck on hold to Poisons Information, as Cort tried to work out a drug dose. He watched Ruby's shoulders tense as Siobhan's bored eyes fell on the student nurse.

'What are you doing, Ruby?' she asked. Ruby was holding a newborn baby and screaming toddler, who'd cut his forehead falling against his toybox and had blood all down his pyjamas.

'Mum's just gone to the toilet,' Ruby answered.

'Well, can't she take them with her?' Siobhan asked. 'We're not a child-minding service.'

'It's no problem.'

'Actually,' Siobhan answered, 'if another emergency comes in, or someone goes off and you're holding a baby, it becomes one!'

'Ooh, that smells nice!' Sheila's only comment was about the smell wafting over as Siobhan stirred her supper. 'What is it?'

'Veal and noodles,' Siobhan said, and just for a second, so small no one, not even Ruby, noticed, there was a shadow of a smile on Cort's mouth as Ruby rolled her eyes and muttered under her breath.

'That'd be right.'

She hated it, Cort fully realised. Behind the smile she was in torture, and given what had gone on, he'd made it much worse for her.

'Thanks so much.' A tearful mum came and took her baby and tried to scoop up the toddler, who was on the floor.

'I know I keep asking, but have you any idea how much longer?'

'We'll get to him as soon as we can,' Siobhan answered before Ruby had a chance. 'Only there are still a couple of patients before him and it will take two staff to hold him down and we just can't spare them at the moment.'

'But you've time to sit and eat,' the mum snapped.

'I'm eating my supper at the desk because I'm on hold to Poisons Information and I expect to be for the next half-hour,' came Siobhan's tart response. 'I'm actually supposed to be on my break, but I'm here to hopefully free up a colleague.'

Yes, she was right, but it could have been handled so much better, because the mum promptly burst into tears. 'There are drunks down in the waiting room. I can't sit and breastfeed...'

And Ruby truly didn't know what to do. There was literally nowhere to put them. Every cubicle was full, all the interview rooms were taken, and though, had it been up to her, she'd have popped Mum into the staffroom, the reality was it was needed for staff to get a break from the perpetual craziness.

'Bring him through.' Cort stood up. He didn't have time, but he'd just have to make it.

'Suture room's not cleaned from the last one.'

'I'll do it,' Ruby said, and glanced at Siobhan. 'And I can hold him by myself.'

Ruby scuttled off and did the quickest clean-up she could, then washed her hands and set up a trolley for Cort.

'You'll need a drawer sheet to wrap him in.' Cort came in, but didn't look at her. 'Mum won't be able to help with holding him.'

'I know.'

He pulled up the anaesthetic so that the little boy wouldn't see the needle, opened up the sutures then told Ruby to bring him in.

'What's his name?'

'Adam,' Ruby said, and flushed, and it was stupid and so, so irrelevant that it was the same name as her brother's, but it just made a point, a stupid point, that they knew more about the other than they ought to officially. 'I'll go and get him.'

'You don't have to come in,' Ruby offered, but his mum was sure that she'd rather.

'Well, if it gets too much,' Ruby said, just as she'd seen the others do, 'just slip out.'

'He's going to struggle and scream,' Cort explained, 'and it will sting for a bit when I put the anaesthetic in, but after that he won't feel a thing.' He explained a little further as Ruby tightly wrapped the little boy. 'It's not fair to settle him down only to stick him with a needle, so once the anaesthetic is in, we'll try and calm him.'

The only way one person could hold him was to practically use the weight of her body over the swaddled child and hold his face with two gloved hands as he screamed loudly in Ruby's ear.

'It will be finished soon, Adam,' Ruby said, and she swore she felt the needle go in as he shrieked even louder.

'That's it.' Cort's voice was loud and deep and caught Adam by surprise. He paused his screaming for just a second. 'All the horrible bit's finished with,' Cort said to the little boy, and then spoke to Ruby. 'Loosen up on him while it takes effect.'

'It's okay.' His mum tried to soothe him, but the baby was crying now too and she was about to as well—either that or pass out. 'I think I'll go out...'

'We'll take good care of him,' Cort said, and then he looked down at the toddler. 'I'm going to make it better in a moment and then you can go home.' He spoke to him in a matter-of-fact voice and maybe all the fight had left him, but the little boy did stop screaming. 'It's not going to hurt now.' He turned to Ruby. 'Go round the other side.' She did so and Cort changed his gloves and put a little green drape over his head, and they were back to where they started, away from the bedlam and shut in the suture room, but there was a whole lot more between them than a patient now. 'You just look at Ruby,' Cort said, which Adam did, and though he did whimper a few times, he was much calmer as Cort worked on quietly.

'Could it have been glued?' Ruby asked, because it would have been much easier.

'It needs a couple of dissolvable sutures—it's a pretty deep cut,' Cort explained. 'And it needed a good clean.' He turned and smiled as a much calmer mum stepped into the room. 'Just wait there,' Cort said, but very nicely. 'He's in the zone. If he sees you he'll think it's over. We shan't be long.' There was one more snip and then as he went to clean it, Ruby could see what he meant by in the zone, because the second Adam sensed it was over, he shot up, saw his mum and not a tightly wrapped drawer sheet or Ruby could have kept him still a second longer.

'Mum!' He burst into tears all over again.

'We're finished!' Cort said. 'You get to choose your plaster now.' And he would have left it to Ruby, but he didn't, took just that one moment to help the little boy select.

'Thanks so much. I'm sorry about before...' the mum said.

'We're sorry you've had to wait,' Ruby said.

'That nurse...' she explained. 'I know she should get her proper break. I had no right to say anything.'

'It's fine,' Cort said.

'I don't know how you do it.' She looked at Ruby, who smiled back at her. 'I don't know how you can work in this place.'

'You get used to it,' Ruby said, because it was either that or fall into the woman's arms like Adam and beg her to take her away from here.

'Take him home to bed and let him sleep, but you need to check him regularly.'

'I'll have him in with me.'

'Good. Stitches out in five days at your GP.' He went through all the head-injury instructions as Ruby found a leaflet then started to clean up.

'Cort,' Ruby said, because it was the only chance she had to do so, 'about—'

'Leave it, Ruby.' Because he just couldn't do this.

'I am sorry.'

So that made it fine, then. Mature he may be, but still it hurt and he just didn't have it in him to accept her apology as easily as that.

'You just concentrate on getting through your work.'

'And that's it?'

'What do you want, Ruby?' He glanced to the door to check no one could hear. 'You've made your feelings perfectly clear.' When she opened her mouth to dispute, Cort overrode her. 'You're right, things would never have worked out between us. I was looking for a diversion, missing Beth. We should have left it at one night.'

And he might just as well have taken a fist and pushed it into her stomach, but somehow she stayed standing.

'I don't believe you.'

'Yeah, well, given the stuff you believe in you might need to take a reality check.'

Yes he was harsh, and perhaps a bit mean, but he couldn't just stand there and accept her apology. It was far easier to push her away.

He didn't want to forgive her, because then he might have to love her, and Cort just wasn't ready for that.

CHAPTER FIFTEEN

'HERE'S to Ruby's last night!' They were all made up, sipping wine, doing each other's hair and getting ready to head down to the Stat Bar. Ruby would have given anything to be joining them and told her friends so.

'We'll take you out tomorrow,' Jess said. 'We'll have a little celebration. Just think—you'll be done!'

She would, Ruby realised.

Somehow she'd got through, not just the work but being alongside Cort. She didn't blame him for not accepting her apology, but she was beginning to realise that it had probably been her only chance to offer one. She was back at uni in a couple of weeks, then exams. There was little chance of seeing him and realisation was dawning that it wasn't just her time in Emergency that would be finally over with by morning.

'Good luck.' Tilly gave her a hug at the door.

'What about…?' Ruby's voice trailed off. She'd been over and over it with Tilly, had been over and over it with herself, and no matter what positive spin she tried to put on it, she and Cort had only known one another for two weeks, which meant not a lot of history to fight for—an elongated one-night stand that didn't stand up to the scrutiny of day.

The full moon was rising as she drove the short distance to Eastern Beaches—the same moon she'd wished on to get her through her time in Emergency, and somehow she knew that it would do its job. Come what may, she'd make it through tonight and then never have to set foot in the place again.

Strange that it made her feel like crying.

God, she hated Adam's car—no matter how she judged it, the seats were so low and she was so short that as she pulled up at boom gates, she couldn't reach to swipe her ID and had to put it in neutral, pull on the handbrake, take off her seat belt and hang out of the open car door to get it to beep. As she turned and gave the queue of cars behind her an apologetic wave, it had to be Cort's car behind hers. Cheeks burning, she promptly stalled and then jerked her way through the gates, but thankfully she found a space easily, cursing quietly to herself as she delved into the tiny boot for her massive bag that contained clothes, shoes and toiletry bag, so she could speedily change for church in the morning. Cort pulled up in the space beside her and she would have dashed off but it was Adam's car, which meant even as she turned to walk, Ruby had to turn back and check *again* that it was locked and that the handbrake was on.

For Cort, it was impossible to ignore her—aside from all that had happened, she intrigued him. What was it with the bag on her shoulder and why had she parked here?

'This is the doctors' area.' Cort saw her tense as his words reached her. 'Senior doctors.'

Ruby spun round, unsure if she was being told off. 'There's hierarchy even in the car park?'

'Especially in the car park,' Cort replied, and Ruby glanced over to see a line of cars all battling for a few spots. 'I think night staff are Area D.'

She drove so rarely it had never entered her head but, come to think of it, she vaguely remembered being given a map when she'd had her security photo taken for Emergency.

'Are you going to move it?' Cort couldn't care less whether she did or not, it was just conversation as he fell into step beside her.

'God, no,' Ruby replied. 'I'd rather face wheel clamps than Sheila's wrath if I'm late. And,' she added, 'it's not for emergencies, just to save your poor legs.'

Cort almost smiled, but falling into step with her, with anyone, came not too readily to him, but he was determined to try, to not just nod and walk on as he so often did. Cort almost admitted to himself that he missed her and if it had to end, he didn't want it to end on the sour note that had played out last night. 'How have you found the nights?'

'Awful,' Ruby admitted. 'But this is the last.'

'Oy! Wait!' Connor half ran to catch up with them and Cort deliberately chose not to make excuses as to why he was walking with Ruby, but to his surprise it was Ruby who offered a reason.

'Mr Mason was telling me I'd parked in the doctors' area.'

'You'll be shot at dawn,' Connor warned. 'Or wheel clamped.'

'Fantastic,' Ruby breathed. 'Then I'll miss out on church and Sunday dinner with my family—it's a win-win.'

'How was the traffic?' Cort asked Connor, when really he wanted to ask Ruby much more.

'Hell,' Connor said. 'All the traffic's diverted for the festival, we're going to have a shocking night—brace yourself, young Ruby,' he warned as they reached the emergency entrance.

'Already braced.' Ruby smiled, but Cort could hear the high note to her voice, could feel, even though he didn't turn his head to look, her back straighten as they walked through the waiting room. As they entered they saw two sets of police officers alongside two soon-to-be patients, and a pumping waiting room. For her last night, Emergency had turned it on and there was a temptation, a strange urge, a protectiveness almost to take her by the hand and walk her out, tell her she didn't actually need to be there.

It was the busiest she'd ever seen it. Inebriated patients lay on mattresses on the floor, every trolley was full and for once Sheila didn't seem to mind Ruby's willingness to trudge up and down to the wards to hand over patients if it freed up a cubicle. Still, when a stabbing came in, Sheila hauled her into Resus to watch as Jamelia inserted a chest drain.

'Excellent.' Cort was encouraging. Ruby could see Jamelia's confidence growing and wished hers would too.

'Can I grab Ruby to do some obs?' For once, Ruby was glad to hear Siobhan's voice, especially when Sheila agreed to release her student. 'He's bipolar, hypermanic, we're just waiting for Psych to come and admit him. Jamelia, can you come and take another look when you've got a moment?'

'Go.' Cort nodded. 'I'll stitch this.'

'Bill!' Ruby recognised the patient as soon as she opened the curtain.

'You know him?' Jamelia asked.

'I do some bank work on the psychiatric ward,' Ruby explained. 'He was in a few weeks ago.'

'How are you, Bill?' Ruby asked. 'How have you been?'

'Not good, not good, not good.' He gripped Ruby's hand as she went to wrap the blood-pressure cuff. 'This isn't, isn't, isn't…' he said. 'I'm not…' Ruby frowned as Bill struggled to explain himself. 'I'm not manic.'

'It's okay, Bill,' Ruby said, carefully checking his obs. She spoke to him some more. 'We'll take good care of you.' She turned to Jamelia. 'His blood pressure's high.'

'I know,' Jamelia said, 'but he's extremely agitated. I've just given him some diazepam. Psych shouldn't be too long.'

'Doctor, doctor, doctor,' Bill begged, but Jamelia didn't understand what he was saying.

'I'm a doctor, Bill,' Jamelia said. 'And you're going to be fine. You just need to calm down.'

'Bill's a doctor,' Ruby explained. 'That's what he's trying to tell you—and he's not normally like this.'

She'd been with him just a few weeks ago during a manic episode, and again during her psych rotation, and he'd been nothing like this. She tried to speak with Jamelia, but Jamelia didn't want a student nurse's opinion and headed off to Resus, where Cort was finishing up suturing in her chest drain.

'Have you done those obs?' Sheila called out to her slippery student. 'You should be back in here.'

'I'll be there in a moment,' Ruby said, torn with indecision, because she had told Jamelia her concerns yet Jamelia didn't seem worried.

But Ruby was.

She went back in to Bill, saw the fear in his eyes and held his hand for a moment.

'Not,' he said once, blowing out air and trying to gather the strength to say it again, spittle at the sides of his mouth and just too ill and too exhausted to state his case further. Ruby knew she had to do it for him.

It was the most nerve-racking thing she had done. Sheila was clearly busy, Connor was in with a patient, so reluctantly Ruby went to Siobhan and explained her concerns, but unfortunately Jamelia came over just as Ruby said that she wasn't sure Bill was manic.

'I've seen him during two acute episodes,' Ruby explained. 'And I really think that there's more to it.'

'Of course he's manic,' Jamelia snapped. 'He's climbing off the gurney, he thinks he's a doctor, he's clanging…'

'He's not clanging,' Ruby responded. 'And he *is* a doctor.'

Jamelia gave an eye roll and went back into Resus,

having clearly decided that Ruby had no idea what she was talking about, and Ruby waited for a shrug from Siobhan as Jamelia headed off. Instead, Siobhan was reading through his obs and calling Reception to ask them to hurry up with Bill's history.

'What's clanging?' Siobhan asked, and saw Ruby blink. 'I don't claim to know everything,' Siobhan said, and maybe Ruby was seeing things, but for a second there she thought Siobhan smiled. 'Just most things.'

'When they're manic, sometimes they do things with words, and it makes no real sense—like not, hot, cot, dot, or…just vague association. He's not doing that now, he just can't get his words out, but they're lucid words. He's trying to tell us that there's something very wrong.'

'Well, bring him over if you're worried,' Siobhan said, and she gave a sigh when Ruby just stood there. 'Ruby? Do you want to bring a patient over to Resus?'

'Yes,' Ruby finally said.

'Then I'll give you a hand.'

And Ruby got it a little bit then. It was indecision that was the enemy in this place, because even if she wasn't sure if it was the right one, as soon as she made the call, whether she turned out to be right or wrong, Siobhan, it would seem, supported her.

So they took off the brakes and wheeled Bill over. Cort was probing an abdominal wound and looked up as they came in.

'Ruby's worried about this patient,' Siobhan explained. 'He's waiting on Psych, but she's looked after him before and says this presentation is unusual for him.' Which was a far more efficient way than Ruby would have described it!

'I'll take a look in a moment,' Cort said, and frowned as he glanced at Bill, who was breathing more rapidly and was much more sweaty now. As Ruby attached him to the monitors the alarm went off loudly as the cuff inflated and blew up higher to get an accurate reading.

'Has he had bloods taken?' Cort checked, and Siobhan nodded.

'He's hypertensive. Jamelia gave him some diazepam earlier as well.'

'I'm not, not, not, not…' Bill begged, and Ruby tried to reassure him.

'We know you're not well, Bill. The doctors are sorting out what's wrong.'

'Ring the lab,' Cort called, 'and ask them to push his bloods as urgent.'

Ruby did so, only to find out that they hadn't got them yet. She looked and there they were, still sitting in the chute basket, so Ruby hurriedly sent them.

'Get Jamelia to come and take another look,' Cort called, but just as Ruby was about to, Bill let out a strange cry and before it had properly registered, she knew, just knew, that he was going to start seizing. Ruby moved quickly, lowering the head of the bed and pulling out the pillow, while Siobhan put oxygen on him as Sheila came speeding over with the cart and a worried Jamelia running in too.

'He's stopped,' Sheila said, but within seconds, even as she pulled up some medication, he was seizing again, and Cort finished up what he was doing, ripped off his gloves and came over.

'He was fine…' Jamelia said, but Cort just ignored her, giving Bill some sedatives. When he continued to seize, he told Sheila to urgently page the medical team.

Bill's blood pressure was becoming elevated and each seizure was running into the next. All Ruby could think was that he didn't deserve this.

'He said this wasn't normal for him.' Ruby heard her own voice, but apparently from the lack of response, she was the only one who did.

'Ring the lab,' Cort said. 'Tell them we need those bloods.' Ruby did so, waiting on the line as they ran some rapid blood tests and delivered the news that Bill's sodium was dangerously low.

'At least we know what we're dealing with.'

They hung some saline, and the medical team worked on him till finally his seizures were halted. But Bill was clearly very sick, and instead of the psychiatric ward he was transferred to ICU. Ruby even went with Siobhan to take him up and hand him over.

'Nice call,' Siobhan said, and gave a compliment in her own backhanded way. 'You have to go with your gut sometimes, even if you have no idea what you're basing it on…'

Though it was nice of Siobhan to say so, Ruby was incensed on her patient's behalf, annoyed at how he had been dismissed, and that anger simmered inside her all night, especially when Jamelia carried on as if nothing had happened.

It was just a horrible, busy, chaotic night, though

there was order to the chaos and, Ruby realised, even if she didn't like the bubbling anger inside her, even if resentment didn't generally suit her, it helped to be carrying some in a place like this. When a group of revellers noisily crossed all boundaries and spilled into Resus, where behind a curtain Ruby had just finished inserting a catheter, to demand when they'd be seen, it was actually Ruby who dealt with them—all five and a bit feet of her. She covered her patient, the poor woman clearly distressed by the intrusion, and Ruby ripped off her gloves and strode over to the three angry men and shooed them out. Sheila, who had been about to summon Security from the waiting room, smothered a smile and replaced the phone.

'You do not come in here!' Ruby was enraged. 'Go back down to the waiting room and when it's your turn you'll be called.'

'Ah, come on, darling…' They made a few comments about her temper and her hair and Ruby just stood her ground, told them that if they took one step further, she'd have them removed, and she meant it. Absolutely, she meant it.

'They're gone.' She went back in and reassured her patient. 'I'll go and get you some water. The doctor wants you to drink a lot.'

'You did well,' Cort said as he made himself a drink, while Ruby banged about in the kitchen where she was getting a jug of water for her patient. For a second there she thought she was about to get to say her piece, that finally the way Bill had been treated was about to be acknowledged, except Cort was talking about something else. With the drunks bursting into Resus.

'It's good to assert yourself,' Cort pushed, but still she said nothing, this mini red tornado in the kitchen, and he wanted her to talk to him, to open up to him, to treat him as she did others, so he pushed a little further. 'You're angry?'

'Yes,' Ruby said. 'I'm angry.'

'Which is fine—'

'Well, I don't like it,' Ruby said. 'I prefer enjoying my work to walking around…' She couldn't say it, couldn't let rip without criticising Jamelia and she didn't want to do that, so she just ignored him, because they'd used up all the free tokens that had come with their first night together. But Cort wouldn't let it slide, Cort wanted the ten minutes of Ruby that her friends and colleagues seemed to get.

'Walking around?' Cort continued. 'Walking around, what?'

'Angry,' Ruby said. 'Is that what it takes to survive this place?'

'For some,' Cort admitted. 'Ruby, it's okay to be angry.'

'That's a joke, coming from you.' She blasted a jug of ice with water. 'I got hurt and the one time I was angry, the one time I let it show…' She turned off the tap. 'Look what it cost me.' She turned on a smile because that was all anyone really wanted from her. '*You* carry on with crabby Cort. As soon as I'm out of here, I'll get back to being happy.'

Except she couldn't quite get there.

The place incensed her, especially when it turned out that no one had bothered to ring Psych and let them know what had happened with Bill. Imran, a psych doctor Ruby knew quite well, came down at two a.m. to admit him.

'Oh, he had a seizure,' Jamelia said. 'Hyponatraemic. He's under ICU for now.'

'Well, thanks so much for advising me,' Imran said. 'I'll get back to bed, then.' But his sarcasm was wasted on Jamelia who just moved on to her next patient.

'Busy?' Ruby asked.

'Full moon,' Imran answered, and Cort, who was on the phone, felt his jaw snap down. 'Have you got time for a drink before I head back up there?'

'I doubt we'll be getting breaks tonight.'

'I don't know how you stand the place,' Imran said, and then he saw a flash of tears in Ruby's eyes. She muttered something about not knowing how she stood it either.

'Can I steal Ruby for a drink?' Imran clearly knew Sheila. 'To compensate for my wasted journey?'

'Ten minutes,' Sheila called over, because no one would be getting a proper break tonight and Ruby clearly needed a short one. Her cheeks were burning with colour, she was tense and angry, and Sheila didn't blame her a bit—she just didn't have time to address it.

As Ruby and Imran headed off to the staffroom, Cort found something out about himself—occasionally he ground his teeth.

Ruby did feel a bit better for talking to Imran. 'What if he'd been still stuck in a cubicle when he'd had the seizure?' Ruby asked as they broke open a bar of chocolate.

'They'd have heard him,' Imran said. 'Bill's going to be fine. They'll sort him out and then he'll be back with us.'

'He's not manic.'

'Of course he's manic.' Imran laughed. 'He does this all the time.'

She closed her eyes, because it was almost impossible. There was just so much to learn, so much to take in, and three years just didn't cut it.

'You'll get there,' Imran said as they headed out to the unit. 'This sort of thing happens all the time.'

'Well, it shouldn't.'

'You'll be back with us soon,' Imran said as they walked passed Cort.

'Thank God,' Ruby muttered, and Cort rather agreed. He needed his mind to get back to work.

CHAPTER SIXTEEN

THERE was a lull about five.

The suture room had a list of patients waiting and there were some still waiting to be taken to the ward, but for a moment they sat at the nurses' station, because a break, Sheila said, was vital. Ruby glanced at the clock. Two and a half hours and her time in Emergency would be over—it couldn't come soon enough for her. Sheila had even said that given she hadn't had her dinner break, if the place was quiet, she could shower and change and be out by seven-thirty.

'Here.' Siobhan waddled in with a laden tray and though Ruby had fully intended to have a strong black coffee with three sugars, she was so touched that Siobhan had filled her little white teapot, it seemed churlish not to drink it, so though she yearned for a hit of caffeine, Ruby sipped on dandelion leaves and chamomile instead.

'He's doing better.' Jamelia came off the phone and smiled over at Ruby, who had no idea who she was talking about. 'Bill,' Jamelia said. 'They're transferring him to a medical ward now.' Then Ruby blinked as Jamelia continued. 'It's good you knew him. I listened too much to his family,' Jamelia admitted. 'They said this is how he got when he came off his medication…'

'He still needed a proper work-up before he was referred to Psych,' Cort broke in, neither judgmental nor angry, just matter-of-fact. 'When a patient's manic, they don't always think to eat and drink properly,' Cort said, 'or they get grandiose and think they can survive on nothing, or, like Bill, start training for a marathon. You don't just label someone as psych till you've done a full work-up.'

He didn't labour the point, in fact no one did, they just spoke about it for a little while, and Sheila regaled them with a few stories from the past. For Ruby it was a revelation and she started to get the place a bit better. Saw that no one was blaming—instead they were teaching and learning.

'Have you heard of clanging, Sheila?' Siobhan said, adding about four sugars to her coffee. Ruby would have killed for a taste. It turned out Sheila hadn't heard the term and they had a bit of fun explaining. Ruby started to see that you were allowed to not know things, you just had to be honest enough to admit it, and it wasn't about scoring points or pulling rank, it was about a group of minds that, when pooled, were formidable.

And finally, when the emergency phone shrilled, whether it was the chamomile or she was just numb from the experience of Emergency, Ruby didn't jolt on her stool when it went off.

If anyone seemed stressed, it was Sheila.

'Yuk!' Sheila put down the phone and pulled a face. 'We've got a penetrating eye injury coming in…' She gave a shudder. 'Siobhan, you'll have to deal with it.' She glanced at Ruby, who couldn't hide her surprise at Sheila's reaction. 'We've all got our things—even me,' Sheila said. 'Mine's eyes. Can't go near them.'

'What's yours, Siobhan?' Sheila asked.

'Dunno.' Siobhan shrugged. 'I guess old people.'

'What?' Sheila grinned. 'You can't go near them?'

'No, they just get to me. Like that woman the other day, moaning about her child not being seen while I was sitting eating—she moaned loudly enough and got straight to the top of the queue and there was poor old Tom who'd been waiting to be stitched since we came on duty and because he's old…' She gave a shrug. 'It just gets to me, I guess.'

Ruby blinked because, even if it had been handled, in Ruby's eyes, poorly, there was a reason—a side to the hard-nosed Siobhan she had never seen. Even Cort looked up in surprise.

'What about you, Cort?' Siobhan asked. 'And don't say kids, because everyone has a thing when a sick kid's brought in.'

He was about to shrug, to say nothing, to get up and walk outside and get some fresh air while they awaited the arrival of the ambulance, but then Cort realised that was what he always did. He closed up and walked off and just dealt with it in his own way, and it wasn't perhaps the best way. He wanted to be part of the solution, wanted more of a team, and he realised that meant taking part on a level that he never had.

'Prolonged resuscitations,' he said. 'I can't stand them!'

'You can't, can you?' Sheila did a double-take as re-alisation hit. 'You get all worked up…comejack booting in and taking over.'

'Yeah, well, I'm working on it,' Cort said. 'My wife was in a car accident, they worked on her for way too long, and she was left with an acquired brain injury…'

'Your wife?' Sheila's face paled and Ruby just sat there quietly and could not have been more proud of him.

'My late wife,' Cort said, and then stood. 'So, yes, I get a bit tense around them, but now you know why.' He saw the flash of blue light come in through the dark window and although he'd missed his chance for fresh air, he was quietly relieved that he'd cleared the air inside a touch, 'Let's see how this guy is.'

It turned out eyes weren't one of Ruby's *things*.

Which meant she didn't mind them.

She was able to talk to the patient and reassure him as Cort carefully assessed, and it was a too serious injury for a general hospital so Ruby sat and monitored him, because he was heavily sedated, as they waited for an ambulance to transfer him to the eye hospital. 'Where did you slip off to?' Ruby grinned, walking back from the ambulance foyer as Sheila returned from taking the last patient to the ward. Connor had agreed to do the escort as Ruby had to get away on time and, anyway, as a student she wasn't able to provide escort.

'Has he gone?' Sheila asked, and Ruby nodded.

'Why don't you go now?' Sheila said. 'It's nearly seven—have your shower and you can be out of here on time.'

'Are you sure?'

'I think you've earned it.'

She smiled all the way to the locker rooms and chatted for a moment to some of the day staff that were dribbling in, but only when she tucked her hair into a shower cap and turned on the taps full blast did she let the tears flow, because that, Ruby had realised, was what this place did to her. It brought every carefully checked emotion right up to the surface, made her confront things, think of things, see things she'd really rather not—and even if the staff did annoy her, even if they were cliquey and rude, now she understood why. And she loved them, every bitchy, horrible one of them.

And now she had to go out there and say goodbye to them, and say goodbye to Cort too—so she cried, where no one could hear her, because it was certainly better out than in, especially as she had to go now and see her family, and heaven forbid she go there all knotty and tense.

Because then she might just say something, speak a little of her mind.

And, as she'd recently found out, that didn't go down well.

Ruby dried and dressed in neutral clothes and brushed her hair till it was straight and shiny. She put on some neutral make-up and instead of putting on bangles and earrings she put her smile back on and headed back out there.

'Where are you off to all dolled up?' Sheila asked, and then looked again. 'Or rather all dolled down?'

'Church.'

Cort glanced up and though, of course, it was Ruby, it wasn't.

She was in a neat brown skirt, with flat brown closed-toe sandals and a neat cream top. Her hair was down and brushed and she was neither prim nor plain. In fact, she looked gorgeous. The only way he could explain it was as if she'd been de-Ruby'd. And he could tell too, just as he had on the first night, that she'd been crying. It was almost indecipherable, she'd put on make-up and her glassy eyes could be from exhaustion, but he knew there was more to it than that.

'At seven-thirty in the morning?' Sheila frowned.

'I'm going with my parents.' Ruby grinned. 'They live out at Whale Beach, which is a good hour away. I said I'd meet them there.'

'You've been working all night,' Sheila pointed out. 'Are you sure you're okay to drive?'

'I'm fine.' Ruby gave a large eye roll as she took a seat on a stool. 'I haven't been to see them for a few weeks. I didn't want to make excuses again.'

'Well, enjoy your Sunday off.'

'I doubt it.' Ruby grimaced. 'A lovely lamb roast…' She put two fingers to her mouth. 'I can't wait!'

'You can't police the world.' Sheila laughed, because she had a daughter who was almost as flaky as this student. 'Let them enjoy their dinner without judging them.'

'Let them?' Ruby swung down her legs from the stool. 'I wish they'd let me. I have to eat the thing. They don't get that if they just let me have vegetables, I'd go and visit them more…'

'You eat it?' Cort frowned, because she had her own fridge, for goodness' sake. She'd guilt-tripped him out of steak and a bacon sandwich, and yet when it suited her, away went her principles.

'They make you eat it?' Sheila was intrigued. 'I'd have to tie Lila down.' Her voice trailed off because she could see Ruby was blushing and a bit uncomfortable.

'They don't make me,' Ruby said. 'It's just…' she gave a tight shrug '…easier. Anyway, I just wanted to say thank you for everything, Sheila.'

'Thank you,' Sheila said. 'We've enjoyed having you. We have!' Sheila smiled when Ruby gave her a disbelieving look. 'I love a challenge. We might see you back here when you're qualified,' Sheila teased.

'Not a chance.' Ruby grinned. 'But I have learnt a lot,' she admitted. 'I really have.'

'I'll see you on…Tuesday, is it? For your final assessment. But don't lose any sleep worrying about it.'

'Don't mention sleep!' Ruby said, and waved. She wanted to say something to Cort but he didn't look up because, as per his instruction, she was just another student.

Easier.

He sat there long after he'd finished writing, blankly staring at his notes, and that word replayed over and over in his head.

Easier to drive for an hour and do family duty after three consecutive nights working.

Easier to dress not as herself.

Easier to eat a roast when it went against every principle she had.

Easier to be happy than to create any waves.

Just stuff down your emotions so *they* don't have to deal with them.

He could see her father in front of him ten years ago—forceps hurled across Theatre and the angry, bullying ways that all the staff tolerated because it was Gregory Carmichael's way.

And he remembered, too, finding a nurse in floods of tears in the coffee room, then blowing her nose and heading back out there, because, well, that's what they all did.

He got her then, got what it might have been like to be the one Gregory was going to sort out.

There was nothing easy about sitting there thinking of her driving that sleek sports car with no sleep and a bellyful of anger, and he wanted to speak to her, to accept her apology and to apologise himself.

'Well, we'll have the next lot of students on Monday,' Sheila said. 'That's it, though, for that lot.'

Was that Sheila's way of letting him know that the rules didn't apply now?

He should go home to bed, Cort decided, not give in to feelings that could probably be put down to lack of sleep. He should wait and see how he felt in a few hours, with a much clearer head.

Yes, indecision was the enemy in this place, and Cort was filled with it now, because he should leave it there, just let things lie, because there was no casual with Ruby, no hope of one night, or two or three—he was thinking of a future and it was way too soon after Beth to be thinking like that.

Anyway, he didn't even know her number to ring her.

He went round to the kitchen and there was her teapot with 'Ruby' written in red and he thought of all she'd put up with, all she'd got through, and he wished he could have had the guts to have been there for her more.

'She's forgotten her teapot.' Sheila walked in and followed where Cort's gaze lingered. 'She'd forget her head, that one. I'll ring her and remind her to pick it up on Tuesday—we've got enough clutter in here as it is.' She opened the off-duty book and pulled out her phone, but Siobhan came in yawning and asking for someone to check drugs, and Sheila did what she never did and left the off-duty book lying there open. It couldn't have been deliberate but Cort, like a guilty schoolboy, wrote a student nurse's number down and actually didn't give too much thought to what would happen if he was caught, or what others would say or think.

All he cared about was Ruby.

He tried her mobile, but if she was driving it was sensible that she didn't pick up, and later when he arrived home and still it went straight to voicemail, he told himself she was in church, so naturally it would be switched off, but there was this terrible dread that woke him around lunchtime—a horrible feeling that he'd left it too late.

He looked over at the picture of Beth, which had been reinstated, and told himself that God wouldn't be that cruel, that two women he loved wouldn't be lost in that way.

Guilt swept right through him, because he was looking at Beth and admitting he loved Ruby as well.

Then you'd better do something about it, Beth's eyes said, because, unlike Ruby, Beth was practical.

It's too soon, Cort implored, but Beth just stared back from a place where time had a different meaning.

He rang again and then again when it was after five, and there was still no answer. And then, even if her phone was off because she was asleep, he just had to know for sure, so he gave in and drove to Hill Street and parked a little way down from the house and waited for the car that was too big and too fast to come round the corner or down the hill, so that he could drive off reassured and could go back to bed and stop worrying. Except it didn't appear.

He could not stand it if anything had happened to her.

Could not go through it again.

Except he was.

He was going through it this very moment, imagining all sorts of things, when she might well be in bed, sleeping, Cort thought. One of her friends might have taken the car out, but he simply had to know—so out onto the street he went, waved to the old lady in the next house when she waved at him, opened the squeaking gate, walked up the garden path and stood on the veranda where he had first kissed Ruby and then, because he had to, he knocked on the door.

'Is Ruby here?' He tried to sound casual.

'No,' Tilly said.

'Do you know when she'll be back?'

'I'm not sure…' And he realised that she was worried too. 'I thought she'd be back a while ago, we were going to throw her a little party…for finishing.'

'She said she was going for lunch at her parents'.' Cort attempted rational. 'Maybe she stayed on there, or she just fell asleep.'

'I just rang her mum and she left ages ago. Her mum sounded upset. I think they might have had a row.' Tilly held open the door. 'Come in if you want.'

'It's okay…' He was about to decline and what? Sit in his car or go home and pace. But he wanted to be with them because they loved her too. For a second Cort closed his eyes, because it was the second time today he'd said it to himself and he said it again for a third time. It was love, that was what it was—too soon, too fast, too much perhaps, but that it was love he was completely certain. 'Thanks,' he said, and stepped into the house that was becoming familiar, and there they all were at the table, the people who loved and cared for her. Feeling a little bit awkward, Cort sat down and joined them.

'We really should know better by now than to worry about her,' Jess said by way of greeting. 'She's always wandering off.' She pointed to a large calendar. 'She's the red one. We know her shifts better than Ruby does. We're always having to dash down to the beach to remind her she's on a late or got a lecture…'

'I might go down to the beach,' Cort offered. 'Take a look.'

'I just went,' Ellie said.

It was a very strange three hours—lots of idle small talk, all pretending not to be sick with worry, and Cort sitting there as if he just happened to have stopped by. Eventually, Cort cracked and rang work to see if they needed him and, oh, so casually asked to go through the admission list, just to see what had come in.

'Nope.'

'Told you,' Ellie said, just back from the beach for the third time.

'There are loads of hospitals,' Tilly snapped, which Cort guessed was unusual for her. 'I'll make a drink.'

'I'll make this one,' Cort offered, because they must have made him twenty. He found the tea bags and mugs and sugar okay, but when he went to the fridge to get some milk, they stopped him.

'Not that one,' Ellie said. 'That's Ruby's fridge.'

'Unless you want rice milk with your tea.' Jess rolled her eyes. 'She has her own fridge so she doesn't get depressed seeing our sausages and things. You do know what you're taking on?'

'Not really,' Cort admitted, but he hoped he'd get to find out.

He was about to suggest that they ring the police, but what could they say? That a twenty-three-year old wasn't home by nine? And then there was the slam of the front door and everyone looked at each other as a cheery call came from the hall.

'I need wine!'

They all just looked at Ruby as she burst into the kitchen. 'What?'

'Where have you been?' Tilly asked in a voice that was just a little bit shaky and not, Cort guess, just from relief.

'At the beach.'

'I looked on the beach,' Ellie said. 'I've been three times and you weren't there.'

'I went to one near my parents' and fell asleep. We had a bit of an argument,' Ruby admitted.

'We've been ringing and ringing you,' Tilly said.

'We've all been worried, Ruby.' It was the first time Cort had spoken, the first words he could manage because the relief that had flooded him was so physical, it had taken a while to find a shade of a normal voice.

'Why are you here?' Ruby blinked in surprise.

'Because I was worried about you.'

Ruby looked at the table, saw the cards and the congratulations cake and the sparkling wine surrounded by mug after mug of tea, and realised she'd missed her own little party. 'I'm sorry, guys. I never even thought.' She went into her bag for her phone. 'It's dead… I just…I didn't want to come home in the mood I was in. I was…' Still she didn't say it and he truly saw then just how guarded she was with her emotions. Happy Ruby was the one she chose to show to the world. 'I just wanted some space. I'm fine now.'

'Fair enough,' Tilly said.

'What was the row about?' Jess asked, but Ruby just shrugged.

'Nothing.'

'Nothing?' Jess frowned.

'It was about something so unbelievably tiny...' Ruby shook her head. 'I haven't got the energy to go into it.'

'Well, we're going down to the Stat Bar—we're the ones who need wine. Are you two coming?'

Ruby glanced at Cort. 'No.' She shook her head. 'Maybe later...' As her housemates walked out, she apologised again. 'I really am sorry. I had no idea you'd all be so worried.'

'It's us overeating.' Tilly hugged her. 'But ring next time you go walkabout.'

She guessed she hadn't got away with it that easily because once alone she looked at Cort and his face was white. She knew that she'd scared him and people didn't get scared if they didn't care.

'I was about to go and get the worry dolls!' He was trying to make a joke, but he didn't have to try with Ruby. 'Don't ever do that again.'

'Why are you here?'

'You left your teapot at work.'

'Cort?'

'Because I was worried about you, because you were upset and angry when you left.'

'I wasn't.'

'Yes, Ruby, you were. And you shouldn't have been driving.'

She opened her mouth to argue then closed it because, yes, he was right, she really shouldn't have been driving. Halfway there the tears had started again and halfway home she'd nearly rear-ended someone, which was why she'd pulled over.

'I had no choice but to go. You don't know what they're like.'

'You could have come back here—got one of your friends to drive and come with you.'

'I didn't want to rot up their day.'

'Well, you did,' Cort said. 'You worried them sick. What was the row about? And don't say nothing.'

Ruby shrugged. 'It was stupid.'

'Tell me.'

'I don't want to talk about it.'

'Why?'

'Because it just winds me up.'

'So,' Cort said, and opened the bubbles that her friends had had waiting. 'Get wound up.' He poured himself a glass and took a seat and Ruby took a mouthful of wine and felt her face burn, not from the wine or lack of sleep but from the stupid row that had hurt so much, from the wave her tiny ripple had made.

'Mum always does a massive lunch. I had cauliflower cheese, pumpkin, roast potatoes and peas, and I thought about what Sheila said about her daughter, and I guess I'd just had a busy night and dealt with all those things, and...' It was beyond pathetic, embarrassing really to repeat it, but he just sat there patiently as she squirmed in her seat and then she came out and said it. 'I didn't have any meat or gravy...' She closed her eyes. 'It doesn't matter.'

'It does.'

It did.

'I just got sick of pretending! It doesn't make him happy anyway. Even if I'd eaten the whole thing, he'd still have something to complain about. I was just trying to be myself…' She shook her head in frustration. 'Now poor Mum's in tears, he's in a filthy mood…. I should have just eaten it…'

'And smiled?' Cort asked, and after a moment Ruby nodded.

'I just want to be myself,' Ruby said, 'except they don't seem to like her very much.'

'Then they don't know what they're missing,' Cort said. And he meant it, because even if he didn't agree with everything, there was nothing about her he would change.

'I try so hard to just blend in, to just…'

'Maybe stop trying.'

'I can't,' Ruby said.

'Okay,' Cort said, and wondered how he'd go, sitting beside her, watching her gag at dinner, and not be able to step in, but he would, if it made things easier, if she ever let him be there for him, if she could ever get past what he'd done.

'I'm sorry that I didn't tell you about Beth,' Cort said. 'You had every right to be angry—to be furious, in fact.'

'No I didn't—I had no right to judge, about how soon… I shouldn't have rushed in. I know everyone is different.'

'Ruby, you had every right,' Cort said, 'because I should have told you that night when I brought you back to my home. I just didn't want to burden you with it all, not till you were through with Emergency. Beth was sick for years and in all that time I couldn't look at anyone else. Every day off was spent at the nursing home. I was married,' Cort said. 'Even if Beth didn't recognise me, I still wanted to do the right thing by her.'

Ruby nodded.

'And I wasn't embarrassed by her. I didn't want visitors or people to see her because I was embarrassed *for* her,' Cort said. 'I didn't want anyone to remember her like that and I still try not to. She was the cleverest, smartest person I've ever met, and there was hardly any of that left. She would have loathed to be seen like that.

'A month after she died, I end up in a bar, and, yep, you were supposed to be a one-night stand. It just never felt like that at the time, or after…'

It hadn't.

Not once had she felt like a temporary solution.

'You're stuck with me, Ruby,' Cort said, and she smiled. 'Even if I am too old and staid…'

She winced at her own words. 'I didn't mean those things.'

'They're all true. I just don't want it to rub off on you.'

'It won't,' Ruby promised.

'I want you to be you.'

'I will be,' Ruby said. 'And you're not boring. You could never be boring.'

'Oh I am—and happily so,' Cort said, thinking about his wardrobe of dark suits and shoes and lack of tattoos or body piercings and smudge sticks and a complete absence of alternative thinking.

'I think we should keep things quiet, though.' She felt

him tense. 'We know how serious we are, I just don't think it would be fair to Beth. Let's just lie low together for a year or so…'

He was more grateful than she could ever know.

Part of him wanted to shout it from the rooftops and to hell with everyone, to tell the world about them, and yet there was loyalty there to Beth that she recognised, promoted, and it only confirmed that loving her was right.

'Someone might come in,' Cort said. As always with Ruby, their kiss was growing out of hand.

'They'll be gone for ages,' Ruby breathed. 'Hang your tie on the door.'

And, boring or not, he was not going to risk an impromptu party descending on Hill Street.

'Get dressed,' Cort said, because he wanted to be completely alone with her.

'I am dressed,' Ruby grumbled, but he took her to her bedroom and she put on her jewels and the clothes that were her, put back all the things that were Ruby, just so he could have the pleasure of taking them off later.

'Text Tilly,' Cort said as they drove past the Stat Bar towards his flat, the bay lit up by a huge moon, music pumping from the bars, and everything right with the world.

'She'll know where I am,' Ruby started, but, yes, given the worry she'd caused today, it would be only fair.

So she texted her friend, told her not to worry if she wasn't home till late tomorrow, that she was at Cort's.

Two minutes later her phone bleeped and Ruby glanced at it and gave a smile.

'What did she say?'

'I'm not telling.'

'What did she say?' Cort grinned.

'That she wants all the details on my return.'

'She'd better not get them,' Cort said, and they drove along the bay and once at his flat he turned off his phone, because that was what he would do now, and Ruby duly switched off hers.

'It's like the start of an exam,' Ruby said, 'when they tell you to switch off your mobiles.'

'Let's find out what you've learnt.' Cort smiled and she was about to make a joke, to smile and dance for him, but she was suddenly serious, because with Cort she could be.

'That you love me.' She couldn't believe she'd be so bold, just to say it.

'Correct.'

'That I love you.' Nor could she believe that she could say that so readily either, but Cort just nodded.

'Correct,' Cort said, and pulled her to him. 'Which, come what may, that we love each other is all we really need to know.'

EPILOGUE

IF YOU were lucky, life went on.

Sheila walked into the changing room before her late shift a few weeks later and tried not to roll her eyes at the sight of a new set of nursing students, some nervous, some arrogant, all about to step right into the front line for the very first time, all naïve about how they would cope.

'Lucky thing!' a loud one said. 'I wouldn't mind being in Bali.'

'I've asked her to bring me back a sarong,' another loud one said. 'But knowing Ruby she'll forget.'

Sheila smiled quietly as she headed to the staffroom, because Bali was so Ruby. She could see her now, drifting along the beach in a sarong or at the markets choosing jewellery, or just lying by a pool, soaking in the sun, knowing she'd qualified and could now follow her heart and study her beloved mental health.

'Postcard from Cort,' Doug said, and handed it to Sheila for a quick read, but her eyes lingered on the words for just a moment longer than they would normally.

Now that they all knew what he'd been through,

Doug hadn't hesitated when Cort had asked for a couple of weeks' unpaid leave—he needed a holiday, he'd explained.

A *real* holiday, for the first time in many, many years. Maybe Fiji, perhaps Bali. And on real holidays, a postcard was expected in a place like Emergency, completely necessary, in fact, because it brought a little bit of sun to the workers, and a little smile to the sender when they glanced up at the cork board in the staffroom weeks and months later. A nice postcard of a stunning view from a stunning luxury hotel in Bali because, Sheila had a feeling, Cort had used the supplied hotel postcards, rather than exert himself by shopping for one.

Cort, Sheila was sure, was rather too busy.

> *Thinking of you all as little as I can.*
> *Clear the board for me* ☺
> *Cort*

And she couldn't be sure, but she almost was. Of course half the students were whooping it up in Bali now, it was a rite of passage almost, and just because Cort Mason happened to be there too…

'Good for him.' Sheila smiled. 'He needed a break.'

It was more than a break, it was a completely new start.

He could hear the click-clack of her hair beads as Ruby, on the second-last day of their holiday, finally wrote her postcards—Cort's had long since been posted.

She'd had her hair beaded the first day they'd arrived and her feet and hands were adorned with henna tattoos and her pale skin was now golden brown. And every day he knew her a little bit more.

'What can I put?' Ruby asked as Cort lay on a sunbed, reading the English papers.

'Who's this one for?'

'Mum and Dad.' Ruby sighed. 'I've said the weather's nice, that the hotel is lovely…' And Cort only wished they could see how much they were missing out on, by censoring their relationship with her. 'And I've written really big…' She added something else then scribbled her name, then got on with the next one, to her house-mates, which would be easy.

Except Cort was right. When it was 'the one', the 'real one', you didn't share the details quite so much. He wasn't on the list on the fridge and there were things that only they two knew.

See you when I'm looking at you x

She wrote that because they were real friends and, as she was working out, she didn't have to pretend to them, didn't have to write about the beach or food or weather. She'd tell them all her news in her own good time.

'I need a rest,' Ruby said, because writing postcards was exhausting work. She turned her head to where Cort now dozed beside her on the sumptuous white lounger. They were a million miles away from drama and she was so relaxed it was an effort to put out a hand

and lift a straw to her mouth. 'I'm exhausted, Cort. I haven't even got the energy to put on some more sun block.'

'I'll put some on for you.' Cort said without opening his eyes, but even if his face didn't twitch, inside he was smiling, because that was how she made him feel.

For Ruby it was different, because this morning when her mother had rung, instead of shrugging her shoulders and smiling and carrying on, she'd actually told him just how knotted up she felt inside, how she could feel the disapproval behind every word, and the world hadn't stopped when she'd voiced her feelings. Cort hadn't crumpled in a heap or accused her of ruining their holiday. Instead, he'd just rubbed her knotted shoulders and let her brood for a little while, because Ruby was finding out she was allowed to be miserable at times.

'Here…' He played the game, sat up and opened the tube.

'I'm too tired to sunbathe,' Ruby grumbled. 'I need a *proper* rest.'

'In bed?' Cort solemnly checked.

'I think so.' Ruby nodded.

She was so tired that he had to peel off her bikini and pull back the sheets and turn on the fan, but she soon perked up.

'I'm feeling better already,' Ruby said, in the cool, dark room with Cort stretched out beside her.

'I thought you might be.'

'How did I get so lucky?' Ruby asked, when Cort was just thinking the same thing.

And then it was just about the two of them, and the lovely click clack of her beads as they made love, followed by the sinking feeling that in one more sleep their holiday would be over, but excitement too at the thought of the real world, with the other one there.

They had dinner on their deck the last night—Cort finally relenting and wearing 'just this once' the sarong Ruby had bought him, and finding it was surprisingly comfortable. Or was it just the company? Sitting there drinking cocktails and eating seafood, while Ruby ate from a huge selection of fruit kebabs. The waiters were waiting, the candles were hissing as one by one they fizzled out, and she didn't want her holiday to end, though she was excited about starting her mental health nurse course and seeing her friends.

'It's been wonderful,' Ruby said, when the sun had long since dipped down over the horizon and the only red glow was from her shoulders.

The waiters took the trays and said goodnight and if she and Cort went to bed then it would be morning and she didn't want it to be, didn't want the magic they'd found to end, quietly wondering every now and then if their relationship would still stand up when they were back in the real world.

'How was your seafood?' Ruby asked.

'Fantastic,' Cort said, then added, 'I won't give up meat.' Because he'd be himself too.

'I'll never ask you to.'

'I'll be eating a lot at work and stopping off—'

'Fine.' Now the waiters were gone she moved onto his lap, kissed his mouth. 'You can do what you like.'

'What about kids?'

'What about them?' Ruby asked, kissing his mouth and running her hands over his lovely brown shoulders. Then she paused because she wasn't sure she was hearing things right.

'Our kids.'

'They'll be beautiful…'

'I meant about food.'

'They can have meat any time you buy it,' Ruby was magnanimous given it was a fantasy. 'And cook it and feed them and wash up afterwards—every night if you want.'

He got up and walked to their villa and Ruby sat and watched as he walked back. He was carrying a thick velvet box and she knew then it wasn't a fantasy, that this was their future they were discussing, and that it was real and would last the scrutiny of day.

'It's white gold,' Cort said, when she opened it. 'I thought it would blend in…'

It would never blend in to Ruby, it was completely and utterly exquisite—a heavy necklace she could wear every day, and only the knowing would see that it wasn't glass in the centre but a deep red ruby, with purple hues when she held it up to the moon, and that the jumble of knots that held it was actually an *R* and a *C* and, yes, if asked, she could say the C was for her surname, but as she slipped it on, it was Cort who rested just above her heart.

'There's a matching ring to follow.' He kissed the back of her neck as her body adjusted to the necklace's new weight, as the cool metal blended till it matched the temperature of her skin, but still she could feel it, their names set in stone, or rather a stone set in their names, and Ruby knew that together was their future.

'There's an M there too,' Cort said, and Ruby traced it with her fingers. 'It stands for Mason—one day when you're ready—that's if marriage isn't too conventional for you?'

'I could think of nothing nicer,' Ruby said, and took his hand when he asked her to dance, even though there was no music.

It didn't matter.

Both of them could hear it.

* * * * *

SURVIVAL GUIDE TO DATING YOUR BOSS

FIONA McARTHUR

Mother to five sons, **Fiona McArthur** is an Australian midwife who loves to write. Mills & Boon® Medical Romance™ gives Fiona the scope to write about all the wonderful aspects of adventure, romance, medicine and midwifery that she feels so passionate about—as well as an excuse to travel! Now that her boys are older, Fiona and her husband Ian are off to meet new people, see new places and have wonderful adventures. Fiona's website is at www.fionamcarthur.com.

To all the fabulous memories I have of Coogee, the friends that made it so, and my husband, who smiled when I flew off for a week here and there.

CHAPTER ONE

TILLY loved Fridays. A leisurely walk down the hill
from the hospital after her last shift before days off, that
first salty sniff of the ocean at the end of Hill Street,
and the bonus of Mrs Bennett, immaculately made up
on her front porch as she waited for her girlfriends to
arrive for Friday afternoon tea.

Tilly adored Mrs Bennett and her friends. Once
famous sopranos in chic dresses, designer shoes and
such lovely smiles, these ladies made Tilly believe in
life getting better and better.

And they never mentioned men. She really liked that.

She couldn't wait to lift her window at the back of the
house and hear the soaring notes of Verdi and Puccini
from the porch at the back of Mrs Bennett's house—it
always made her smile.

Tilly wondered if Mrs Bennett pulled her window
shut when Tilly and her friends had their more rowdy
parties.

Maybe she was strange to prefer the company of
older ladies to boys her own age but risking your heart

to a fickle man in the scramble to find 'the one' seemed much more insane to Tilly. Of course, she'd been a slow learner with *two* bad experiences in twelve months until Ruby had pointed out her 'pattern of disaster'.

Older men. She'd always been attracted by the big boys in senior school while she'd been a junior, then those in university while she'd been a senior, and now those who were out of their twenties when she'd just reached them. Searching for approval from the father she'd never known perhaps? That's what Ruby said.

Tilly sighed. Boys her age just seemed a little…insubstantial. She would just stay away from them completely.

The waft of real scones and Mrs B.'s Sydney Royal Easter Show winning marble cake dissipated the tendrils of regret and Tilly shook herself. It was Friday. Yay!

'Afternoon, Mrs B.,' Tilly called as she approached.

'Matilda. Lovely to see you.'

'Is that window sticking again?' Tilly drew level and Mrs Bennett smiled. 'No. I think you've cured it this time, dear. There's another one just starting to squeak and I'll let you know when it gets bad.'

More practice. Excellent. Tilly's last infatuation had been with a mature carpenter who'd turned out to be a secretly engaged control freak who liked to keep several women dancing off the end of his workman's belt. She was determined to never need his skills again. Just like the interior decorator who'd had so many rules and preferences on her behaviour and had then turned out to be married.

'No problem.' Tilly glanced up at the two bay windows, one each side of the veranda, and noted the one only a quarter pushed up. 'Girls coming soon?'

Mrs Bennett glanced at her watch. 'Any time now. I'll save you a scone.'

'Say hello for me.' Tilly swung open her gate and mounted the tiled steps. Home. And not a man in sight. Good.

Seventy-One Hill Street stood tall and thin with a decrepit Gothic air in need of even more TLC than Mrs Bennett's house.

Those tall eaves, all four bedrooms at the back upstairs and the main bedroom downstairs that belonged to the absent owner, could do with a good strip and paint. Tilly decided she might have a go in her holidays.

It was a real party house. The three other girls were the sisters Tilly had never had. She couldn't imagine life without their chaos and warmth and the fun they brought to out-of-work hours.

Tilly smiled to herself as she thought more about the girls. There was Ruby, a mental health nurse who didn't appear nearly as chaotic now she'd found Cort, a senior emergency registrar from the hospital they all worked at.

Tilly's need to provide a willing ear, and the occasional emergency alcohol, had decreased exponentially the longer Ruby and Cort had been together.

Ellie, an orphan, spent most of the week in sterile

operating theatres, but still managed to regularly fall in and out of love, searching for Mr Right to be the father of her longed-for family.

While Jess, children's nurse at Eastern Beaches, broke her heart every time Ruby's gorgeous brother, and incidentally their landlord, flew in from Operation New Faces with a willowy brunette or blonde on his arm.

Funny how her flatmates gave her plenty of scope for that thwarted older-sister tendency she could finally admit she had.

Then there was her job. Tilly ran up the stairs and threw her bag on the purple quilt cover on her bed. Tilly loved being a midwife.

Women were incredible, babies so instinctually amazing, and she could mother the mothers to her heart's content while they mothered their babies.

That's what she told Mrs Bennett later in the afternoon. They were clearing up after the girls had gone. Tilly's singing lessons by osmosis seemed to be working and she and Mrs Bennett were trilling away in the kitchen when the conversation came around to men.

'To sing that aria you need to be able to sing the love.' Mrs Bennett never joked about her music.

Tilly sighed. 'Then I'll probably never be good at it.'

'Of course you will.' Mrs Bennett's finger pointed skywards to the future. 'One day you'll find your man. You can't go on forever being single.'

Tilly laughed. 'You are. You're happy.'

Mrs Bennett twinkled. 'I'm certainly content. But

in a different way from when I was married to the love of my life.' She looked at Tilly. 'You can't miss out on that.'

Tilly shrugged. 'I always seem to go for the wrong guys. Seriously, I've nothing against men as friends but after the last two I guess I'm not really geared to be answerable to a man.'

Mrs Bennett fixed her with a stern look. 'They were too old for you, dear. And they lied.'

'You're right. That's what Ruby said. But look what falling for men does to my girlfriends. Even my mother was another casualty. I'm going to stay the sensible one cruising as a single woman for a few years. Travel the world. There's a lot I want to do and it's much less stressful.'

'Very wise,' said Mrs Bennett, and she smiled.

On Sunday morning, when Tilly caught a glimpse over the fence of a tall, black-haired stranger lurking around Mrs B.'s back window, her heart jumped at the recognition of danger.

She glanced back at her own house but the other girls were out and not due back for a while.

Her hand slid up to rest on her chest, ridiculous thought he'd hear her heartbeat, but for the moment it was up to her—someone had to protect Mrs Bennett.

Dry mouthed, she glanced around for a weapon, something, anything for protection, and then she saw it. Tilly's fingers closed around the pointed red beanie hat of the small but stalwart garden gnome at her feet and she eased him out from the damp earth under the hydrangea. The cold concrete sat heavily in her hand.

She chewed her lip. She really didn't want to maim the man, just slow him down a bit so he couldn't get away before the police arrived. With her other hand she flipped her phone and dialled emergency. At least she had a back-up plan.

Mrs B.'s ground-floor window screeched in protest and the material of the man's T-shirt stretched across his broad back as he tried to ease the window up quietly. A tall, well-built man should be throwing bricks on a truck for a living, not trying to rob defenceless old ladies. Tilly refused to be distracted by the tug of nervous suggestion that flight might be a better option than fight, judging by the ripple of musculature under the thin fabric.

He was trying to get into the house and Mrs Bennett was in there. Tilly felt a swell of pure rage surge with a helpful dose of adrenalin and she heaved the gnome with a straight-arm throw over the fence towards the backs of his legs. The gnome flew horizontally like an avenging angel and took out both backs of his knees in one blow.

Because the burglar had stretched up, his legs were locked and the muscles contracted with the blow.

Tilly stifled a nervous laugh when Goliath sat awkwardly back on the wet grass on top of the gnome and swore loudly.

Great job, Tilly congratulated the gnome, and backed back around the side of her house out of sight as she flicked the damp earth off her hand. She couldn't help the big grin on her face and the hormones rushed around her body until she fanned her face with her phone for relief.

The police call centre chattered and her hand froze as she remembered. She brought the phone to her lips and murmured quietly. 'Yes, I'm Matilda McPherson. I'd like to report a burglar at 73 Hill Street, Coogee. Mrs Bennett's backyard.'

'What the hell do you think you're doing? I'm fixing the window, not breaking in.' Like an avenging archangel the man had found her and his dark blue eyes blazed. 'I'm her nephew.'

He reached his long arm out, snatched the phone, threw it on the ground and for one horrible moment Tilly thought he was going to stamp on it.

Instead he drew an enormous breath, which incidentally did amazing things to the ripples under the front of his T-shirt, and glared at her with the most virulent disgust and even loathing.

Shame, that, a tiny, impressed voice whispered as Tilly quaked just a little at his ferocity.

Now she could see his face it wasn't the face of a criminal. He was very angry but he wasn't going to physically assault her. She didn't know how she knew that but despite Tilly's brain chanting 'Good time to leave' in an insistent whisper, and despite the thumping in her chest that agreed in rhythmic beat with her brain, she couldn't allow him the satisfaction of thinking he intimidated her.

Before she could say anything he ground out, 'I should sue you for assault.'

Yep. Daunting up close, especially with steam coming out of his ears, and Tilly blinked as she rallied. Maybe it was sensible to leave. 'Assault? A little woman like me? With a gnome?'

She tossed her hair to disguise the tensing of her muscles as she prepared to fly. 'Should look good in the local newspaper. Maybe they'll take your picture with the weapon?'

She watched with interest as his mouth thinned—might have been a better idea to keep her smart mouth closed—and then the moment when she was about to run was lost when Mrs Bennett poked her head over the low fence. 'Ah. Children, I see you've met.'

Mrs B. smiled beatifically as she came around the corner. She carried the gnome close to her chest and handed it gently, like a tiny baby, to Tilly.

'Look who came to visit at my house,' she said just as a siren began to wail in the distance.

Tilly glanced at the man's face. Apparently the siren just topped off his day.

By the time the police sergeant had laughed his way back to his patrol car Marcus was considering climbing back upstairs to his bed and pulling the lavender-scented sheets over his head to start the day again.

Instead he closed his eyes. Mainly because it removed the smart-mouthed redhead from his sight before he strangled her. From the fond look on his aunt's face the redhead was clearly a 'favourite person', and, to be fair, he supposed it was a good thing she looked out for Maurine.

'I am sorry.' The woman stood beside him on his aunt's veranda to see the policeman off. Didn't she have a home to go to?

He almost groaned. That's right. She did. And it was far too close to his at the moment.

To add insult to injury, she then said, 'Do your legs hurt?'

His lashes lifted only slightly as he glared at her. He forced the words past his teeth. 'I'm fine, thanks. If you'll excuse me.'

Marcus closed his eyes and sighed. If the rented flat fiasco hadn't happened, if the closest hotel hadn't been solidly booked for a week-long conference, if he didn't start work on Monday, if, if…

He ground his teeth and then decided it indicated a lack of control. Marcus liked control, relished it, had seen what could happen when it was lost, and he needed control to breathe.

He wasn't sure how he and his aunt would rub together, but if he remembered correctly from that one Christmas after his sister had died Aunt Maurine had been a safe haven in a sad world.

It would only be a week or two until he found a new flat. He'd buy one if he had to. Control. He rubbed his chin. Hmm. In fact, he liked that idea. Nobody could interfere with his plans then.

* * *

Tilly watched him go. Limping. Oops. She'd say that was a fair case of alienation there. Mentally she shrugged. Shame. He'd have made a gorgeous gene pool for Ellie's future children. Tall, good bone structure, great body, and even related to a delightful old lady. But he had no sense of humour. And that was the most important trait as far as Tilly was concerned.

Not that she was concerned. She frowned at herself. It had nothing to do with her how cleverly amusing Ellie's children could be.

Tilly went back inside her own house just as her flatmate Ruby arrived behind her, drifting up the stairs with a serene smile and a filmy scarf floating behind her.

'Hi, there, Tilly.' Ruby looked her up and down. 'You not ready? Sunday brunch at the pub?'

'I'd forgotten.' She glanced at the old grandfather clock in the corner. 'Give me ten.'

Twenty minutes later the girls were perched on stools looking out the Stat Bar window at the park full of football-kicking young bloods and the sea beyond. Another glorious blue-sky day in paradise.

Tilly weighed the words in her mind before she said them. She wasn't sure why she felt the need to curb her usual method of blurting stuff out. 'Mrs B. has a nephew.'

'Next door? Oh, my goodness, Tilly. That's so exciting.' Ellie sat blonde and beautiful and suddenly buoyant on the stool. 'Is he gorgeous? Does he like you? Would he like me?'

Tilly glanced at Ellie. Blonde, petite, beautiful. Who wouldn't? 'Not sure about you but he can't stand me. I took him out with a garden gnome.'

Three pairs of eyes swivelled to full interest. She certainly had their attention now, Tilly thought ruefully. 'I had the notion he was breaking into one of the windows at the back of Mrs B.'s. He was actually fixing it.' Tilly listened to herself, surprised at the glum note she hadn't expected, and injected more bravado. 'It was a good throw, though, sideways to the back of the legs.'

There was a stunned silence followed by a howl of amusement from the girls.

'What did he say?' From Ruby.

'Was he hurt?' From Ellie.

'What did Mrs Bennett say?' From Jess, who liked the older lady next door as much as Tilly did.

Tilly pulled the slice of lime out of the neck of her bottle of light beer and sucked it. 'He swore, he's got a limp, and Mrs B. got the giggles. So did the police officer who arrived.'

Ruby was impressed. 'You called the police as well?'

'I thought he was a burglar.'

'Very sensible.' Jess nodded. 'I doubt a real burglar would be happy with being hit by a gnome.'

'I'd bet he wasn't happy. What's his name, Till?' Ellie asked, clearly feeling sorry for her future partner.

'Marcus.' Tilly could see him in her mind as clear as day. 'He's six-four, blue eyes, dark curly hair and built like a brickie's labourer. Great genes.'

'Ohhhh.' Ellie's eyes shone.

'You sure you don't fancy him, Till?' Ruby was watching with those knowing eyes.

Tilly swallowed the rest of her beer and dropped the lime skin in. 'Not my type.'

Ruby and Jess exchanged amused glances. Ellie wasn't included because she was still off in dreamland, populating the world with miniature dark-haired brickies. 'Sounds like everyone's type to me,' Jess said.

'So how long's he staying?' That was Ruby.

'No idea. Conversation flagged after the police car drove off.' Tilly looked up and saw the laughter in her friend's eyes and she had to chuckle. Parts of the encounter had been funny. But the fact that he obviously hated her—would like to see her boiled in oil probably—wasn't amusing at all.

CHAPTER TWO

Monday morning sunshine streamed into the open bedroom window as Marcus towelled his shoulders. As he turned away from the streaky mirror he caught a glimpse of the purple bruises on the backs of his legs.

At least he wasn't limping today, no thanks to the red-headed witch next door. He hadn't gone for a run today just to give his legs a chance to heal. But he could have done with one to rid himself of the snatches of nightmares that had included dear Matilda. He didn't know why she'd made such an impression on him— apart from the physical imprint of assault.

He hung the towel evenly on the rail and walked naked into the bedroom. His aunt had been twinkling at him most of last night because it was all *so-o-o* funny. And he'd heard enough about Matilda with the legendary handywoman skills to make him dislike her even without the gnome.

But he wasn't wasting thought on annoyances because today was a big day. His mobile phone beeped twice, an appointment reminder that he had an hour until work, and as usual he was on time.

He'd worked hard for this. Not just the early stuff, sweating over a restaurant stove between uni classes, extra shifts right through his internship, and the study he'd put in for his O&G exams—it was the effort put in to give him the right to make policy changes.

To have a say.

To protect women and babies from idiots and poor outcomes and poor practitioners. An oath he'd sworn as a heartbroken child.

Now finally to be the consultant in charge of an obstetric unit, a small one by city standards but one with a brilliant reputation, and he knew exactly how he wanted it run. His mothers and babies would be the safest in Australia.

A snatch of song, a woman's voice drifting up from the garden below with a soft Irish melody that made the hairs prickle on the back of his neck. He lifted his head. The tune was pure and incredibly seductive and Marcus slung the towel around his hips and leaned out of the window.

His head whipped back in when he saw who it was. St Matilda in a bikini top with a towel around her waist. Long red hair crinkled wet from the sea like a siren's.

She was like a gnat, buzzing outside his conscious decision not to think about her, and he wanted to swat her. And that delicious backside of hers.

Whoa! Where had that come from? Heat descended

to his groin and he backed farther away from the window.

He'd been working so hard these past few years he hadn't had time for anything but brief flings. It was obviously just a physical need he should think about addressing again. Maybe he'd have time soon but certainly not in that neighbourly direction.

Plus she was too young for him. Though he had to admit just then he'd felt younger than he had in a while. He grinned then his leg twinged as he reached for his clothes and he thought of the gnome. Best to avoid the pain.

Two hours later Marcus surveyed his two residents, his registrar, and the MUM, Midwifery Unit Manager, in his new office as he outlined his plans. And it felt good.

They'd had a ward round on each floor, the gynae floor on top and antenatal beds next down with the antenatal clinic. Then the neonatal nursery floor and on the ground the birthing units and theatres.

He'd done a double take when Gina, the midwife in charge, had proudly pointed out the new large baths in the labour ward for pain relief in labour. Apparently they'd been put in from fundraising by one of the new graduate midwives but he hadn't commented as yet on that. No doubt she'd noticed her announcement hadn't been greeted with shouts of joy.

'Diligent observation with strict documentation, a medical officer for each birth if possible, though I do understand sometimes babies come in a rush. But I'd like admission foetal monitoring on all women until the baby's wellbeing has been proved. Risk assessment on every woman will be an area I'll scrutinise thoroughly.'

The medical officers all nodded, though Gina didn't look impressed. Well, tough. The buck stopped with him. 'Any questions?'

Gina spoke up. 'This isn't a training hospital for midwives. My girls are all qualified and very observant, up to date and extremely diligent already.'

'I'm sure they are.' But… 'Not all midwives have the same level of experience.'

Gina wasn't finished. 'I thought the studies said admission foetal monitoring increased a woman's risk of unnecessary intervention?'

He'd heard it before. 'I'm glad you asked that.' He knew what could go wrong. 'I've seen the studies but I'm not convinced. I'll leave some less publicised clinical trials for you to look at.'

When Tilly walked in for the afternoon shift handover there seemed an unusual quietness over the ward. There were a few gloomy faces from the students, the senior midwives were in a huddle with the MUM, and the other new grad, her friend Zoe, who'd almost finished her shift, drifted across.

'Why so glum?' Tilly looked at her with raised eyebrows.

'Dream's gone,' Zoe said sadly. 'Our new broom has arrived and we're not happy, Tilly. Ward meeting in five.'

Tilly frowned. At least she'd hear the worst instead of imagining it. They'd been so excited about the new consultant, too. With a younger man appointed to the post there'd been great hopes of a shift away from the medical model of over-monitoring and early intervention. How come the basic concept that women were designed to have babies had been lost somewhere in the teaching of new doctors?

Their previous consultant had been old school and a bit dithery, so you could almost understand his reluctance to change, but now it looked like they were worse off.

She followed Zoe into the meeting room. 'So he's not young and modern?'

Zoe pulled a face. 'He's young, majorly good-looking in a serious way, but not much of a sense of humour.'

Sounded like someone she'd met recently but this was not the time to think of social disasters. This was work and the thought of going backwards into a more medical mode of midwifery sucked big time.

Gina called them together and outlined the new directives. 'Full electronic monitoring of babies on admission for the moment, please, where possible. And he doesn't like the idea of the baths, but will tolerate them for pain relief as long as no babies are born in there, until we've reassessed the policy.'

Tilly couldn't believe it. 'After all our work? What's to assess? New South Wales Health said, "Make pain relief in water an option."'

Gina sighed. 'I hear you, Tilly. Just make sure your

women have been well informed, have signed consent, and agree to a land birth before they get in. We don't want that option of pain relief taken away until we can change his mind about the actual birth.'

That double-sucked. The last thing most women about to give birth wanted was to move, especially out of a warm, buoyant bath into a cool room and a hard bed.

Tilly chewed her lip and as the meeting broke up Gina drew her aside. 'This probably affects you most, Tilly. I know you put a lot of work into the fundraising. You have the same passion and instincts as your mother and all I can say is go slow.'

Tilly sighed and accepted she'd have to pull back. 'Doesn't sound like he'd appreciate Mum's philosophy.'

Gina smiled. 'Perhaps not that enlightened yet. We'll work on him.'

It didn't occur to Tilly not to grind her teeth. Control was overrated. 'It's offensive that we have to work on anybody. Back to being handmaidens. We should all be here for the women—including him.'

'Give him time.' Gina was always the voice of reason—a woman aware that passion needed nurturing and sometimes steering into less controversial paths. 'We'll show him we can provide safety and support as well as an optimal environment. Then he'll understand.'

The shift passed quietly, two normal births who arrived at the last minute, no time for excessive monitoring or to call for medical help, Tilly thought with satisfaction, and no sight of the new head of obstetrics.

Tilly went home consumed with curiosity and not a little disappointment. She wanted to see this man that had everyone quaking in their boots but she'd just have to wait.

The next morning, like most mornings since she'd moved into Hill Street, Tilly headed for the ocean. She couldn't help her glance up at the guest-bedroom windows in Mrs B.'s house.

Her dreams last night had been populated by a particular tall, dark and dark haired policeman who seemed to catch her speeding every time she drove onto a particular country road. No doubt there was something deep and meaningful in there somewhere but Tilly had been left with a feeling of anticipation and the wish that she actually owned a car to give her the chance of it coming true. Shame he wasn't younger than she was and she could try for a fling.

Maybe she should just paint the hallway. And refix the falling picture rail. That would keep her mind where it should be.

As Marcus jogged back up the hill after his run he saw three young women leave the house next door. The annoying one wasn't with them.

The crash and muffled scream happened as he passed her gate and the repeated swear word, not a bad one in the scheme of things, floated out the window towards him. He sighed.

Obviously she was alive, but his Hippocratic oath

demanded he at least check she wasn't about to do more damage. 'Hello?'

The swearing stopped.

He called out again. 'It's Marcus from next door. Just checking. You all right?' Marcus tilted his head and listened at her front door, which he could see was unlocked. Typical. Why'd she do that? Didn't she read the papers? Foolish woman.

'Um. I'm okay. Thanks.'

She didn't sound it. In fact, if he wasn't totally mistaken he had the feeling she was almost in tears. 'Can I come in?'

He heard the scrape of furniture and a muffled sob. Nothing else for it, he had to check.

'I'm coming in.'

She was sitting on the floor, the ladder was on its side and the annoying one was sitting beside it with her foot in her hand. He hoped to hell she hadn't fallen off the ladder.

He crouched down next to her. 'Matilda, isn't it?' As if he didn't remember. 'What happened? Did you hit your head?'

'Hello, Marcus.' She brushed a long tangled spiral of hair out of her eyes and his hand twitched at the unexpected desire to catch a tendril she'd missed. How did it spring all over like that and still be so soft?

'No. I wasn't up the ladder when it fell. But the hammer was. It landed on my toe.' She bit a decidedly wobbly lip.

He looked away, not because he wanted to gather her

up in his arms and comfort her, certainly not. He looked away to professionally assess her injury and saw one already bruising big toe. He glanced at her woebegone face then back at her toe.

Her gaze followed his. 'It throbs.'

'I imagine it would. I won't touch it until you get a bit of relief.' He glanced around the open room towards a doorway that looked like it led to the kitchen. 'Do you have any ice?'

She almost smiled and he almost melted. 'Always.'

He stood up. Quickly. 'I'll grab some from the freezer then.' Marcus stepped around the ladder and righted it before heading for the kitchen. He couldn't help a little peek around as he went. The house was very tidy.

He guessed that was one thing in her favour, though he supposed it could be any of the girls who had the clean fetish. He wasn't sure why he didn't want to stack up good things in Matilda's favour and refocussed on the task at hand.

Freezer. He saw the unopened bag of frozen peas and decided it would mould better around her foot. He grabbed a tea towel that was folded on the bench.

When he crouched back down beside her she looked more composed and he mentally sighed with relief. He mightn't have coped with her tears. 'I've brought the frozen peas. Less square.'

She took them and lowered them gingerly onto her bruised toe. They both winced. 'Ow-w…' she murmured as the green plastic bag settled around her foot.

'Where would you like to sit? Somewhere comfortable, maybe. With your leg up?' She couldn't stay there on the floor, which was cold tiles.

Her big green eyes, still shiny with unshed tears, so completely captured his attention he wasn't sure what she was talking about when she answered. 'Um…I'll try for the sofa.'

So far? So far so good? Sofa. Right. Move somewhere more comfortable. What the heck was wrong with him this morning? She lifted the ice and he helped her up and he saw her grit her teeth to take a step.

This was crazy. 'Here.' He picked her up easily in his arms and took the few strides to the three-seater lounge. She felt decidedly pleasant against his chest and it was with strange reluctance that he put her down.

Not sensible. He knelt down and looked quickly at her toe again as she prepared to replace the ice. The bruising was mainly below the start of the nail and he ran his finger along her slender, cute phalanges. He cleared his throat. 'I don't think anything's broken. Just bruised.'

She nodded then looked away from him and he suddenly realised he was still holding her foot. He almost dropped it in his haste to stand up. 'Well, if nothing else is hurt, I'll be on my way.' He unobtrusively wiped his hand on his trousers to rid himself of that warm and tingly feeling.

Big, solemn eyes looked up at him. 'Thanks for checking on me.'

The sooner he got out of here the better. 'My aunt would kill me if I didn't.'

She nodded. 'Of course. Thanks anyway.'

Marcus left. Quickly.

Tilly watched him go, her toe a dull throbbing ache that was being replaced by a dull throbbing ache from the cold peas, but the rest of her was still dazed from being picked up and carried as if she were a baby.

Scoop and go with no effort at all from him. It had been a very strange feeling to be held against that solid, manly chest and one she would have liked to have savoured for maybe a little while longer just for interest's sake.

Only to see why women liked it, of course. She almost got the reason. She could still smell the faint scent of virile man. Maybe guys did have some short-term advantages.

She glanced around at the flat-headed copper nails that had spilled out of the box and the hammer lying beside them. No more repairs this morning. Her toe was feeling better already and she'd be sensible to keep it up before work that afternoon.

She needed to remind herself that this guy qualified as an 'older man' and he pressed too many of her attraction buttons to be anywhere near safe as a platonic friend.

CHAPTER THREE

TILLY'S toe wasn't too bad by afternoon, probably that quick packet of peas, because she squeezed into her shoe with only a little tenderness before she caught the bus up the hill to work, rather than walk.

Tilly, along with the rest of the afternoon staff, had just finished their walk around the ward to meet the patients and for clinical handover when the phone rang.

Gina picked it up, listened, and then waved. 'There's a patient with foetal distress, first baby, coming in by ambulance.' Gina assessed the staff on duty. 'Home birth. Probable emergency Caesarean. You take her, Tilly.'

'Yep. Thanks.' Tilly felt the clutch of sympathy in her stomach and glanced at her watch. 'How far away?'

Gina looked at the wall clock. 'Ten minutes. Josie Meldon's the mum, from Randwick, and the midwife is Scottish Mary.'

Tilly was already moving. 'Who's the doctor on call?'

'The new consultant.'

So she'd get to meet the man. 'I'll page him and get the papers ready for Theatre.' More than anyone, Tilly understood the efficiency and reliability of home-birth midwives. And Mary was one of the best.

Tilly's mother and grandmother had both been heavily involved in the home-birth movement all their lives and Tilly had been born at home, naturally, as well as growing up holding placards at dozens of home-birth rallies.

She'd known Mary for years and if Mary said Caesarean, which she hated with a passion, that was what was needed.

She dialled the pager number for the new consultant then scooped a pile of preprepared theatre papers from the drawer on her way to the filing cabinet.

The cabinet held all the bookings of pregnant women in their catchment. Eastern Beaches Maternity Wing, or EB as it was known, had great rapport with the local independent midwives and in the last six months since Tilly had graduated she'd made extra efforts to liaise between the two areas of maternity care.

Tilly's goal had been to increase the mutual respect between hospital and private midwives, and while not missing, rapport hadn't flourished either.

Gina, a progressive manager and long-standing friend of Tilly's mother, had encouraged her. Now EB had brief admission papers of even the home-birth clients in case of emergencies such as this to streamline unexpected admissions. This benefited everybody, especially the incoming mums.

As Tilly lifted Josie Meldon's file the phone rang and Tilly picked it up. 'Maternity, Tilly. Can I help you?'

There was a brief pause and Tilly glanced at the light on the phone to check the caller was still on the line. Then a voice. 'Dr Bennett. You paged?'

'Yes.' She frowned at the fleeting illusion that she recognised the voice and then shrugged it off. 'We've a woman in need of emergency Caesarean coming in from home. Full-term baby. Foetal distress and her midwife is with her. I'm about to ring Theatre.'

'A failed home birth?'

The thinly veiled scepticism in the new doctor's response scratched against Tilly's nerves like a nail on a blackboard and she wouldn't have called the words back if she could have.

'Not really the time for labelling, do you think?'

He ignored that. 'She hasn't arrived for assessment yet? Hold the alert to Theatre until I assess her.'

Tilly frowned fiercely into the phone. 'That's your call but I'll still prepare the theatre notes.'

Another pause while he digested that and Tilly's flushed face glared at the phone. She wanted to get Theatre going.

'Who gave you permission to instigate a theatre call?'

'The midwife in charge of the case has called it. We're all working for the mother and baby, but just a moment,' she said sweetly, 'I'll put you onto the midwifery manager.'

Tilly held the phone with the tips of her fingers as if

she'd just discovered it was covered in horse manure. No wonder everyone detested this guy. She carried it at the end of a straight arm and handed it to Gina. 'I think this is for you.'

To Tilly's surprise Gina smiled wryly as if she'd seen this coming. Gina shooed her away to other preparations and Tilly gave no apologies for possibly upsetting the consultant. It was her job to help protect the women in her area. Thank goodness Gina knew that.

Marcus put the phone down after the brief discussion with Gina. He measured his steps to the door because what he really wanted to do was swoop down to birthing and shake his nemesis.

He couldn't believe the gnome thrower from next door was a midwife in his ward but he had no difficulty believing she'd champion home birth.

Home birth. The taste of it was metallic in his mouth, his least favourite association with his job, but even he could see that was personal and he shouldn't let it colour his judgement.

But he'd sort that after he assessed the new admission. 'Page my resident and registrar to meet me immediately on labour ward, please, Sheryl.' He spoke as he strode out the door and his new secretary nodded at his back. She was used to obstetricians in a hurry.

He briefly considered the shock he'd received when Matilda had been on the end of the phone. He tried not to think about the fact she would have told them all about the incident at his aunt's house. He was above out-of-school gossip and could ignore that the staff would snicker at the idea of him being hit by a gnome. And that he'd picked her up from the floor that morning.

Tough. He had more important things to think about.

The midwife in charge, thank goodness, was a sensible woman, but he wouldn't tolerate lack of respect from anyone, no matter how many windows she'd fixed for his aunt.

Marcus didn't wait for the lift and loped down the stairs two at a time, each step more forcible than the last, until he realised what he was doing. Calm. Control.

Tilly didn't give Dr Bennett another thought. She used a different phone to get a gurney over for her patient to transfer immediately to Theatre as soon as she had 'his' permission.

The ambulance arrived with her patient a minute later and Tilly directed them into the empty birthing room where she had the set-up for a catheter and IV ready to go.

Mary looked calm as usual but her hand shook slightly as she handed over her patient. 'This is Josie. We spoke about having a Caesarean on the way in, and that we'll have to put in a drip and catheter before surgery.' Mary's lilt was more pronounced with worry.

'Hi, Josie. I'm Tilly. One of the midwives here.' Tilly handed Mary the pre-jellied sensor from the electronic foetal monitor so they could all hear how Josie's baby's heart rate was.

The monitor picked up the clop-clop of the baby, a little faster than average rate but as soon as Josie started to get a contraction it slowed quite dramatically and

Tilly looked at Mary. 'I'll just pop the drip in while we wait for the obstetrician. Dr Bennett is our new consultant and he'll be taking over Josie's care while she's here.'

Tilly smiled sympathetically at the worried woman and her husband, and they all listened as Josie sighed heavily at the end of the contraction. When it was completely gone and her baby's heart rate had slowed even more they all waited with held breath until the rate slowly picked up and finally returned to the rapid rate of a compensating baby.

Okay, baby was coping and doing a good job of conserving energy, but not for long.

Tilly went on. 'It's rotten luck this has happened to you, but we'll try and keep you up to date as we go, and Mary and your husband can stay with you whatever happens.'

The door opened and a group of three doctors swarmed in like big white moths. Tilly didn't think it was fanciful to think they seemed to shrink the room.

The tallest moth was more like an avenging angel. An archangel she'd met before. 'I'm Dr Bennett. Fill me in, please.'

Mary stepped forward. 'I'm Josie's midwife.' That was all Tilly heard for the first frozen second or two because she was staring at the disaster that stood in front of her.

She felt like slapping her forehead. Dr Bennett. Mrs Bennett. Gnome man. This was a pearler. Wait till she told the girls at home. He didn't even look at her but somehow she knew he knew she was there.

Mary's voice drifted back in and Tilly listened distractedly as she went back to hanging the IV flask.

'Josie was doing beautifully, seven centimetres dilated, when we had a sudden dive of the fetal hearts with a good recovery the first time and then a repeat with a slower response.'

The chief white moth didn't say anything and Mary hurried on. 'Then the foetal tachycardia you can see on this graph. I'm not sure why, the response isn't dependent on position, but in case it was a true knot or something sinister we opted to come in. Each contraction has seen a slower recovery of the deceleration in heartbeat.'

'Of course.' His voice gave nothing away. 'What time did you notice the first deceleration?'

Mary glanced at her watch nervously. 'Maybe twenty minutes ago.'

He didn't say anything but inexcusable delay was the message everyone in the room heard. He looked away from Mary and his face softened into a reassuring smile as he leaned down and met Josie's eyes.

'You did the right thing, coming in.' He nodded and rested his hand on Josie's as she clutched the sheet. 'We'll have your baby out very quickly. Hang in there.' He glanced around at the rest of the people in the room. Tilly included. 'I want Josie on the table in ten minutes.'

Tilly felt the tiny slip of her leash and gave up on her silence. Didn't he have any idea how attuned Mary was to her women? She struggled, but thankfully her voice came out mildly, for her, as she gave in to defence. She waved the catheter in her hand. 'Thanks to Mary's pre-warning, the gurney's here and Josie's almost ready now, Doctor.'

His glance barely acknowledged her existence as he swept out.

'Holey dooley, thanks for the bat.' Mary caught Tilly's eyes and rolled them as she regathered her composure. 'Now I know what court feels like.'

'You do an amazing job, and have better statistics than a dozen hospitals, Mary. I don't mind telling people. He's new and doesn't understand but my manager says he's one of the best,' she said to Josie with a grin, 'and we'll have you there in under ten, Josie, so bear with us.'

Josie was in Theatre in eight minutes, once she was there a very quick spinal injection that numbed her took five, and her son was born ten minutes later.

Marcus peered over the green drape that separated Josie's upper chest from the operation site. 'A true knot in the cord, slowly pulling tighter as he descended the birth canal.'

At least he had the grace to nod at Mary, Tilly thought. 'You were right. Well done.' Then he looked back at Josie. 'A bit too dangerous for baby for a normal birth this time but he looks great now. He'll be with you in a sec.'

At the other end, waiting to take the baby, Tilly had to admit his technique was amazing. Swift, yet sure, and by far the most gentle Caesarean she'd seen since she'd started her training.

Sometimes the tugging at the end of the operation, that time as baby's head and body were removed after opening the uterus, could look almost brutal, but this baby had been scooped seamlessly and with a birth almost as serene as vaginal birth in water.

Tilly had to grin under her mask. No doubt another tussle she'd be having with this man.

Now that baby was safe, just waiting for his cord to be clamped and cut, Tilly could allow herself a little flutter of anticipation for the ongoing battle as she waited for Marcus to pass across their patient.

He looked calm. Calmer than he had when she'd taken him out with a gnome. Calmer than when the police car had rolled up. And to be fair, he'd been very calm and concerned and even kind when he'd come to her rescue that morning.

The surgical team had been quietly courteous and extremely efficient. The scrub sister was smiling her heart out at the pleasure of scrubbing in with him. And Tilly couldn't help notice his eyes glance Sister's way with a twinkle when she spoke. The silly woman was blushing over a smile and a few curling hairs at the V of his loose scrubs.

Marcus ignored the fact that he knew Matilda was watching him. He reached across and carefully laid Josie's baby on the sterile sheet on the resuscitation trolley and stepped away from the risk of contamination as she leaned forward.

It was Marcus's turn to watch. From the safety of his sterile field he watched the little boy wriggle on the sheet as she wiped him dry and murmured to him. It seemed she was good at her job. How annoying. He frowned at himself. That was ridiculous. That was a good thing.

He watched her as she assessed heart rate and breathing, along with colour and tone as she finished drying him.

Baby looked perfect, not distressed and she gathered him up with a deftness that spoke of experience and well-founded confidence. As she carried him around the screen to his mother, Matilda's pleasure shone and lit up the room. He glanced away because he'd almost smiled himself.

He saw the home-birth midwife's eyes mist as she sat beside Josie's head on the other side of the screen, not something he would normally have noticed, and he was left with a little disquiet at how abruptly he'd dealt with her. Hopefully he'd have a chance to reassure her before she left the hospital. Had he been insensitive? At least she'd known when to call it.

The next time he looked up it was because the little boy had begun to cry loudly as Tilly unwrapped him and draped him across his mother, baby chest to mother's breast, skin to skin. Tilly tucked one of his hands in under his mother's armpit and settled a warmed bunny rug over both of them.

He'd got over his shock and wasn't feeling quite as annoyed with her. But he'd have a word later. She was a militant little thing. He'd picked that up from the one comment she'd made in the birth suite. He should probably tell her he wasn't a fan of home births.

'Hello, my little darling. You scared us.'

Marcus heard the words as he began to suture the uterus back together. Such heartfelt relief, and he caught the moment when Josie's husband kissed his wife's cheek with a shuddering sigh. This was why he did this job. To keep families safe.

Half an hour later they were almost done. Baby had just let out a roar. 'Good set of lungs,' Marcus said as he looked over the top of the screen again and smiled warmly at the new parents, then his gaze skimmed Mary and settled on Tilly.

Tilly saw his eyes rest on her. We'll talk later, the look said. Now baby and mum were safe he appeared to be thinking of a little discussion about her phone manner perhaps. Good.

Tilly couldn't help the flutter under her rib cage, the flickering nervousness of a battle of wits and practice preferences, and she turned her head away from him. She looked forward to the challenge but perhaps it would be wise not to let him know.

On the return to the ward, Tilly sponged and settled Josie and her baby so Mary could go home much relieved. The rest of the ward was so busy Tilly didn't have a chance to wonder when Marcus would come to find her.

Which was just as well because he didn't get a chance that night, and apart from a few over-the-shoulder

glances that came up empty Tilly went home with unfinished business lying between them.

Marcus woke at dawn. He didn't know what had woken
him, but he knew it was hopeless to attempt further
sleep.

He rolled out of bed and stretched, seeing the sun
was tinging the horizon of ocean with pink and the
promise of another beautiful day. The lure of the salty
tang of a sea breeze had him swiftly change into his
trainers and let himself out of his aunt's house at a slow
run towards the beach.

A woman dived into the surf as he reached the sand
and he couldn't shed the ripple of anxiety as she disappeared under the waves. Her head popped up again and
he shuddered as old memories surfaced as well. Swimming hadn't been attractive since his sixth birthday.

Irresponsible, that's what it was, to swim so far out
and alone, he said to himself, then grimaced for sound-
ing like a grumpy old man. Well, for goodness' sake,
there were no others on the beach and the lifesavers
wouldn't start for another hour so who would help her
if she ran into trouble?

He turned his gaze to the sand in front and increased
his speed until the slap of his runners on the sand beneath him banished the memories and soothed his soul.

Out past the waves the woman swam parallel to the
beach from one side of the bay to the other and he sent
one brief glance her way as he turned to run up the cliff
path and onto the headland.

As he returned from his run he closed in on another girl, one he recognised, as she walked up the hill towards the house. One he'd meant to catch up with last night and hadn't had a chance to.

Unfinished work business lay between them but maybe that should keep for work. All he could think of was how amazing her wet siren's hair was, that wiggle of her walk under the towel wrapped around her that did uncomfortable things to his libido, and the strains of a haunting Irish lullaby, this time drifting backwards towards him.

Now, here was a dilemma.

He could run past and pretend he didn't recognise her and hope he made it into the house before she called out to him.

Or he could stop now, hang back, and not catch up.

Or he could fall in beside her and pretend he didn't care either way—which he tried but it didn't quite come off. 'Morning, Matilda.'

The lullaby abruptly ended and she glanced across at him. 'Good morning, Marcus. Or should I say Dr Bennett?'

'Only at work will be fine.'

Tilly grinned at him and he couldn't help his smile back. Not what he had intended at all. Neither was the slow and leisurely perusal of all she had on display above the towel. But what was a man to do when she looked so good?

She had the body of an angel, now that he had a chance to admire her up close, and the long line of her neck made his fingers itch with the impulse to follow the droplet of seawater that trickled enticingly down into the hollow between her perfect breasts.

Good Lord. His mouth dried and his mind went blank. Not a normal occurrence.

'Join me for breakfast?' He frowned. Now, why had he said that? It was the last thing he needed before work and gave the opposite impression of what he wanted to get clear between them. 'To discuss yesterday.'

She hesitated and he thought for a moment he'd get out of the ridiculous situation he'd created. Much more sensible to discuss work at work—like he'd decided before he'd been bowled out by his middle stump.

'Where?'

His stupid mind went blank again. 'Down at the beach? Pick somewhere to sit. I'll find you. Say fifteen minutes?'

'Something quick and light? Sounds good.'

A quick one. That's what he fancied all right and it was a damn nuisance his sleeping libido had decided to wake up when she'd gone past.

No. This was an opportunity to clear the air. About work. Maybe find some common ground on their perceptions of theatre calls and lines that were drawn. That was the sensible thing to discuss.

Fifteen minutes later theatre calls were the last thing Marcus wanted to discuss. She'd taken him at his word and waited for him by sitting on the steps of the white wrought-iron rotunda, a picturesque place of summer bands and vocal touters, and quite a fitting place for a mischievous midwife who drove him mad but a little public if anyone from the hospital walked past. He couldn't help glance around but nobody seemed particularly interested in them.

She *almost* wore an emerald sundress and up close the way it fitted her body took his breath and his brains away. Again.

He handed over the dish of fruit and yoghurt he'd chosen without thinking but thankfully she looked happy enough with his choice.

Then his mouth let him down. 'You look gorgeous.' He almost slapped his hand over it. *No-o-o-o.* Quick recovery needed. 'But I'm not a fan of home births.' The words hung starkly, like the family of swallows under the scalloped roof of the rotunda.

Her sudden smile faded. 'I noticed. Why?'

Good. She'd heard him. At least he'd said what he had to. 'Too dangerous. Poor outcomes if something goes wrong.' He looked away. 'And personal reasons. I really don't want to discuss it.'

To his surprise she nodded with more understanding than he'd expected. 'I can see that.' She glanced away to the waves.

When she said, 'Do you run most mornings?' ridiculous relief expanded inside him. He caught her eye as she looked back.

He could laugh now. 'When people don't cripple me with gnomes, yes.'

She bit her lip and blushed delightfully. 'I'm sorry. And I didn't mention it at work.'

He couldn't pretend that wasn't a bonus. Not the most glorious way to introduce the new consultant. 'I'm over it.' Actually, he was—surprising even himself—and Matilda looked happy to hear it. He let her have a full-blown smile so she could see he was telling the truth. 'I do have some sense of humour. Eventually.'

She looked down and smiled at the steps and he felt a frown on his forehead. Had he sounded self-indulgent? Forgotten how to talk trivia to a woman? Not usually. Maybe it was just this woman.

He forced himself on. 'So you like to swim in the mornings. And sing.' Her eyes lit up again, like they had in Theatre last night, and they smiled at each other like two loons. Then he remembered they worked together and he needed to keep distance. He glanced around at the people in the park. No one was looking.

There was an awkward silence and he patted the rotunda they sat on. 'Do you sit here often?'

She glanced around, encompassing the grass of the park, the sea, and finally the rotunda. 'When it's empty. I can see right out over the ocean. In the spring they have white daisies around the bottom. I pretend it's my castle and I'm a princess.'

Not too far-fetched even for his prosaic imagination. She looked like he'd always imagined a fairytale princess looked. He'd never had a thing for tiny blond-haired dolls, always dark, willowy Rapunzel-type ones, and red was close enough.

Problem was she so easily enmeshed him, like those nets hanging off the boats down on the beach, and he had to disentangle himself. A liaison with a junior midwife was the last thing he needed.

He just hadn't wanted misunderstandings at work and especially when his aunt thought so much of her. Really his only reason for being here.

He finished his breakfast in a hurry and stood up. 'Sorry to rush off.'

'No. You go. I'll stay a little longer. I often eat down here when I'm working the late shift.'

Tilly watched him go with his strong brown legs eating up the distance and the incline to his aunt's house. He didn't look back and his spine stayed straight and tall as he moved like a well-oiled machine, though actually he was a bit of a machine, with his running and his rules for the ward and the world. Marcus The Machine. A control freak. Which was sad.

Yet somehow she didn't think he'd planned the invitation to have breakfast with him. She smiled to herself. She'd bet that had come out of nowhere.

CHAPTER FOUR

WHEN Tilly walked into work that afternoon she didn't even get a handover. Gina shooed her straight through to Birthing as she arrived and briefed her on the way. 'There's a teenage mum in birth suite four. I'd like you to look after her.'

'Yes, please.' Tilly was happy with that and Gina grinned at her enthusiasm.

'India Ray. Her mum's in South Australia and the boyfriend's outside on the street at the moment. She has a nasty history of abuse and of course she's terrified of the birth and anyone touching her. The seniors will cover the ward until she's delivered so concentrate on her. She's had her monitoring done, so you can see the trace in the chart—all's well there.'

Tilly nodded, she could almost hear her mum's voice, 'If a girl's had a rotten childhood, past abuse can seriously affect the way she labours.' It had been a passion of her mother's that she'd passed on to Tilly, to be especially supportive and aware that labours could suddenly stop when women felt vulnerable. Privacy and actual physical contact were huge issues.

'Good luck.' Gina left her to finish handover with the others and Tilly knocked on the door and slipped into the darkened room. She could hear rapid breathing coming from the bed.

'Hello, there, India.' Tilly peered through the dimness and waited for her eyes to adjust. 'I'm Tilly. I'm the midwife looking after you this afternoon.'

There was no response from the young woman on the bed. Tilly tried again. 'How's it going?'

A sniff. 'My belly hurts.' India shot one agonised look at Tilly then stared back down at the sheet she'd drawn up to her chin as she lay on the bed curled up like a baby herself.

Tilly glanced around until she found the small mobile stool and her mind searched for ways to connect with the frightened young woman as she crossed to the stool. She sat, lowered the stool as far as it would go, and glided in at a much lower height than she'd been as she'd stood near the bed.

Her eyes were almost level with India's as the wheels stopped beside the clutched sheets.

She kept her voice quiet and conversational. 'It's hard work, this labour business. But worth it.' Tilly paused, in no hurry, letting India get used to her.

India grunted and Tilly bit her lip to stop a smile.

'Perhaps it's the bed.' As if the suggestion had just occurred to her. 'If you lie down with contractions they

make your baby's weight crunch your back and hips.
They say you feel the pain about ten times worse.'

India gritted her teeth. 'I don't want to move. I can't.
And I hate needles.'

Tilly nodded. 'Sure. I understand.' She picked up
the hand-held Doppler from the chest of drawers beside
the bed and squeezed gel onto the end from the tube of
conducting jelly. 'When you have the next contraction,
can I listen to your baby, please? When we change staff
for a labour we like to hear and say hello to your baby
right at the start.'

She waited for India to nod that she understood.

The girl finally shifted her head slightly on the
pillow in agreement and Tilly went on. 'After that I'd
like to feel your tummy and the position your baby is
lying in if that's okay with you?'

India shifted on the pillow again.

Not a lot of connection happening yet, Tilly thought
ruefully. 'I could wait till after the next contraction for
that bit, if you like, and then we'll see?'

Two thin shoulders shrugged under the sheet and
Tilly smiled. 'Where's your boyfriend?'

'Outside. He won't stay with me.' India's lip quiv-
ered, 'Since I gave up smoking he smokes ten times
more than he ever did. Today he's smoking a hundred
times more.'

'That's hard. He'll be sorry tomorrow and feel rotten,
though. Good on you for giving up. You need to keep
healthy because this little person is going to keep you
on the run.'

India defended her absent hero. 'Grant says he's trying to give up.'

Tilly held up her hands. 'No judgement from me. He'll quit one day then. Every time he tries to quit smoking he learns something that'll help him in the end.' Tilly nodded. 'Sounds like he's nervous and probably needs something to hold today.'

India glared at the empty doorway. 'He should hold my hand.'

'Yep.' Tilly looked down at the childlike hand clutching the sheet and felt a pull of sympathy. Support was so important in labour. She felt like nudging Grant wherever he was. 'He should.' Tilly glanced at the clock on the wall so she could watch the time between contractions and see how long it took until Grant came back. 'But when he's not here, if you need a hand you can use mine.'

Then she changed the subject so India didn't have to accept or decline the offer. 'Have you seen those cyber-cigarettes? They're rechargeable. Crazy. You use them like a real cigarette and they glow blue on the end when you breathe in. You even puff out smoke, but it's really just water vapour and nicotine replacement therapy.'

The first smile was always the hardest to draw but Tilly could feel the lessening of tension in the girl beside her when she finally smiled back.

'Do they work?' India was a very pretty girl when she didn't scowl. 'Sounds silly.'

Before they could follow up on that, a new contraction chased away any thought of humour as India hunkered down in the bed and screwed her eyes shut as the next wave rolled over her. Tears squeezed out beneath her clenched eyelids and Tilly slid one hand gently in next to India's fingers in case she wanted it.

Convulsively India's hand opened, grabbed Tilly's, and squeezed hard down on Tilly's fingers with her rings. Oops. She should have asked her to take the silver off first.

Tilly winced quietly until the contraction began to ease. 'I'm going to listen to your baby as the contraction ends now.' She extricated her blanched fingers and slid the little Doppler under the side of the sheet and onto India's round tummy.

The baby's heart rate echoed around the room in a galloping rhythm that made even India smile. The sound continued merrily as the contraction eased right away and after a minute more Tilly took the ultrasound monitor away.

'Baby sounds great.' Tilly wiped off the gel that was left behind on India's skin. 'Can I feel your tummy now, please?'

'Okay.' This time India looked more interested and Tilly smiled. 'Lovely tummy. Love your belly ring. Is that a little dragon?'

She nodded. 'My boyfriend wanted me to get a tattoo but someone said you shouldn't while you're pregnant.'

'Good choice. Not a great time to get an infection in your blood.' Tilly palpated the top of India's belly for the uterus with her hands and then the sides, and finally with both hands felt how deep into the pelvis

India's baby's head had descended. 'She's well down and pointing the right way. Looks like she's all ready to go.'

'How'd you know it's a girl?'

Tilly smiled. 'I don't. That's me being silly. I just call them all girls till someone corrects me. The other midwife said your mum is in South Australia?'

India brushed the hair out of her face. 'If she's still there. She's always doing a bolt.' India looked across at Tilly and her eyes narrowed. 'I'm going to be there for my baby no matter what.'

Tilly met her eyes and nodded. 'It sounds like you understand how important that is. Good on you. Is your dad around?'

'Is yours?' The answer shot back before Tilly realised she'd overstepped the boundaries.

'Sorry.' Word choice was so important. She owed India the truth because she'd expected it from her. 'No, not one who's there for me. I never even met him.'

She could almost see India's hackles subside. 'Neither have I.' And that was all they had time for before the next pain.

During the contraction India's boyfriend drifted in on a cloud of secondhand cigarette smoke and the room suddenly felt musty and sad.

India moaned noisily and Grant winced and picked up the remote control for the TV. 'Can't she have an epidural or something?'

Great support person, Tilly thought, but she didn't show any disapproval. Grant was all India had and less than perfect was better than none. 'We're think-ing about a change of position first. I'm Tilly.'

After the introductions, Grant shrugged and then sat slumped in the chair and flicked the channels on the television. Tilly eyed the bathroom door with some hope.

'After the next pain how about you try the bath, India? The heat from the water and the weight off your back could be really helpful for the pain. You wouldn't have to have a drip in your arm like you would for the epidural if you decided on that.'

India's slim white shoulders shrugged. 'If you like.' She turned her head away and closed her eyes. Well, that was better than not wanting to move, Tilly thought, and went ahead to fill the bath and gather the towels before she went back to the bed.

'While we're waiting for the bath to fill, you could try standing up and leaning on the bed?' Tilly was nothing if not persistent. 'Just to get the weight off your back?'

India gave Tilly a long-suffering look that Tilly smiled at. 'Yeah, I know. I nag.'

Grudgingly India accepted the necessity. 'Guess you have to.' With much huffing and puffing, and no help from Grant, India was finally standing beside the bed.

The next pain came and she breathed noisily through it with a little more control. 'That was still terrible,' she said with a sideways glance at Tilly, 'but a bit easier to breathe with.'

Tilly smiled with satisfaction. Every little bit of

movement helped. 'Wait till you feel the water take all the weight off you and wrap you in a warm hug. It's worth the hassle of getting undressed.'

India's eyes widened with sudden comprehension and Tilly saw the girl's recoil at the thought of being naked. She was pretty sure Gina was right about past abuse. Tilly promised herself then and there she'd keep India safe and her privacy respected.

India didn't meet Tilly's eyes. 'I want to leave my top on.'

Tilly nodded enthusiastically. 'No problem. That's a great idea and you'll relax better. I'll give you a towel you can pull up in the water, too. It keeps you warm as well as covers you.'

India lowered her voice even more. 'If I had my baby in the water, nobody would see my bits.'

Tilly sighed. 'I know. And it's a great way to have a baby but at the moment we're not allowed to have the last moments of birth underwater. But you could be in there almost until the end.'

India scowled. 'Why not the birth?'

Yes, why not? Tilly thought mutinously, but kept her face bland. 'New doctor. New rules. But we can have the pain helped until the end at the moment.'

India looked sideways at Tilly. 'What if I don't get out?'

Tilly met her look. 'My head will roll and they might pull out the baths.'

'Oh.' India looked away

No more was said and Tilly acknowledged philosophically that India owed her no allegiance. So be it.

She was willing to take the consequences if it helped India realise her body was an amazing part of her and not something to be ashamed of. Tilly had a sudden vision of the look Marcus had sent her in Theatre yesterday and she'd bet a water birth would get more than a look. But maybe he'd get it if she explained.

Tilly helped the girl into the almost full bath and the dropping of tension from the young woman's face made everything worth it. 'Oh, my,' said India. She sighed blissfully. 'The bed was dumb.' India had power now.

Tilly couldn't help the pleased glow that made her smile. She loved this job. 'You can only do what feels right at the time.'

Tilly draped the towel over India's belly and legs and the water seeped into it quickly to create a warm, wet blanket over her bare skin.

'When you have the next contraction, towards the end of it can you lean a little over so that your belly comes up out of the water? I need to listen. It's good for baby to meet your germs but the fewer people who put their hands in your bath water the better,' Tilly explained. 'I still need to keep an ear out in case baby gets tired as we get closer to the end.'

India's eyes stayed closed and already she sounded more drowsy and relaxed. 'Okay.'

Tilly dimmed the lights. 'When you're ready to push, we can get you to stand up and have your baby. That way you can sit down again later.'

She heard a knock on the door into the main room and glanced down as India's eyes flew open at the noise.

India clutched the wet towel in a convulsive protective gesture.

They both watched the doorway widen to admit Marcus and his entourage until it seemed the room was full of men and Tilly sensed the tensing of India in the bath.

If she could just stall them long enough. 'I'll talk to them first,' she said quietly, and India nodded gratefully.

Before Tilly could say anything Marcus had seen her, absorbed the impending scenario, and already a frown crossed his face. There was no doubt he was unhappy with his patient in the bath. Or maybe any Tilly state of affairs.

His voice wasn't loud but it was definitely firm. 'I hope you're not thinking of a water birth in here?'

'No. Unfortunately not.' Tilly lowered her voice until he had to bend to catch her words, an unsubtle reminder that he'd still spoken too strongly for the quiet room.

More softly but with no less firmness he replied, 'Good.'

She stepped closer so she blocked out his assistants and the discussion continued between the two of them.

She used his comment to open for hers. 'Though the privacy and lack of contact would very much suit a frightened and self-conscious young woman.' She met his eyes and waited.

When he didn't say anything she said, 'I have no plan to flout ward policy and India's been told that we need her to stand up before the end of her labour. Would it be so bad if she did stay in the bath?'

'Yes.' His eyes bored into hers. 'I want her out before second stage starts, Sister.'

Now not even early second stage. Tilly chewed her lip. 'Such a shame when pushing in the bath would progress her labour more.'

His face tightened and Tilly knew she was skirting close to the edge. Obviously they'd already lost the rapport they'd shared that morning at the beach. Did she think they wouldn't?

It seemed two very different people faced each other now. She raised her brows. 'Is that the new policy? Out of the buoyant water at the beginning of pushing?'

They both knew it wasn't. Yet. 'If it's not, it will be.' They were both speaking very softly. It would have been funny if it hadn't been so serious. 'So tell me, Sister, how far dilated is my patient now?'

Tilly gave an infinitesimal shrug. 'Exactly, you mean?'

He raised his brows at her deliberate obtuseness and nodded. Like a terrier on a bone.

She shrugged again. 'I don't know. I'd say she's three-quarters of the way there. But as India's baby's heart rate is fine and she hasn't asked for pain relief, I haven't assessed her dilatation exactly.'

Marcus narrowed his gaze and the sudden coldness in his blue eyes drifted down her neck like a cool breeze. Uh-oh. Too far. It was him standing over her after the gnome all over again. Well, she hadn't run then and she wasn't running now.

He was seriously displeased and she wondered fleetingly what his problem was, but for the moment she was more concerned about her patient's problems.

He said, 'Shouldn't that information be available before entering the bath?'

Tilly only just prevented herself from rolling her eyes. Seriously. The guy had no idea. Water wasn't an invasive procedure. It was a heat pack. A drug-free heat pack.

Of course she couldn't not answer. 'Why? It isn't rocket science. A warm bath is a comfort measure that promotes relaxation, which helps progress in labour. Isn't that what we're after? Without drugs and side effects? Would you be happier with an epidural?'

'At least I'd know where she was up to.'

Tilly glanced back at the half-open door into the bathroom. 'My instinct tells me she's progressing rapidly now she's in the bath.' They were still whispering at each other and it must have looked strange to the other people in the room, though Grant was absorbed in the television and Marcus's residents continued to talk among themselves.

Tilly persisted. 'Unlike an uncomfortable vaginal examination, which only satisfies the curiosity of the caregiver and can change in a minute anyway.'

'And if something goes wrong and nobody has checked to find it?' Marcus was back to trying to contain that urge to strangle her again. Nemesis was right.

But he could do a war of whispers if that was what it took. And he would win. 'Please ask India to leave the bath and I would like an examination to indicate her progress.'

Then he let her know she was moving into dangerous waters in case she was as unaware as she appeared. 'I'm not happy with your attitude.'

'And I'm not happy with yours.' He really shouldn't have been surprised she'd said that. He'd watched her struggle to keep it under her breath. Pointless struggle.

The little witch. But a tiny part inside him had to admire her temerity, her dogged protection of her patient, but this was one fight he would win.

'Unfortunately I'm ultimately responsible for the safety of all the mothers and babies in my care.'

Still she wouldn't back down. 'And you think I'm not?'

Okay. Enough. 'We'll discuss this at another time.'

Her eyes gave it all away. 'I'll look forward to it.'

India's voice floated drowsily from the half-closed door into bathroom. 'Tilly?'

'Coming.' Tilly switched from combat mode to comfort. Maybe they'd wasted enough time to get what they wanted anyway. Tilly threw a glance over her shoulder at Marcus and closed her eyes briefly as she turned to her patient. She knew that tone. Not only were they going to have a baby in the bath, it was going to happen under the consultant's nose.

A tiny whisper from India that Tilly hoped didn't carry. 'I think it's coming. I can't move.'

'Get her out and onto the bed.' Marcus was behind her and when Tilly lifted the towel they could both see the time for moving was almost past.

If only he could see how easy and straightforward it all was, he'd have to change his mind. 'We're all here. It's safe. Can we just have the baby here, Doctor, then we'll move? Nice and calmly?' Tilly didn't pressure him. It was enough she'd asked. Just asked with a tiny hope he'd listen. It would be so much better for India in the privacy of the bathroom.

Marcus hesitated. 'It'd better be smooth.'

'I agree,' Tilly said as she knelt down beside the bath on the cushion. 'Just listen to your body, India. The doctor's here as well. Keep baby's head under the water until he's all out and then I'll help you lift him up and lay him on your tummy.' She looked around for India's boyfriend but he wasn't there. 'Do want me to call Grant?'

'No.' India shook her head vehemently. 'He doesn't like anything gross.'

Marcus heard it all. Watched Tilly settle herself. Suddenly he felt the familiar panic rise at the thought of a baby being born underwater, even though his brain told him it happened every day. Hundreds of them. If not thousands. But not under his very nose.

He couldn't believe this was happening. After all he'd done to avoid this very scenario. His head was telling him that babies had been born in water all over the world with no complications, some of his colleagues even encouraged it, but he hated it.

All he could see was his little sister floating face down in the pond. A picture that haunted him still. His fault. He should have seen she was missing. He'd sworn to protect her. What if this baby looked just like all those years ago.

He could still hear his own scream. He couldn't stand by and watch this. He turned and grabbed the towels Tilly had placed earlier.

'Pull the plug. Stand up, please, India. Now.' There was something in his voice that had Tilly scoop the plug and India rise to her feet before either of them thought about disagreeing.

'Now, step out and we'll get you to the bed.' His voice seemed strangely too calm as he wrapped the towel around the young girl's shoulders and between them they almost frogmarched her to the bed, where she climbed up awkwardly and sat back against the high pillows just in time for the birth of the head.

Marcus pulled on the gloves his resident handed him and he calmly cradled the rest of India's baby as she eased her out and up onto her mother's chest. Baby mewled like a kitten as Tilly dried her and India relaxed back into the bed with an incredulous gasp. 'My baby. That was so quick.'

It was all over in minutes, third stage complete, no damage, no problems, and a stunned India clutching her baby with a dazed look on her face. Tilly twitched the towel over India's waist to cover her lower half as Marcus stood back. Even Grant looked impressed.

'Congratulations, India,' Marcus said, and he still hadn't looked at Tilly. That had been so close. Too close.

As he left there was a tinge of irony only Tilly heard. 'I'll leave you in Sister's capable hands.'

Tilly fought to keep her face calm. He just didn't get it.

She forced a smile at a stunned India and Grant as they looked at their baby. India's face glowed as she stroked the little fingers that rested on her neck. 'Oh, my goodness,' India said, astounded she'd done it. 'It's over.'

'She's beautiful. And you are incredibly clever. You okay if I come back in a second?'

India nodded. 'Sure.' She smiled shyly at Tilly. 'Thank you so much.'

'You were fabulous. I'll be back.' She hurried after Marcus and shut the door to the birth suite behind her.

'Excuse me, Dr Bennett.' Her voice while quiet was anything but conciliatory and Marcus nodded at his residents to keep going.

When the young men were out of earshot he raised his brows. 'Yes?'

'That was bad,' she whispered. 'You got away with it but you've no idea how close you came to destroying her confidence.'

Marcus had assumed Matilda wouldn't like the loss of a water birth but he hadn't expected this. What was up her nose? He wasn't at all keen on her tone either. Young midwife Matilda was back to being a gnat.

He tightened the control. He wasn't going to lose

it. 'I'm sorry you think that.' His tone held a thread of steel. 'I see a well mother and baby with no ill effects.'

Tilly had her hands hovering near her hips, though she didn't go all the way and plant them. 'Did you also see a young woman with a history of child abuse sitting up on a bed with three strange men looking on?'

Marcus played back the scene. India hadn't seemed to mind at the time.

'If the birth hadn't been absolutely imminent so that she didn't have time to think of it, that exposure could have destroyed her.'

'I think you're over-dramatising this.'

'You burst into the bathroom and ordered her out of that bath like a bully. She didn't need to be on display on a bed. She could have just stood up in the bath.'

Marcus had never considered himself a bully, or been accused of it, and the idea was abhorrent to him. Despite the denial on his lips, he wondered if there was any truth to Tilly's angry accusation.

He hadn't known about the previous abuse. How could he? He'd evicted India from the bath for her own safety! Or had it really been for his own peace of mind? He shrugged all that off. It was something to think about later. For the moment this wasn't the time or the place. He wasn't happy being spoken to like this.

'That's enough. When you've cooled down we'll talk about this but not until you've recovered your temper.'

She glared at him and shook her head. 'If you'd thought more about the patient than your rules, you'd understand why I'm so upset!' Tilly spun on her heel and marched back to the birth room.

Marcus watched her go and then shook his own head. That was uncalled for. A certain midwife was in for a stern talking to in the privacy of his office. He used the stairs to go up to his office to get rid of the excess energy he suddenly had and arrived there much sooner than he'd have liked.

Tilly was on autopilot as she helped India enjoy that first hour after birth skin to skin with her baby and no interference as mother and babe bonded.

For India, Tilly knew it was important that she take her time and allowed Mia to find her own way to her mother's nipple, as Tilly had assured India she would. Thankfully, little Mia bobbed her way across her mum's chest and latched on by herself in under an hour. The less handling and help, the better India would feel about breastfeeding. Judging by the ecstatic smile on the new mum's face, and the sleepily replete blink of her daughter, India's life was about to change for the better.

Afterwards Tilly helped India shower and dress her baby, and even Grant seemed to turn over a new leaf and be supportive.

Two hours later mother and baby were asleep, tucked up in their respective beds side by side, and Grant had gone to celebrate.

The birthing suite stood clean and ready for the next arrival and Gina crooked her finger as Tilly put down the paperwork she'd just completed.

'Finished?'

Tilly nodded.

Gina smiled regretfully. 'Then Dr Bennett wants to see you in his office before he goes home, Tilly. Sailing a bit close to the wind, I fear, my dear.' Gina nodded, not unsympathetically, towards the lifts. 'Come and see me when you get back and we'll have a coffee.'

'Thanks, Gina.' Tilly stood up and squared her shoulders. Bring it on, she told herself, but the idea of putting anything in her stomach, let alone a coffee, wasn't a pleasant one.

She ignored the lift and trod lightly up the stairs to the consultants' rooms. Sheryl waved her to a seat and a minute later waved her through into the inner office.

She knocked and opened the door. Marcus stood with his back to her as he looked out the window.

'Please close the door,' he said without turning, his ramrod-straight back solid against the light, and Tilly felt the slow burn of irritation. Still, she did as she was asked.

Though if he didn't turn soon, she'd walk out. That sounded like a really good idea. 'Perhaps I'll come back later,' she said finally.

That shifted him. He turned and looked at her. 'Please sit down, Matilda.'

Nobody called her Matilda except Mrs Bennett and her mother when she'd done something wrong. Well, she hadn't done anything wrong except try to make her patient feel as comfortable as possible and she was blowed if she'd be raked over the coals for it.

Her chin went up and he didn't miss the moment. Typical. And dangerous. But she wouldn't care about that.

'Living precariously again? More will fall on you than a hammer on your toe.'

She lifted her chin higher. 'I don't know what you mean.'

'I'm in a quandary.' He gestured to the seat and he could see the reluctance as she sat. Trying to be fair, he sat, too, and studied her across his desk.

He fixed his eyes on her determined little chin, which was pointing so high he wondered if she could actually see him. That was part of his problem. She distracted him. Infuriated him. Made him lose the control he prided himself on, and he would allow no one, especially a little red-haired midwife with self-destructive tendencies, to ripple his hard-won equilibrium.

He'd never had this type of problem with a midwife before. A voice inside said he'd never been as dogmatic as he seemed to get with Tilly but it didn't really matter. He had to draw the line.

'You know why you're here. I need to reprimand you for disputing my orders, and in front of my assistants, and then taking me to task. That wasn't professional and I won't have a junior midwife tell me what to do.'

Her chin dropped a little and for a horrible moment there he thought it wobbled. He held his breath, suddenly terrified for a moment about what he'd do if she cried, but thankfully she didn't. But she didn't answer.

He couldn't help his voice softening a little. 'Do you agree?'

Finally she said, 'You had your own way in the end anyway.' He could hear the thickness in her voice.

He frowned. 'That's not the point.' That was too close. He'd actually wanted to stand up and pat her shoulder—or more.

But that would be weak.

Then she said, 'The point should be what's best for the patient.'

'Precisely. And I haven't seen enough medically based studies that prove water birth is as safe as land birth. I'm the one in charge.'

'I can show you studies.' It was as if she ignored the bit about him being in charge and his concern about her becoming upset dissolved rapidly. She was so annoying.

And still going on. 'I have well-documented hospital trials, though usually by midwives—because science isn't much involved. There's no uptake of drugs to measure just shortening of labour and lack of intervention. That's a bit harder to measure.'

He'd had enough. Protect him from zealots. 'I'll look into it more. In the meantime, I won't have any babies risked by birth underwater until we discuss it again.'

'Some rural hospitals have fifteen per cent of their births in water. I know of one that's over fifty per cent.'

'Matilda. Stop! I don't want that situation to arise again. Is that clear?'

She looked at him as if she'd suddenly remembered

where she was. She looked quite shocked actually and then put her head down. He wasn't sure he liked that.

'Yes, Doctor.' No apology but no defiance either. He could have said more. Could have cited worst-case scenarios, demanded a more detailed agreement. But he didn't. He needed this to end, too. 'Thank you, Sister.'

They both stood and she left with enough speed even for him.

Marcus sighed as he walked over and shut his door again. That hadn't gone quite how he'd planned and he wasn't sure he knew where it had gone wrong. Maybe it was because he could see that she was just as passionate about helping her patients as he was, only from the opposite side of the spectrum. He closed his eyes and massaged the stiffness in his neck. A damn shame the only fly in the ointment of his dream job lived next door and affected him like no other woman had before.

Tilly hit the stairwell at a run and she was halfway down before she slowed, sniffed, and thanked the universe she hadn't cried in front of him.

Why on earth had she felt like crying? Probably because she'd been mad. She'd been mad all right, thinking they could have a water birth in front of him when she'd been told it was off the agenda. But India had been so vulnerable and Tilly had wanted her to feel proud of what her body could do in her birth. It was only luck they'd got away with India not noticing the people in the room at the time.

She just hoped he didn't take it out on the rest of the

ward and ban the baths outright. Gina would be well within her rights to chastise her if that happened. She felt like slapping her forehead. What on earth had possessed her to push him so far?

CHAPTER FIVE

'AND then he just ordered me to pull the plug and India to move. When we could have had the baby easily in the bath.'

'Poor Till. But I bet you gave as good as you got.' Jess could be as militant as Tilly when it came to her passion for her own patients in the children's ward.

Tilly swallowed the tiny particle of guilt that tickled her throat. 'To top it off, I had to go to his office and get hauled over the coals as well later.'

It was midnight. All four girls sat around the kitchen table and sipped hot chocolate before they headed to bed.

'Didn't you say there's a no water-birth policy at the moment?' This from Ruby, usually the most alternate of them all. And that was not what Tilly wanted to hear.

'It's not in writing yet. And surely not when the birth was so imminent.'

'But he still got her to the bed in time?'

See what happened when Ruby fell in love with a doctor, Tilly thought mutinously. She changed sides.

Tilly knew that wasn't fair. Ruby had a point, but Marcus drove her crazy.

'Maybe something happened and he has a reason to hate water birth.' Ellie wasn't slow on the risks of this conversation deteriorating. 'Why don't you try and talk to him out of work time?'

Jess nodded. 'Yep. Good idea. Maybe drop in next door at his aunt's or maybe one morning? I think he runs—you might pass him one day.'

It felt strange to be on the receiving end of advice. She'd always been the one with the sympathetic ear. Tilly felt heat creep up her cheek. She'd never been a good pretender and didn't know why she hadn't wanted to mention the fact she'd had a little chat with Marcus this morning.

Before all this had happened.

Maybe because after the first brief mention they'd both avoided discussing the hospital, and what did that mean anyway?

'Tilly! You're blushing.' Three pairs of eyes swivelled to look at her and Tilly rolled her own at the inevitability of being caught out.

'I sort of had breakfast with him this morning.'

Now she really had their focus. To Tilly's relief, Ellie burst out laughing. 'With the father of my prospective children? Darn. I'll have to find another one now.'

They all laughed and Tilly relaxed. So silly, trying to hide such an event from her friends. 'It was just like you said. We met outside after his run and he asked me to breakfast.'

Ruby leaned forward. 'So how'd you get on? Did he flirt?'

Jess nudged with her elbow and a big grin. 'Did you?'

'Cut it out. It was fruit and yoghurt in the rotunda at the beach for a whole ten minutes. We talked about work and it cleared the air after that first disastrous time.'

But not the second.

She thought of the recent battle of wills, which had been a little too public for a junior midwife and the consultant. That might take more than Greek yoghurt and a light sea breeze.

Ruby laughed. 'So is he nice when you're not throwing gnomes at him?'

At least Jess was trying to keep her face straight. 'Has he any sense of humour?'

Of course he did. She didn't know why she was so sure about that when she'd been so doubtful. 'Well, he laughed a little about the gnome so that's a start. And he has a nice smile when it actually works. But I doubt we're friends after today.'

Ruby didn't agree. 'If he can forgive you a gnome he can forgive you a heated discussion. Besides, he didn't drag in the nurse manager, which he had every right to do. He dealt with you himself. I reckon that means he wants that episode finished and done and no leftover angst.'

Tilly thought about that. Maybe Ruby was right. She

didn't know how Marcus's mind worked. She wouldn't mind a bit more information on that mystery herself.

Something dark lingered over his view of water births and maybe one day she'd find out what it was. She'd gained so little insight into him but it was early days yet and she didn't want to know too much. She could guess where that would leave her. It was all very unsettling.

Ruby sighed and picked up her mobile. 'Well, as much as I'd like to delve deeper into Tilly's reasons for not telling us immediately that she had breakfast with the hunk next door, I have to go and soak in some beauty sleep for my own gorgeous man. I'm on the early shift tomorrow.'

Ruby turned back. 'But I think we should have a party this weekend and invite Marcus so we can all see what makes him tick.' She looked at Tilly. 'If you want him to come?' Ruby smiled at them all as she drifted away.

Jess yawned. Ellie unconsciously copied her and they both laughed.

'Party's a good idea. 'Night.' Jess gave Tilly a quick sympathetic hug and followed Ruby out of the sitting room and up the stairs towards her own room.

'Watch him, Tilly. Early days, though.' Ellie had the most experience of men and their foibles and knew how to bounce back. 'Take it slowly and look after yourself.'

Take what slowly? She'd just had an argument with the man. Been reprimanded. She wasn't looking for a relationship, not for years. It was unlikely there was any way she could have Marcus as a friend anyway, even out of work hours. Tilly rinsed her cup and switched out the light.

It was all very well for them. Ask Marcus to one of their parties? They were barely speaking to each other.

If she did ask him, it would definitely have to be a morning invitation and not done on the ward. He could only say no and she could live with that. Might be a whole lot easier if he did.

But what about her rule not to get involved with anybody? Still, she wasn't planning to get involved, it was just the possibility of an off-duty friendship that could be surprisingly pleasant. Nothing else.

Marcus saw the light go out next door as he lay with his hands behind his head and stared at the dark ceiling. He wondered which room was Tilly's and what it was like.

Then he squeezed his eyes shut for a second and dragged his mind away from next door and back to his own room. He could just make out the deeply sculpted cornices and the ceiling rose around the tiny chandelier above his head. He needed to get his own flat, somewhere away from here. Away from her.

Finally he fell asleep but his rest was anything but dreamless. Sleep gave way to another glorious sunrise, which helped banish the darkness of his latest dream.

He was six again. The house seemed full of people, talking in low voices, everyone busy as they fluttered around the bedroom, and those quiet moans his mother made that swirled in his tummy and made him feel sick.

Marcus wished this baby would just come out now but there was nothing he could do. He wanted to hold his mother's hand but nobody would let him near her. He couldn't do anything he wanted to do to make himself feel better. He had no choice in the matter. No control over anything.

'Your mother's fine.' His father gave him a quick pat on the head as he shooed him away from the bedroom door. 'Keep an eye on your sister, Marcus. I need you to be a big boy now.'

He didn't want to do that either. When the screams started he forgot all about Nell, could only put his little hands over his ears and close his eyes, until finally a faint baby's cry could be heard and everyone started to talk at once.

It was an hour later before he was able to see her. 'Where's Marcus and Nell?' he heard his mother ask in a weak voice, and he turned to the toy box, the last place he'd seen his sister.

Marcus shook himself and dressed quickly. The blue of the ocean reflected the cloudless sky and helped to dissipate the heaviness he'd woken with. Marcus sucked in a huge breath of salt-laden air when he hit the path outside and set off down the hill towards the beach.

This was good. The slap of his feet on the path, the freshness of an ocean breeze, and out in front an ocean liner crawling across the horizon with twinkling lights ablaze. Now, that was the last thing he'd ever consider doing—a cruise across a deep ocean. He shuddered and increased his speed.

The woman was swimming across the bay again and he suddenly realised it was Matilda. Of course it was. How on earth had he missed that yesterday? Risky behaviour was her bread and butter.

He couldn't get that picture of her wobbling chin out of his head. Which was ridiculous. He could understand if he was obsessed by her delectable breasts, but a chin? He really needed to get a grip. Get a grip. To his surprise a wide smile crossed his face.

An hour later he came up behind Matilda's towel-wrapped person as she walked up the beach and he couldn't deny his reaction was pleasure. Shame he wasn't some beach-dwelling surfer Joe with no issues and responsibilities. Maybe just for today he could pretend because he'd been pretty hard on her yesterday. 'Hello, there, Matilda.'

She stopped and turned his way, and to his relief she smiled at him without any hesitation. It seemed work stayed at work. He was ridiculously happy with that. She glanced behind herself and stepped back to sit on the sandstone wall that surrounded the beach. He followed her and they sat there and squinted back out at the waves.

'You really shouldn't swim so far out, you know.'

She looked at him quizzically and he knew he had no right to try to tell her what to do. 'And watch you don't fall off a cliff while you run,' she retorted.

'Touché.' They smiled at each other.

She hesitated and then fixed her gaze on his face

with a little of that jut of chin he could even become fond of. 'Actually, I should apologise about yesterday.'

Her cheeks went pink and he wanted to stop her. Let it all go, he thought, but she was right. His authority couldn't be questioned or it wouldn't work. He didn't say anything in case he ruined her effort at apologising but he genuinely admired her for bringing it up again.

'Anyway. I'll try to remember you're the boss.' She slanted a glance at him. 'At work anyway.'

To his surprise he laughed out loud. Not something he'd done a lot of lately and she joined him with a touch of relief. Was he that much of an ogre at work? The thought sat uncomfortably.

'Fair enough. Open season out of hours.' He changed the subject. That one had been done to death. 'So how was the water?' It looked cold and deep to him.

'Gorgeous.' Her eyes glowed and he thought the water wasn't the only thing that was gorgeous. 'I love it. Do you swim much?'

Not on your life. 'Not at all. Never learnt.'

She blinked at him and he felt like blinking at himself. Not something he usually volunteered.

'Then pleasure awaits you,' she said, and it pleased him she didn't utter the usual expression of disbelief.

'One day,' he said, and for the first time ever he wasn't one hundred per cent sure it wasn't true.

Absently she tucked damp hair behind her ear and he could feel his own fingers twitch with the urge to help. 'I've never tried to run for exercise,' she said. 'Too jarring on my knobbly knees.'

He glanced down, and the delightful length of really quite incredible legs made him think of anything but knobbly, but he teased her with a wise nod. 'I can see why.'

She flashed him a glance, saw the amusement in his face and burst out laughing. 'I wasn't fishing for a compliment.'

'I believe you.' He twisted to glance at the shops behind them. 'I thought I might try a fruit smoothie for breakfast to eat on Maurine's veranda this morning. Like me to order one for you?'

'Sure. I'll show you the best place for any type of crushed juice.' They crossed at the lights and walked past his usual breakfast place. He got the feeling she was trying to say something and he hoped it wasn't work related. He looked down at her but she was staring straight ahead.

'We're having a party on Friday night.' Now she looked at him as if relieved to get the first sentence out. 'Four of us live in the house. We all work at the hospital. You're welcome to come if you're free.'

Not what he'd expected but he didn't think so. He didn't do parties. Never had time. He'd be hopeless at it. 'I'll be tied up late Friday.' The words came out easier than the idea of attending. Plus it would be full of hospital people and he didn't want his friendship with Tilly to be a source of gossip. It would be easy for people to get the wrong idea.

Now he'd have to figure out where to go, though there was always plenty of work if he wanted it.

He realised Tilly had already moved on. 'No problem.' She shrugged and smiled at him and he wasn't sure what the feeling was he had now. Relief it wasn't a problem? It certainly wasn't disappointment that she didn't care. Was it?

'Come if you can.' She gestured with her hand at a fruit shop. 'This place here. They do the most amazing juice and smoothies.'

Ten minutes later they carried their drinks up the hill, and Marcus felt lighter and happier than he had for years. She was so relaxing. No pressure. Great to look at. Fun to be with. When not at work anyway.

He smiled to himself. Tilly didn't pressure him like other women had. She hadn't been worried at all that he'd declined her invitation. She was just a female friend and he couldn't ever remember having one of those.

Then his pager went off and with the noise he changed back into who he really was.

He lifted his phone and Tilly saw his expression change.

'See you later.' He took off and jogged the rest of the way to his house and disappeared inside.

Tilly sipped the creamy juice as she watched him go. With one phone call he'd looked like a battle-worn soldier going to fight. That was sad. For Tilly her work wasn't a battle: it was a watching game and a privilege. She guessed it was different for an obstetrician because they were called on when the chips were down. She wished she could show him how it should be.

CHAPTER SIX

IT WAS Friday night and Marcus heard the party as soon as he parked his car. He'd been trying not to think about it all day. No way was he going. He had a hundred reasons why he shouldn't.

There seemed to be an extra dozen cars, half on and half off the footpath up the street, and light and sound spilled out of the downstairs windows. He hoped it wouldn't go on all night. He wondered what his aunt said about this. It seemed pretty thoughtless. Bah humbug.

'Good grief, no, it doesn't bother me,' Aunt Maurine said with a laugh. 'I love the sound of the singing that comes later. And they put up with my girls on a Friday afternoon.'

She peered at him. 'You should go. Loosen up. You're a nice man, Marcus. I wouldn't like anyone to think you were a bit of a stuffed shirt.'

That straightened his shoulders. 'I'm not worried what they think.'

She glanced at him sympathetically and he didn't

like that either. 'And don't mind you haven't been given an invitation. The girls won't care if you just turn up.'

Marcus wrinkled his nose. 'I have an invitation, thank you.'

She raised suddenly haughty brows and he saw the lead soprano younger singers would have quaked at twenty years ago. 'Then why are you still here, talking to a woman twice your age?'

It seemed he had no choice. But he wasn't going like this in a shirt and tie. He'd stick out like a doctor surrounded by young nurses.

Ten minutes later he knocked on the door and discovered there were as many medicos as nurses dancing on the lounge-room floor and none of them cared.

He'd missed out on this at uni.

Always working, saving, studying. So this was what parties were like. It didn't look too wild. Noisy and colourful and someone had dug out a revolving colour strobe that painted everyone red and then green and then pink and back to red again. It was a wonder they weren't all having epileptic fits with the flashing lights.

Even the senior registrar from A and E he'd met yesterday, Cort someone, was there with his arm around an attractive redhead whom he thought perhaps lived here. It seemed he was right because she tilted her head back and called up the stairs.

'Tilly. Marcus is here.'

Then Matilda appeared. There was a big happy smile on her face and he could do nothing but smile back. She looked gorgeous again in black tights and a lime-green skirt with 1960s-style earrings that stroked her neck in the way he wanted to.

She drifted down the stairs like a debutante, slow and sinuous with a touch of shyness, and he held his breath until he realised what he was doing. He caught a sympathetic look from the A and E reg. but she looked too good to pretend he wasn't bowled over.

'I'm so glad you came,' she said loudly just as the music finished, and her voice fell into the silence. Everyone turned and looked at them both.

Marcus felt himself flush, and a shaft of regret and the wish he'd stayed home flashed through him for a moment, but then the music started again and she put out her hand and dragged him through to the kitchen where it was quieter.

'Sorry about that.' She even laughed and he realised she was unperturbed. Maybe he was a stuffed shirt but someone had to be responsible and he'd hate anyone to get the idea they were an item.

When he didn't answer she shook her head. 'It will be all over the hospital tomorrow.' She shrugged. 'Not a lot you can do about it. Just treat me like the annoying midwife you always do and you'll be fine. Everyone will think you're just slumming.'

She was teasing him again and he'd never realised she had a little dimple to the right of her mouth. He'd always known she'd had a mouth, a smart one. Tonight it was luscious and he had the sudden urge to taste her just a little.

He slipped his hand into hers where she'd dropped

it and pulled her in behind the edge of the refrigerator so that they were shielded from the door and he could back her up against the wall very gently but firmly until she was trapped.

By him. It felt remarkably good to have that power over her for a change. He put a hand on either side of her head against the wall, and they both knew she could duck under and out if she wanted to. But she didn't. Hmm.

'So,' he said softly and rubbed his cheek against hers. She felt like silk and no doubt he felt like sandpaper because he hadn't shaved since that morning, but she didn't seem to mind. If he wasn't mistaken, she almost purred.

'I like your perfume.' It was flowery and light and seemed to sing of summer.

'I like yours,' she said cheekily, and his smile widened.

He had another sniff and fought back the urge to crush her into his chest. He spoke to distract himself. 'It seems a good party.'

'All our parties are good.' And the way she looked at him said she had no problem with the standing arrangement they had at the moment. He felt his mouth tilt as he looked at her. Glorious skin, determined little chin, and that mouth. His eyes dropped.

He moved in until his chest flattened her breasts delightfully against him and she slid her arms up and around his shoulders. He liked the curl of her fingers against him and he pushed her earrings off her neck with his nose and brushed his lips along the line of her jaw like he'd hungered to do before. Her scent and the satin feel and the subtle pulse beneath his mouth felt more erotic than he'd expected.

Then their mouths touched, and joined, and he liked the taste of her even more. She made him feel like a parched traveller in a desert with a sense of homecoming and a caress of recognition. A taste of discovery and suddenly a taste of madness as they both learnt the other and found exactly what they'd never realised they'd looked for.

The perfect kiss, the perfect taste, the perfect fit and feel and depth, everything was right when it should have taken time to recognise and bond—yet instead they fitted together as if they'd waited for this moment.

Both pulled back at the same time, and if he wasn't mistaken, she was just as stunned and wary and not quite sure what had happened as he was. 'I'm sorry,' he said, 'I got carried away.'

The darkness of her pupils drew him. 'Funny. I thought there were two of us.'

Their gazes locked. He smiled. 'Were there?' They'd felt like one entity to him.

She laughed. It sounded a little nervous because this was moving too fast for an improbable relationship and at that moment the crowd surged through the kitchen door and into the room and they were surrounded by people looking for food and drinks. Tilly broke away, opened the fridge and began handing out platters.

Marcus leant back against the wall and watched her, and tried to figure out what had just happened.

Every now and then she cast him a quick glance, a shy smile, and he could see she was just as confused as he. He guessed that was something.

But he was strangely content just to watch her for the moment. The shift of her arms, the swing of her earrings against her neck, the pull of her shirt across her breasts.

When the crowds had been fed, he and Tilly moved back with them into the lounge, where the music had changed to a slower beat with a less deafening volume, and people lay around on cushions with at least two to an armchair and six along the floor, leaning back on the lounge he'd lifted her onto the other day.

'Give us a song, Tilly,' said a thin fellow Marcus recognised as the radiologist he'd spoken to earlier that day at the hospital, and a few more voices joined in.

Tilly shooed a young male nurse off her chair and pushed Marcus into it. Then she sat on his lap as if she did it every day and picked up a guitar from beside the chair.

He was trapped, pleasantly squashed, and wrapped in a surreal ambiance he'd never experienced before with this mystifying young woman and her friends. Suddenly he was a part of the crowd, instead of looking down on it, and it felt pretty good.

Tilly began to sing, quite unself-consciously, with that beautiful lilting ballad he'd heard before as she strummed the guitar. One of the male nurses joined in and within seconds a few more had joined.

Someone suggested a well-known song and suddenly the walls were bouncing with noise and laughter and Marcus looked around in wonder.

They sang a couple more and then people drifted out to refuel and recharge their drinks.

The sound system came back on and Tilly put the guitar down and leaned back against him, her face flushed and smiling. He kissed her neck. 'You're enjoying yourself?' He could see she was.

'Aren't you?' she said.

Actually, he was. Not a stuffed shirt at all. 'Very much. Thank you for asking me.'

A tiny smiled curved her lips and he wanted to kiss her again. 'It's not free. You have to sing. Your aunt has a glorious voice. You must have some inherited talent.'

He listened to a lot of music but he didn't sing. He didn't even sing in the shower or the car. But he wanted to please her. 'I could probably do a really mean "Poke Salad Annie".'

'Never heard of it.' She shrugged those delectable arms and his hand strayed up to curve over and cup the warmth of her shoulder. Her skin felt like satin beneath his fingers.

He sang 'Gator got your Grannie' in a Deep South baritone and she giggled. 'Oh, I like that. Do it some more.'

'That's enough, you two.' A pint-sized blonde grinned at them. 'Are we out of ice, Tilly?'

She nodded. 'I fear it's a tragedy.' She looked at Marcus. 'You're not drinking, are you?'

Not alcohol anyway. He was certainly imbibing something as she sat on him and he thanked goodness he had his shirt untucked. 'Nope. On call.' He patted his shirt pocket because he hadn't given his phone a thought in the last two hours. Thankfully it was still there.

She prepared to climb off him and parts of him mourned. She was oblivious, of course. 'Would you give me a lift to the pub and we'll get some ice, please?'

Ice sounded like a good idea, though he wasn't sure about dripping iced water in the tiny boot of his car. His mouth twitched. But he could think of worse things than having Tilly to himself in the close confines of his car in the dark. 'I guess I could. I'd been hoping to catch the submarine races anyway.'

She frowned. 'How do you see submarines race? Aren't they under the water?'

She was so naive. He liked that about her. 'Another name for parking in the dark. In a car with a girl.'

She slapped his hand away from her waist and stood up. 'There'll be none of that, sir.'

He tried to look crestfallen. 'Now, that's a shame. Do we get to put the ice in the refrigerator when we come back?'

He saw the moment she realised he was talking about the last time they'd been in the kitchen. Tilly looked at him from under her eyebrows and suddenly they were both laughing.

He captured her hand and dragged her out to his car. He felt like he was sixteen again, which was ridiculous when he was twice that age.

'So, you're enjoying your new job?' They were in the line-up of cars a few minues later to drive through the hotel bottle shop, and Tilly suddenly remembered the look on Marcus's face when his mobile had rung the other day. A soldier into battle.

He smiled at her. Tonight he looked a man happy with his world.

'Very much. And I enjoy private practice. It's satisfying to monitor a woman's progress through her pregnancy.' He drummed his fingers on the steering wheel. 'To know I've taken every precaution and been vigilant for the safe arrival of their precious baby.'

'Vigilant sounds like a force against evil.'

His hands tightened and she saw that his knuckles had whitened. 'Someone has to take the responsibility to ensure the safety of women and their families.'

Tilly mentally sighed. 'Okay, but healthy birthing women aren't at risk. You're not a control freak, are you?'

'What?' He didn't look happy with that.

Oops. She should have stopped there. Any progress they'd made tonight was about to go out the open window, and the warmth they generated between them cooled quickly when work became involved. Maybe that was a good thing if she was going to stay his friend and not anything else.

But, unfortunately, she couldn't stop. He was still

seeing birth as a battle. For most women it wasn't like that. 'Do you think perhaps you're treating pregnancy like an illness? As if a healthy mother is at risk for nine months and needs constant testing in case.'

'Probably.' His hands stilled and he glanced at her. 'Because some women do. It's a fact. Pregnancy increases risk. Things go wrong.'

She sighed. 'Sure. Some women need watching and expertise. But not all the time. Over-watching and interfering can draw bad outcomes, too. I guess what I'm trying to say is that normal pregnancy is not a disease.'

She saw the battle he was having with himself not to get heated and she felt sorry for him. They'd never agree on this and it wasn't fair to do this to him. She backed off.

'Anyway, I love watching the expectation as the due date appears. Meeting a woman's family, answering questions, and afterwards the glow of a new mother.'

She saw the relief he had something he could agree with or maybe it was just relief because the car in front had moved through and he'd be able to get out of the car away from her soon.

She'd done a good job of destroying their rapport anyway. Tilly rolled her neck in the dark. Dumb. Or deliberate subconscious sabotage?

CHAPTER SEVEN

THE morning after the party it was blowing a gale and the white caps on the sea were blown off the tops almost as fast as they formed. There were several strong rips dragging the foam on top of the water out to sea. On days like this Tilly opted for the women's pool for her swim.

Marcus ran past Tilly with a wave of his hand and she waved back. She was talking to a wizened old gentleman with faded blue swimmers emblazoned with 'Coogee Lifesaver' across his skinny buttocks.

The old bloke must have been swimming in the sea for seventy years at least, Marcus decided, or maybe eighty because his skin was as leathered and wrinkled as that of an anorexic sea lion.

The guy seemed to know Tilly well but, then, Tilly seemed to know everyone well.

Except him. He couldn't get a handle on her.

His feet slapped the sand as he crossed the beach and he reviewed last night in his mind.

He'd thought they were fine at the party but then

they'd gone for ice in his car, even though he hadn't been real keen to put wet bags in his car's boot. Tilly had seen his reluctance and teased him about it but he'd been brave about that.

He'd still been fazed by that kiss and the closeness of her on his lap in the lounge. He should have shut down that conversation about low-risk women earlier. Maybe kissed her to keep her quiet. That sounded much more fun. Her views on pregnancy and birth continued to jar him.

Soon after they'd arrived back he'd been called out and lost his chance to back her up against the wall again. Even now he could feel his body stir at the thought and he doubted he'd be able to look at a refrigerator in the same light ever again.

Before he could get to the top of the cliff path his phone rang and that was the end of his run. But that was okay. Diversion was a good thing. He turned round and jogged back to the house to get changed and go in to work on a Saturday.

The next morning they both reached the front path at the same time because he'd thought she might have slipped away yesterday to avoid him.

Tilly's brows drew together with mock suspicion and she looked up at him. 'Are you stalking me?'

He was trying hard not to but he'd actually missed talking to her yesterday. 'Could be.'

'Lovely,' she said, and they both smiled as they walked down to the beach. An easy silence sat comfortably on a sleepy Sunday morning. Even the waves were small against the beach now that the wind had died, and as they got closer the sun had already begun to warm the air.

'I was wondering if after our exercise you'd be interested in a long, leisurely Sunday breakfast.' There went his mouth again. It seemed he had it all worked out subconsciously. 'A table for two at the Beachside Bistro, browse the papers, enjoy the sun?'

She smiled at him and he was damned if he didn't feel like he'd just won a prize. 'Sounds wonderful.'

Excellent. 'Good,' he said out loud. He pulled his phone out of his pocket. 'I'll book a table by the window for eight.'

'Of course you will.' She shook her head and laughed at him. 'Leisurely, but with a timetable.' She reached up and kissed his mouth, a soft, promising kiss that almost had him flat on his back in the sand.

Then she patted his arm and left him where the path veered away from the water. He watched her drop her towel and then she was diving into the surf without a backward glance.

He stood there watching her as she swam and savoured the imprint of her sweet mouth against his. He almost wished he could dive in after her.

'Don't let her get away.' The old lifesaver from yesterday watched him with a quizzical lift of one snow-white eyebrow. 'She's a keeper, that one. Swim after her.'

'Love to.' He watched her lovely arms drive through the water. Then surprised himself again. 'Can't swim.'

The old man glanced at Tilly as she struck out through the surf until she reached the quieter waters of the bay. 'Then you'd better learn.'

In what spare moment of his day? 'I'm a bit old for arm floats,' Marcus joked, ready to move on.

'Six in the evenings. At the sea pool. I'm Duggie. Always there so it won't matter if you don't come. Might take a week or two. We'll see.'

The old man sniffed and moved on and Marcus stared after him. Good grief. He cast one last glance at Tilly then turned his face to the sand and began to run. He didn't want to think about the idea of putting his face in the water but thinking never hurt anyone.

An hour later Marcus's breakfast table was marked with a 'reserved' sign. Shielded by a palm in a window alcove perched above the beach, the table sat in the striped shade as the sun climbed up over their heads.

A tall black-eyed waiter placed a napkin across Tilly's lap with a familiar flick of his fingers and a wide smile. She laughed up at him. 'Were you scared I'd tuck it into my neck?'

The man raised one eyebrow and nodded. 'Absolutely,' he said, and Tilly laughed again.

Marcus thought it a bit strange, and a little intrusive for a waiter. 'Know him, do you?' He hoped so or he'd be having a word with someone.

'He used to go out with Ellie.' She glanced around

with a smile. 'Actually, most of these waiters used to go out with Ellie.'

Good grief. 'How many of them went out with you?' Now, why had he asked that? He certainly didn't want to know the answer.

'None.' She shrugged. 'I'm keeping it light. More of a looker than a participant. Burnt twice with ones who didn't work out. I'm saving up to do a study tour around the world in a year. Very happy being single.'

He raised his juice. 'Me, too. Here's to uncompli-cated friendship.'

Tilly clinked her glass against his. 'Happy to have fun as long as it doesn't get serious.'

Perfect. An unexpected voice inside him wondered how much fun she'd agree to. Uncomplicated sex?

'I'll drink to that.' They both sipped as their eyes met and a smouldering frisson of awareness flickered across the table between them.

Tilly raised her eyebrows and smiled. He had to admit it was a strange conversation to have with a woman and laden with undertones. She dropped her eyes to the breakfast she'd chosen so far.

They started with tropical fruit and she licked her lips at the first taste of the most glorious cinnamon yoghurt. He'd had some before and he'd thought she'd like it.

'What is this? I have to find out.' She waved enthu-siastically at her friend the waiter and the man came scurrying over with a big smile. It was almost as if she wanted to confirm she could flirt with other guys if she wanted to. No problem. Marcus tried not to frown, though he could have told her the brand.

He looked out through the windows and away from the two of them. The curving crescent of sand stretched both ways to the cliffs on either side of Coogee Beach.

He certainly understood why people thought Coogee was paradise. He could see the bay and other swimmers striking out like Tilly had across the blue water, then suddenly a flash of grey broke the surface.

'Look, dolphins.' He leaned forward and pointed and she craned her neck and upper body until she saw them.

Her breasts seemed to heave out of her top and he dragged his eyes away before she caught him looking but his good humour had been miraculously restored. The picture was imprinted indelibly on his brain and he'd pull it out and look at it again later. He grinned into his juice. 'Ever swum with dolphins?'

She sat back and it was safe to look again. 'Only once.' She smiled at the memory. 'They brushed against me and I nearly died of shock. Thought it was a shark.' She shuddered at the memory. 'But once I'd realised it was a dolphin, I remembered dolphins kept the sharks away so I felt better. I often see them a few waves away. Playing with each other. I know the day's going to be special when I see that happen.' She grinned at him. 'Dolphins mate for life, you know.'

Nobody mates for life. 'It's a lovely fairytale.' He returned to the previous subject. 'I can't imagine what you must have felt like when it brushed against you.'

He shook his head. 'I have enough trouble imagining the water underneath me let alone the sharks.' Marcus tapped his neck. 'If I was meant to swim, I'd have been born with gills.'

She disagreed. 'I was born to swim. I find it soothing to strike out through the waves. My mind wanders with the rhythm of breathing and using my arms and legs. It starts my day well.'

He could see that bit. 'That's how I feel about my run.'

She raised her brows. 'Don't tell me we have something in common?'

The rapport was back. And it felt good. 'I think perhaps we have a lot more in common than I thought— just a different way of looking at things.'

She gave him one of those smiles that felt like a precious gift. 'Marcus. That sounds very liberal for you.'

He grimaced. 'Let's not go there.' He stood up. 'Shall we try another course?'

The open buffet tempted them, and they piled their plates with mushrooms and tomato and a crispy rasher of bacon each. When Tilly saw they'd chosen almost identical breakfasts she laughed. 'Oh, no. An old couple with the same breakfast.'

'This once. Well-deserved appetite after our exercise,' Marcus said virtuously, and they carried their laden plates back to the seat with only mild guilt.

Back at the table they could see the dolphins were closer to shore and excited children pointed out to the waves. The sun was warm on his neck, the woman opposite was brown and gorgeous, and the sea and sand looked idyllic.

'I can see why my aunt loves it here,' Marcus said. 'I may have to change my plans of location if I decide to buy instead of rent.'

She nodded enthusiastically. 'Coogee has a great feel. It's young and vibrant, with a core group of great older people like your aunt and Duggie, and most of the houses and flats have so much character.'

'Duggie? The lifesaver. I spoke to him this morning.' He looked at her and remembered the kiss. He remembered it very well and it must have shown on his face because she blushed. 'He told me to dive in after you.'

She didn't meet his eyes. 'Duggie thinks everyone should be able to swim to Sydney Heads and back.'

Fat chance of that. 'He offered me swimming lessons.' That made her face him, he thought with satisfaction.

She zoned in on him with real attention. 'I could teach you.' Now he wished he hadn't mentioned it. What sort of man didn't swim?

She went on like a crusader and he didn't know how to stop her. 'I could. I used to teach the Nippers.'

Please change the subject. 'Nippers?'

'Junior lifesavers. Little ones. Most could swim but there were a few who weren't real happy about the surf.'

He could understand that. 'Sounds like me.'

Her face glowed and he couldn't tear his eyes away even though he wasn't happy about the reason for it.

'I love watching people learn to swim. I'm a good teacher.'

He could believe that but it wasn't happening. 'Not sure how I'd be as a student.'

She shrugged in that easy way that he really liked about her. 'If it doesn't happen, that's okay.'

Suddenly he was almost tempted. 'But time is against me.'

She sensed the opening he hadn't meant to give. 'If you got up a little earlier, we could do twenty minutes after your run.'

She was nothing if not focussed. Terrier-like. It was too much to ask. 'You'd have to get up earlier, too.'

She brushed that off. 'I'm a midwife. My kind got burned at the stake for doing what they love. Getting up earlier is nothing.'

Did he want to accept? He had a sudden vision of Tilly, in her bikini, directing his arms, and holding him to keep him afloat, lots of contact possibilities, much more fun than Duggie. 'I'll think about your generous offer. Maybe one lesson to try. I promise I won't burn you at the stake if it doesn't work.'

She grimaced. 'But happy to burn me for my mid-wifery.'

He looked down at his eggs. 'Pass.'

She raised her eyebrows and picked up her own fork and knife. 'Typical. Then pass the salt, please.'

The next day, back to reality on the ward round, Marcus hoped the time they'd spent together over the weekend wouldn't make it awkward at work—but she had said at the party he could treat her like the annoying midwife she was.

The thought made him smile. There was no doubt his little midwife did cause some measure of agitation in his manly chest and he was thinking of her more than he should. He'd really not planned to be distracted by anyone for a while but he had the feeling there wasn't a lot he could do about it now.

Tilly intrigued and amused him and turned him on with just a glimpse of her.

Later in the day he wasn't feeling quite so warm and fuzzy.

He'd gone down to the ward again to see his private patient, a woman who'd had a previous Caesarean because her induced labour had gone on too long, and now her second baby was due in two weeks.

Stella's repeat Caesarean operation had been arranged for the next day and he'd ordered a foetal monitoring session in the ward to check on her baby. Instead of a woman preparing for surgery he found that after an hour of exposure to Tilly, his patient had suddenly decided she'd like to cancel the operation, wait to go into labour naturally and try to have a vaginal birth.

Marcus suppressed a sigh. He'd had no idea Stella would prefer that. Had he missed something in their previous conversations or had Tilly swayed her?

He glanced at Tilly who looked back innocently. 'That's your right, of course, Stella,' he agreed. 'And, yes, it's true this baby may not be as big, although the ultrasound says a reasonable size.'

Stella peered at him as if to discern his own feelings about it all but that didn't help him figure out what she really wanted. He wasn't sure whether to blame Tilly or thank her.

Suddenly Stella burst into speech. 'If anything changed and I needed a Caesarean, would I still be able to have it?'

He tilted his head and frowned. It was a worry if he gave that impression. 'Of course you would. No problem. If you want to try a normal birth again, I'm with you all the way. Is that what you want?'

He didn't hold grudges with pregnant women. 'I thought you wanted the Caesarean because you were so exhausted from your last labour?' If that did happen again to her he'd quite happily strangle Tilly for encouraging her to go through a long first stage again.

'Tilly says if I go into labour naturally hormones are released that help my baby breathe better after birth. And Caesarean babies have a much greater risk of ending up in Neonatal Intensive Care.'

It was a risk they took every day but Caesareans were so common they didn't include that in pre-talks any more. 'That's all true.'

'You didn't mention that.' Her brows creased and Marcus kept his face neutral.

'I'm sorry. I thought you'd decided on the operative birth. I didn't want you to feel I was being negative about your choice.'

'Oh.' She looked a little shamefaced and he didn't want that either.

Sometimes pregnant women's emotions were a minefield but he got that. 'It's okay. Really. Whatever you want.'

In a less combative tone she said, 'So why do so many women have booked Caesareans?'

He really would have to spend more time with his ladies. It seemed it was too easy to assume they understood. He'd have to take that on board—it was just a little hard getting it from the junior midwife. Again. God bless Tilly. Not!

He looked at Tilly and raised his eyebrows. He hoped she could read the message. You started all this, his brows said, help me reassure her.

Tilly kept quiet. She probably thought she'd said enough, which he might agree or disagree with later, but for the moment he just continued because it seemed he had the stage.

Marcus pulled a chair over and sat down. His body language said he had all the time in the world to talk and Stella responded with a little drop of her shoulders. He focussed on her face, determined to ally her concerns. 'Because, as you said, operative deliveries have risk and we can't do all of our Caesareans in the middle of the night. It's safer when everyone is awake, full staff, and a mother hasn't any food in her tummy. That means booking them in advance.'

Stella frowned. 'Okay. But I might just go ahead and have a normal birth and not need an operation at all.'

He smiled at Stella. He really hoped she did. 'And I'll look forward to that.'

She chewed her lip. 'If I go overdue, can you induce me?'

Marcus shot a look at Tilly. Cat got your tongue? So you didn't tell her about that, he thought.

'Not usually. Because of your previous Caesarean it's better not to force the uterus to contract with drugs. Even with a natural progression of contractions you'll be closely monitored for any signs of the previous scar in your uterus coming apart.'

He hadn't spoken of that either, because he'd thought she wasn't going to have a labour.

'But we do have a special monitor that you can wear in the shower or walk around with,' Tilly offered, but Stella was on a roll with working herself up.

'Does that make my baby at more risk if I have a vaginal birth?'

Marcus shook his head. 'No. Only if your labour becomes complicated. You have no other risk factors. Baby's growing well, no medical problems. Statistically your baby is safer if born during normal birth.'

Stella nodded, satisfied, and smiled at them both. 'Then I'll go home and wait for that.'

'Fine.' He glanced at Tilly then back at Stella and dug in his pocket for his card. He wrote on the back. 'Here's my mobile number if you have any worries or more questions. I'll let Theatre know to cancel the case. It's honestly not a problem.'

'Thank you. I do feel better now. I'm going to do it

naturally.' Stella left, and Marcus waited for Tilly to come back from showing her out.

Tilly knew he was waiting and wanted to take a right turn and hide in the sluice room but she didn't. It wasn't her style.

'Um. Sorry she gave you the third degree.'

He raised his eyebrows. 'That was fun. Not.'

Tilly shrugged. 'She really had a lot of questions and once I started to answer them it just went on from there.'

He was partially to blame and that Stella might have been upset wasn't good enough. 'It's okay. I should have covered more in the rooms. But you were very quiet. I could have done with a bit more help to calm her down.'

He was right. Even to Tilly, her voice sounded sheepish. 'I thought I might have said enough.'

She looked relieved when he half laughed as he turned to go. 'Probably.'

'Are we still swimming tomorrow?'

He glanced at her with wide eyes. 'Am I going to have to do it naturally?'

It was Tuesday morning.

'Let your body float. Trust the water. We're designed to float.' It was seven in the morning and the first of the lessons with Tilly. 'The water's not even up to your waist and you can stand up any time.'

She definitely had a thing about trusting water. They were poles apart.

Sitting in this position, the water was up to his

nipples. It was cold and very salty. Funny, he'd never tasted the salt in sea water before 6:00 p.m. last night.

Thank goodness he'd come and at least become a little more comfortable in the water. Duggie had been very matter-of-fact about his reluctance and this morning he could sit in it without shuddering. No way had he been going to make the first attempt in front of Tilly.

But he didn't know if he really wanted to do this. Thank goodness there wasn't anyone else around. 'This is ridiculous.'

Tilly's voice was in his ear. Comforting. 'Just lean back on me, Marcus. I've got you. If anyone sees us they'll just think we're having a cuddle.'

That was the only reason he was still there. Tilly's skin against his in the water, satin with an underlying strength, and the softness of her breasts against the back of his head. It could certainly be agreeably erotic if he wasn't so unhappy about the water and the chance of people looking at them.

Her hands were around his chest loosely as he leaned back and she shifted farther away as he stretched out. He wouldn't have minded rolling the back of his head around that lovely cleft but she might drop him. He snuggled a little with an internal smile. She never lost contact. He knew she was there. Reliable.

Her voice went on. Warm and wonderful and he could see how she helped women in labour. 'Close your eyes and just feel it. Spread your arms out. Let yourself relax and I'll hold your shoulders.' He closed his eyes. Actually, it was better with his eyes closed. Like a cold bath. Suddenly he could feel his weight shift and his legs lifted as he stretched right out. He was floating!

His eyes flew open and he stiffened, and as he sank water nearly ran into his mouth. He gasped just as Tilly's arms came around him and kept him above water level again.

'Nearly.'

This was pathetic. He made himself sick with this stupid fear. Something shifted in his mind and he forced himself to trust her this time as he leaned back against her. This time he relaxed his body into the sand on the bottom of the sea pool.

His legs drifted towards the surface and he fought the urge to stiffen. His head leaned back more as she shifted away, still with her hand under his shoulder blades but that was all.

His ears submerged and then he was floating. He kept his eyes shut and pointed his toes until he stretched out fully. She had the tips of her fingers under the back of his head but he was doing it all himself. It wasn't too bad.

When he sat up and looked at her with a grin—darn it, he was pleased with himself—she grinned back. Even more delighted than he was. 'Okay. You're a good teacher.'

Her eyes opened wide, innocently green. 'That wasn't what you said when Stella changed her mind about the Caesarean.'

Cheeky. 'Ouch. Nasty woman. I'll remember that next time at work.'

'Ouch, yourself.'

Fifteen minutes later they were walking back to Hill Street. 'What are you scared of, Tilly?'

Tilly shot a look at him. 'What makes you think I'm scared of anything?' She flicked a stray hair out of her eyes. 'Apart from trusting men, of course.'

He laughed. 'Can't help you with that one. But seriously?'

I was serious, Tilly thought. 'Um. Suturing?'

She saw his incredulous look. 'Suturing?'

What was so bizarre about that? 'Yep. I did the suturing module and passed but I'm a terrible seamstress with real sewing and I'd hate to do a botched job on a lady who's just given birth.'

He pursed his lips. 'Fair enough. So we could practise that. I learnt on foam. Then we could do steak. Neat little stitches. I'll teach you on the weekend. Then I'll feel I'm repaying you for the swimming lessons.'

'There's no debt, Marcus.'

Maybe she didn't see one. 'I'd like to do it.'

She tilted her head. 'I think I have issues when you're nice to me.' Then she smiled at him and it ran down his body like a bolt of liquid heat. 'Okay. Thanks. But not till before lunch. I have something on during Saturday morning.'

He nodded. Satisfied. 'Brunch at your house. I'll bring supplies.'

She paused at her gate. 'We'll have a barbeque after

with our carpetbag steak.' They grinned at each other. 'Ruby's a vegetarian. She'll hold her nose when she smells the meat.'

CHAPTER EIGHT

THEY managed to get through the rest of the week without any major confrontations at work, and even some sweet moments during births, when he tried to be as unobtrusive as possible and observe rather than direct. He'd had a few memorable smiles from Tilly.

By Saturday morning, after his swim, he was looking forward to brunch. There seemed to be some type of rally going on and it was pretty noisy. The beach park was full of baby strollers, toddlers, militant mamas, doting dads and purple-dressed women whom Marcus finally realised were home-birth midwives. He could feel his lip curl.

Placards abounded. 'Home birth is a choice.' 'Babies birth naturally.' 'Midwives hold the future.'

Marcus rolled his eyes. He'd gone for his run late because he'd been up half the night with a tricky delivery and subsequent emergency Caesarean. All had turned out well but it had been touch and go for a while there for mother and baby and his eyes felt like sandpaper.

Imagine if that woman had been at home. These were

exactly the sort of people his parents had hung around with. Hard as it had been to accept after his sister's accidental drowning, he'd never really come to terms with any parents' decision to have their baby's birth outside the hospital in a non-structured environment.

'A well mother and baby can be safer at home than in a hospital. Leave medical care for sick mothers and babies.' The words penetrated his heated thoughts and he froze. He knew that voice.

'Midwifery care is safe care. Everyone wants well mothers and babies. Tell your local member of parliament that you want the choice of safe home birth.' Why was he surprised? But he wondered if the hospital allowed their midwives to promote such dangerous practice.

He tilted his neck past the dreadlocked hair in front and now he could see her. Dressed in a purple sundress, her height raising her face slightly above those on the old-fashioned park bandstand, the gazebo they'd sat and had breakfast together in, as she gazed earnestly out over the sea of faces.

He pulled his head back behind the woman in front in case she saw him. There was a smattering of applause and nodding heads as she left the dais.

He felt let down, back-stabbed, incredibly hurt— which was ridiculous. He'd known she was passionate about natural birth. But he hadn't known she was a radical.

He put his head down and turned away but it was

slow moving through the suddenly dissipating throng of onlookers.

'Marcus?' Tilly touched his hand and he straightened but he couldn't look at her. He stared into the distance where an oil tanker was crossing the ocean out on the horizon past her left ear.

His voice was flat when the words came out. 'You're part of the home-birth movement, aren't you?'

She straightened her shoulders. He saw the shift, but couldn't look at her while he waited for her to confirm it. He didn't want to see the truth. Just watch the damn ship crawl across the waves, he told himself.

'Yes, I am. Absolutely.' Straight up. No flinching. Of course she was.

He looked then. Stared straight into her eyes. Said goodbye to her eyes, her nose, that mouth. The features he'd come to like a lot. Not love, it couldn't possibly be love, but definitely feel attached to. But whatever they had between them was over. Had to be because she stood for everything he distrusted.

'Well, I disagree with all of it. And I'd rather not become involved with someone who is. I'd consider it professionally hypocritical.'

Her fine brows were raised and for the second time since he'd known her she was angry. 'Spending a little time together doesn't make us involved. But I'd hate to make you a hypocrite, Marcus.' A lot of irony accompanied that comment.

Her emotion practically singed his eyebrows as her eyes bored into his. 'You're a big one for generalisations, aren't you? Why are you so closed off and negative about something that should be every woman's right?'

Why? Did she have an hour? 'Because it's dangerous. Because people die or almost die.' Now he was angry at himself for making it personal.

He saw her face change. Soften instantly at whatever had crossed his face but he didn't want her sympathy. She said, 'I'm guessing something happened.'

'That's not important.' He wanted her to understand he could never encourage a birth at home for one of his clients.

'To me it is. Can't you tell me?' Caring eyes looked into his and he didn't want that connection.

And he really didn't want to remember that day. He'd been six and his baby sister had drowned. That's why he'd never learnt to swim, but he didn't say it. He looked past her to the ship that was almost gone. 'Nothing happened. Goodbye, Tilly.'

He'd go to his consulting rooms and put the whole thing from his mind. There was plenty to do there. He could do that. Because he had control.

She watched him walk away with his shoulders straight and his head up but she knew how much he was hurting. She'd wanted to tell him that the unexpected happened in hospitals, too.

That home birth had evolved and midwives were trained, skilled, updated more than ever before. Professional women doing a professional job. And women at risk were share-cared with a doctor when they should be. But he was gone and she had a lot to think about.

She guessed there was no suturing lesson this morning or carpetbag steak.

When she went home his car wasn't there. Mrs Bennett was sitting on her front veranda, drinking a cup of tea.

'Hello, Matilda,' she called, before Tilly turned into her own gate. 'Fancy a cup of tea?'

Tilly stopped and went up the path in Mrs Bennett's and joined her on the veranda. She glanced at the little table beside Mrs Bennett's knees. 'And scones? Yum.'

'There's plenty in the pot. I thought Marcus was joining me but he's torn off somewhere in that car of his.'

Tilly wondered if she was the reason he'd 'torn' off. 'It must be nice to have him here for company.'

'Yes. It is.' Mrs Bennett poured for Tilly. 'Strange, when I'm used to my own company, but nice. He's a good man and easy to live with. It was lovely to see him go over to your party the other night. I don't think Marcus's done much of that sort of thing. Takes things a bit seriously, I think. He used to be such a happy little thing. Singing made-up songs all the time until the tragedy.'

Tilly couldn't help the soar of interest those words provided. 'Did he?' This was sneaky but no way was she leaving. She settled into her seat.

Mrs Bennett nodded. 'His mother almost died during a birth at home. Not something a child should watch. Silly woman. She had a bleeding disorder, never told the midwife or they wouldn't have allowed it, and should never have had the babe at home.'

Home-birth horror story. She should have known. 'He never said.'

'You might need to give him a bit of leeway if he seems serious. I don't mind telling you, Matilda, that boy was hard done by. His parents didn't make enough effort to make him see it wasn't his fault.'

'How could his mother's birth problems be his fault?'

'Not his mother's. His little sister died the same day. There should have been other adults there looking after those children while his mother birthed, not putting a six-year-old in charge of a three-year-old.'

Tilly felt the cold clutch her belly. Water, she'd bet. 'Poor Marcus.'

'Of course the boy was too young to be responsible with all the screaming that I'll bet went on. His little sister wandered away and drowned in the fish pond they had out the back.' Mrs Bennett bit her lip and wiped away a tear.

Now she'd upset her friend. Tilly felt terrible. 'I'm sorry if talking about this made you sad, Mrs Bennett.'

Mrs Bennett sat up straighter, pulled one of her immaculately ironed lace handkerchiefs out of her pocket and dabbed her eyes. 'It was a very sad time. But I don't mind tears. Might be the actress in me.' She gave a watery smile.

'Tears always make you feel better, that's their job.'

She sniffed delicately. 'They were all so airy-fairy in those days. Flower children twenty years after the movement finished.' She snorted. 'Well, they nearly lost two flowers that day by not being responsible and poor Marcus was saddled with the guilt.'

Tilly could see a solemn little Marcus bowed under the horror of that day. How devastating. She wanted to pick him up and hug him. No wonder he was so serious sometimes.

'Anyway...' Mrs Bennett straightened in her chair. 'He worked his way through uni the hard way, determined not to ask for anything from his parents. Not that they ever saved a penny in their lives, despite being very intelligent people. Not practical, you know. Luckily Marcus was very independent even then.' She sighed. 'Still, he turned out well.'

Except for control tendencies, mistrust of women, and an aversion to water. Tilly picked up her cup. And she'd bet he'd be horrified his aunt had shared that with her, not that she'd break that confidence. Tilly hoped Mrs B. wasn't trying to set them up together because they were just too different.

When Tilly went next door an hour later she certainly had a lot to think about.

Ellie was setting the table and she looked up when Tilly entered. 'What's happening with you and Marcus? Thought he was coming back today for suturing lessons?'

'Not today. We've agreed to differ. Again.'

Ellie studied Tilly's face. 'That's a shame. I actually felt you could suit each other.'

Tilly turned away. 'I thought you wanted him for his genes.'

Ellie grinned. 'Plenty more fish in the sea.' She looked down at the plates on the table. 'Which reminds me, Jess gave up on your barbeque. She's bringing fish and chips. Should be back any minute.'

Tilly groaned and held her stomach. 'Mrs B.'s been filling me up with scones. Small plate for me.'

After four days of avoiding Tilly, late one afternoon Marcus dried his back and grinned at Duggie. 'I can swim.'

'Not a bad stroke.' The old lifesaver was standing on the beach beside the lifesaving shed after their lesson.

Marcus nodded and allowed the concept to sink in. He should have done this years ago. 'Yep. It's not pretty but it works.' And he was happy with that, too. He could do a slow, solid freestyle that was anything but flashy, and it had come out of nowhere and didn't tire him at all.

It seemed that Tilly, along with Duggie's pithy help, had conquered his fear well and truly.

He studied the ocean in front of them and out to where a man was swimming across the bay, and he thought of Tilly again. Something he did with monotonous regularity despite telling himself to stop. 'But I'd hate to have to rely on my own steam to save someone out there.'

Duggie nodded. 'Best not to try without something

to help you float. Gotta have a plan. But get one quick because people do drown.'

He followed Marcus's glance. 'Always think what you're going to do when you get there. You don't fight with the ocean. Or the person you want to help.' He pointed to a young man battling through the waves on his way out to catch a wave on his board.

'See that!' He shook his grizzled head. 'He's got his head up, he's daring the waves to slam into him. If he stayed low on the board, sliced through the waves, allowed it to flow around him, he'd find it much easier.'

Marcus could see what he meant. 'Can we give that a go one day?'

Duggie nodded. 'Now's as good as any. Rescue boards just here. Grab one.'

Marcus nodded. He was a little nervous but keen to try. He hadn't told Tilly he could swim yet or that he'd done the last few evenings with Duggie. He'd avoided the mornings and her since their home-birth discussion. But each day he found he missed the rapport between them more as time passed. It seemed he'd enjoyed her company a lot.

Not to mention the fact that his body remembered the feel of her skin in the water. He missed that very much. Almost worth pretending he couldn't swim. She'd probably think they'd still need arm and leg movements in sections. He frowned at himself. Morally he couldn't do that.

He picked up the board. 'So who taught you about the ocean, Duggie?'

Duggie laughed. 'I learnt the hard way. The youngest of five brothers, they just threw me in.' His amusement split his face into a hundred weathered wrinkles and Marcus couldn't help smiling back. 'If I didn't learn, I went under. Was the youngest surf lifesaving champion in Australia thanks to those brothers.'

His craggy face saddened for a moment. 'Lost 'em all in the war. Didn't like being young then.' He picked up his board as if it were a feather. 'Come on. I'll show you how not to drown when you go to help someone.'

Marcus winced at the 'D' word and tucked his board under his arm. If someone had told him a month ago he'd be doing this he would have said they were mad. But one rise of Duggie's bushy white eyebrows and he was nodding his head. It was crazy how much confidence the old guy inspired.

The sea was warmer than the pool and the feel of the board under him as he paddled out after Duggie felt curiously liberating. His hands dug satisfyingly through the water and every few seconds he skimmed up a wave and down the other side. He could feel the stretch of his smile, the salt tingled on his face with the wind and he sucked in the sudden freedom of endless ocean in front of him. So this was why Tilly swam.

'Come alongside,' Duggie called back, and Marcus dug deeper.

Duggie slipped off the board and they practised the way to load victims and paddle back to the beach by riding a wave or kneeling. It was a little bit precarious and Marcus hoped he'd never need to use the knowledge, but it all gelled with Duggie's wisdom of being prepared.

CHAPTER NINE

AVOIDING Tilly at work was easier as time went on.
That was a good thing. Dr Bennett and the midwife
would never see eye to eye. He was busy, she was busy,
and he could avoid her quite easily if he saw her in the
distance. Something he'd mastered recently. He had no
doubt she was avoiding him, too.

Mornings still lacked something, though. As if his
brain refused to join the two Matildas and insisted
on two different identities, and one of them he sorely
missed. Mornings with Matilda were gone and it didn't
feel right.

He'd achieved the reality by the simple expedient of
running in another location but there was no doubt he
felt the loss of the rapport they'd fallen into. He'd never
felt that need with a woman before. To sit, talk, laugh.

The other was easier to understand because apparently the subtle sexual tension since that first kiss and
during their one swimming lesson had been highlights
of his year. He could tell because those memories in-

truded far too often into his thoughts when he ran. Even at the new beach.

Even now he could imagine the tangle of legs they'd ended with as he'd learnt to float, the softness of her breasts against the back of his head, and the feel of her hands against his skin. He wanted it back. He wanted Morning Matilda back but he had to come to terms with the fact that work dynamics played a part in how he handled the progress or lack of progress in their relationship.

Did it really matter that she had radical beliefs as long as he had control at work? Was he sabotaging a blossoming friendship, a different kind of relationship from anything he'd ever had, for the sake of work when it didn't have to cross over to there?

The next morning Tilly walked up the footpath towards Hill Street and she could see that Marcus's car was still there. So he hadn't gone to work yet. He'd been leaving really early this week. And she hadn't seen him out for his run. She'd swear he hadn't run at all the past few days since he'd abandoned her after the rally.

Well, she wasn't chasing him. He was the moth and she was the flame—Ellie's mantra echoed diligently in her head. Not that she wanted a relationship, but she'd enjoyed his company. Outside work anyway.

'Hi, there.' Tilly jumped, almost guiltily, as the object of her thoughts came up behind her.

Tilly didn't comment on the fact he'd been missing at this time for the last few days. 'Hello, there, to you.'

'Are you still keen for swimming lessons?' He stopped and walked beside her.

She shrugged. 'I thought you might not want to do them any more.'

He was looking at her strangely. 'I have some good memories. Maybe tomorrow if you're not busy?'

It seemed she wasn't *persona non grata* any more. That was nice. Confusing, but she wasn't going to get excited about it. 'If you'd like. The water's been lovely the last few days.'

She wanted to tell him she knew about his mother and his sister but it wasn't the sort of thing you could drop into a conversation. Maybe she'd just leave it to mention in another lifetime.

He glanced at his watch. 'See you then. I have to go in early today.' He jogged off again and she watched him cover the distance to his house with his long strides.

The guy was like a roller-coaster but she couldn't deny she felt that extra spring in her step that had been lacking the last few days. She told herself it was just because she didn't like being at outs with anyone.

The next morning Marcus kicked with his feet hanging onto the side of the pool.

He couldn't believe he was there despite his misgivings, ignoring his professional beliefs to be with her. He was like one of those stupid insects drawn to the blue light. He knew it was going to hurt but he couldn't resist. The only good thing was that now he had the confidence he could swim, everything felt easy. He assured himself that kicking practice would strengthen his freestyle.

Some folks might say he was a bit devious after his successful lessons with Duggie during the evenings but he enjoyed watching Tilly being teacher too much to resist.

And so far it had been as delightful as he'd imagined and it hadn't taken much, some skin, a little laughter, and he'd felt strangely at peace again. They were both kicking side by side as they hung onto the pool edge when the question popped into his mind. 'So, tell me about your family.'

'I have my mum.'

'Tell me about your mother.' Splash, splash, splash. Her splashing slowed. 'Why?' It took him a minute to realise.

Two big kicks from Marcus. 'Because I sure as heck can't figure you out. Maybe if I can understand your mother then I'll understand you.'

Her kick increased and she didn't say anything for half a minute. Water flew into the air as if she was trying to kick the water to death. 'You'd hate my mother.'

Good grief. He let his feet sink and stood up to look at her. 'How can you say that?'

Tilly stopped too and they faced each other, wary, like kids who'd splashed each other too much. 'She's a home-birth midwife, very militant, but also very caring of the women in her care.'

Okay. Maybe he would. No. Of course he wouldn't because she'd be like Tilly and he couldn't hate her if he tried. He had tried—and failed. 'Where does she live?'

'Wollongong. South of Sydney.'

His breath eased out of the side of his mouth with a little hiss he hoped she didn't hear. He turned away and rubbed the back of his suddenly stiff neck. For a horrible moment he'd thought she was going to say up where his parents had lived. Even thinking about it made him shudder. Her mother would be too young to be the one anyway. He dropped his shoulders and sighed.

That shone a little light on why she was how she was. She went on. 'We lived with my grandmother and the only men I really knew were partners of the women my mother and grandmother cared for. She was a home-birth midwife, too.'

Of course she was. And her great-great-grandmother was probably a white witch who delivered at home, too. He couldn't help it —he still had issues with that. But it didn't make him want to get out of the pool and leave her. He had come a long way.

'What about your father?'

She shrugged. 'Never met him. Didn't want to know about me. There's some irresponsible men around.'

Yep. Like his own father, and he wasn't enjoying the conversation any more. He really should work on those issues.

It was Matilda's turn to be curious. 'What about your family?'

'I don't see my parents much. They're not the most responsible people. My sister drowned when I was young and I don't think I ever really forgave them or myself.'

He'd never verbalised that in his life. Why on earth would he bring it up now? His phone rang from the side of the pool and Marcus decided it was a great excuse to drop the subject. He stubbed his toe on the uneven rock of the pool in his haste to get to it. He wiped his hands on the towel, picked up his phone, and almost said thank you instead of hello.

Tilly watched him. Something had happened there. At least he'd mentioned his past but she could see he still had issues to resolve about his family. Silently she thanked Mrs Bennett for the heads up. A stark warning this man wasn't ready to be emotionally involved with anyone.

And she was a little worried she was forgetting she didn't want that either. Maybe it wasn't worth trying to keep their friendship.

He blew hot and cold so much she was getting a chill. She should be used to his fluctuations by now. She was getting way too obsessed with this guy. Tilly ran back over the strange conversation and the shift when she'd mentioned…what?

Tilly climbed out, well aware there'd be no more lesson today, or maybe any day if he was going to give off the vibes he was shedding at the moment.

'I have to go,' he said. She could tell he wanted to say more. Maybe even so she'd understand there could never be anything between them. Well, that was okay because she got that. But apparently he couldn't get the words out. Instead he waved as he turned away.

'And you have to go because of the phone call, too,' she said to his back.

His car was gone when she arrived in Hill Street and Mrs Bennett was sitting on her veranda.

Tilly chewed her lip and decided she couldn't stand not knowing. 'Mrs Bennett?'

'Yes, Tilly, dear.'

She leaned on the gate. 'Can I ask you something?'

'Of course.'

'I've just had a strange conversation with Marcus.'

Her neighbour laughed. 'Only one, dear?'

Tilly smiled. 'Actually, we've had a few, but today was right up there.' She looked at Mrs Bennett and wondered if she really wanted to know more things that would make her care about Marcus.

'Does Marcus ever see his family?'

Mrs Bennett smiled wryly. 'I think I've seen more of him this month than they have for the last twenty years.'

Tilly tried not to let her confusion over Marcus affect her at work the next few days. Keeping distance between them helped but it became impossible when Stella Trainer came in on Wednesday evening.

'I haven't felt my baby move.' Stella and her husband appeared at the desk at the start of Tilly's shift.

Tilly came round the desk and nodded with a sympathetic smile. 'Then let's go and have a little listen, shall we? That way you can feel reassured. Babies often slow down as they get closer to birth.'

She ushered Stella into the assessment room and pulled her notes. 'When was the last time you saw Dr Bennett?'

'Yesterday.' She smiled tremulously. 'We heard the heartbeat then.'

'Okay. That's good.' Tilly smiled again but she had this horrible sinking feeling drawn from the absolute fear that radiated from the mother in front of her. This was more than concern, this was terror at an instinctual level, and Tilly didn't like it.

She helped Stella lie down and lifted her floral maternity top to palpate her tummy to establish the lie of the baby. There was no movement with that stimulation so she applied a little more gel than she normally would and placed the Doppler over the spot where the baby's shoulder, and under that, baby's heart, would be situated and searched for the sound they both strained to hear.

Nothing. Tilly checked the other side and then back where she'd first listened. Still nothing.

'The heartbeat's not there. Is it?' Stella said flatly, with a horribly tight face and an anguished glance at her husband.

Tilly swallowed the fear in her own throat. 'I can't find it at the moment, Stella. I'm sorry. I'll get Gina, the midwifery manager, she's more experienced, and I'll page Dr Bennett to come down.'

Stella looked at her with bleak eyes. 'Thanks, Tilly. Yes, please.'

Tilly's mind raced as she almost ran out of the door. She found Gina talking to a relative and she tapped her shoulder. 'Excuse me. I'm sorry. I need you, please.'

Gina nodded to the relative and as she turned away Tilly whispered what had happened. Gina patted Tilly's shoulder. 'I'll go in while you ring Dr Bennett.'

When Marcus picked up the phone he almost hoped it was Tilly, even though he'd promised himself he was going to avoid her like the plague. But this was a Tilly he'd never heard.

'Dr Bennett. Stella Trainer has arrived with no foetal movement. I can't hear a foetal heart.' Her voice broke.

'I'm on my way.' No. Not Stella. He'd seen her yesterday. He should have done that bloody Caesarean last week.

The next two hours were tragic. The ultrasound proved that Stella's baby had died, though it couldn't say why or when. There was no signs of foetal distress, no apparent problems with the cord or placental separation. Just an unexplained cruel act of nature.

Stella and her husband perched on the edge of their chairs in stunned silence while Marcus sat helplessly, unable to give them a concrete reason or any hope that they were mistaken. All he could give them was sympathy and try to answer any questions the best he could.

He offered a Caesarean or an immediate induction

of the labour but gently recommended they wait a few days for Stella to go into labour naturally. Tilly silently nodded her agreement of this plan, too, and with trepidation the grieving parents decided to go home and wait for contractions to start.

Tilly gave them her mobile phone number if they needed to talk. Marcus had already done that.

Tilly glanced across at Marcus, his face a tight mask as they both watched the parents leave. He opened his mouth to say something, thought better of it and shook his head. Then he walked away. Tilly knew what he was thinking and her heart was breaking for everyone.

The next morning, after a night spent dozing in fits and starts in her bed, it was with relief that Tilly saw the streaks of dawn finally appear. She'd worried at the idea that her encouragement to Stella and Rob had cost their baby her life, though the fact that all had been well the previous day disputed that.

She knew it wasn't rational, she knew she was being unfair to herself, but common sense didn't help.

What if their baby had been born earlier? If she hadn't been on shift, would it still be alive? The horrible self-recriminations wouldn't go away. She dragged herself out of bed and pulled on her swimmers and then Tilly beat the water of the bay with tears streaming down her face. Instead of looking for dolphins, she almost wished a shark would gobble her up.

Despite her brief maudlin death wish, after her swim

she felt a little better and even a little calmer as she pushed through the breakers to the beach.

Until she saw the man doing slow laps in the sea pool. Marcus? Swimming? It wasn't graceful but it was strong. The slow strokes mechanical, repetitious, as if they could go on all day without effort. As if he was trying to exhaust himself and couldn't.

When had he learnt? Had he always known and he'd just lied to her? And the fact he was practising there in front of her was a message. She shook her head. She didn't understand but it was another blow to her morale. Tilly hurried past the pool and up to her house. She didn't want to see him because she'd just burst into tears.

Stella went into labour that night. She spoke to Tilly on her mobile and told her she wanted to stay home as long as she could because she didn't want medicated pain relief.

'If this is all I'm going to have when my baby is born, I want to feel the labour and remember it all.'

Tilly nodded into the phone and cleared her throat. 'Of course.' She could see that made sense. 'I'll have everything ready when you come in.' Tilly arranged for one of the other midwives to be available to take unobtrusive photographs if Stella wanted them.

Tilly was there waiting with the bath full and the lights dim when they arrived.

Stella's husband, Rob, had brought music they wanted to play. The lullabies they'd chosen with such anticipation for their baby's birth would still greet their little girl as she came into the world, even though she wouldn't hear them.

Tilly bit her lip and closed her eyes to get a grip. It was okay—maybe somewhere their baby would hear them.

Tilly checked Stella's observations and settled her into the bath, and even thought briefly about Marcus's preference for assessment of labour before Stella stepped in, but the mother preferred not to be disturbed and of course Tilly agreed.

'I need to ring Dr Bennett. Let him know you're in.'

'Okay. Thanks, Tilly.' Stella lay back with her eyes closed as she breathed through a contraction.

Tilly pulled the door shut gently, leaving them with the other midwife.

Tilly dialled Marcus's mobile and he answered at the second ring. 'Dr Bennett. It's Tilly.' She nearly said Sister McPherson but decided that was silly. 'Stella has arrived in established labour.' She thought she'd better tell him. 'She's in the bath.'

She heard the sigh. 'I don't suppose you examined her first?'

Tilly closed her eyes. 'She said she'd prefer not to be disturbed.'

'How convenient.' More irony than anger but still Tilly didn't need it.

'Don't do this, Marcus. We're all hurting. I'll ring you when she's pushing.' Tilly put the phone down gently.

Marcus snapped his phone shut. Well, he'd deserved that. But he was having real problems coping with Stella's loss. And it was even harder because he'd done everything right.

He'd monitored, scanned, checked the foetal growth and mother's health consistently. He'd done every conceivable blood test to ensure she was well. It wasn't fair. It wasn't right.

It didn't matter when people said some babies died. He knew what it was like to lose someone and he'd chosen this career to keep babies and mums safe. He'd failed. And he didn't know where or how not to do it again.

How could her baby have died? And the cancelled Caesarean only made it a hundred times worse. The ultimate case of 'if only'. He didn't think he'd ever forgive Matilda for talking Stella out of that, even though he knew it wasn't her fault. He began to dress to go up to the hospital.

His phone rang again and it was Tilly. 'She's pushing.'

'I'm coming,' he said, but the phone was dead. Tilly had already gone. Of course she wouldn't leave them long at this time.

When Marcus arrived he expected to find them out of the bathroom and pushing on the bed—but of course they weren't.

They were in the bathroom, the mother submerged in the water and Tilly on her knees, peering into the gloom. Stella was gently breathing her baby out.

He shut his mouth. What was he going to say? Get out or the baby will drown? Marcus drew a slow breath in and sighed. He nodded at Rob, who was in the bath, too, but seated behind his wife and holding her gently as Stella leaned back against him.

Marcus quietly moved to the only vacant seat in the room—the toilet. He vaguely noticed the other midwife in the corner with a camera.

He may as well watch and learn. In fact, when he thought about it, despite the muted sadness, it was very peaceful in here, pleasantly warm, and the light was dim but enough to see by. He noticed Tilly had a torch by her feet in case she needed to see, but otherwise not much was happening, and apparently that was fine.

'Keep breathing like that, Stella,' Tilly whispered. 'Now put your hands down and feel baby's head as she comes out.'

Good grief, they were at that stage? He couldn't tell by Stella's face.

'I can feel her,' Stella whispered.

'That's lovely. Keep breathing with the contractions until she glides into your hands.' Tilly gestured to Rob to stretch his hands around and feel if he could.

Tilly peered into the water. 'Here she comes.' She still hadn't put her hands in at all. It was all the parents. Marcus was spellbound. A little horrified but spellbound.

Then his brain suddenly remembered that this was in water. He hated water. Water had taken his little sister and it had been his fault. He should have looked after her.

But he'd been so small. Too young to have that responsibility. The voice came from nowhere. Never his fault. The voice was repeating it like a litany in his head and while his eyes watched the parents lift and greet their eternally sleeping baby, in some unexplained and mystical way he said goodbye to his own baby sister, and finally left her to rest in peace. Of course his parents had never blamed him. It had been beyond his control. As this was beyond his control.

This wasn't his fault. What Tilly said was true. He'd done everything he knew to keep mother and baby safe. It hadn't been enough, but it wasn't his fault. Or Tilly's. It wasn't anybody's fault. It was a tragic turn of nature.

He looked across to where Stella was holding her baby between her breasts in the water, tears in rivers down her cheeks and Rob's arms around them all.

Tilly had sat back, tears on her own face, and he didn't know when he moved, just that he did. He knelt behind her and put his arms around her waist until, after initial stiffness, she leant back against him.

They all stayed, in a tableau, as Stella held baby Katia until it was time to move.

Marcus left them a little while later. He'd checked Katia for any obvious reasons why she'd passed away inside her mother but none were obvious. There was nothing more he could do.

He left a remarkably composed Tilly to deal with

the touches he knew little about, wrote an initial brief comment in Stella's notes, and went back to his office.

He couldn't erase in his mind the view he'd had from where he'd sat. The tableau of composed grief set amidst the subdued wonder of an amazing birth. In this situation he could even be an advocate for delivery in water—yet he couldn't call it anyone delivering anything. It had been a mother aware of her body's force and capturing the moment to welcome her child into the world.

Such a tragedy the child hadn't been able to breathe the air when her face had lifted to the surface. He scrubbed his face as if to lose the frozen expression he knew was on there and sat down to write a detailed consultant's report which he would drop down later when he went to see Stella again.

Two hours later, Marcus went to see the parents. Stella and Rob were settled in a private room with Katia, whom they were keeping with them tonight while Stella stayed in hospital. He arranged to see them in his rooms when the results came back from the examination of Katia in a week's time and again offered his number if they needed to talk.

When he left them he couldn't see Tilly anywhere and the ward seemed remarkably quiet for a place that delivered half a dozen babies a day. He passed two other midwives but not Tilly, and he tried not to look for her but in the back of his mind he'd realised that such gentle strength for the parents would come at a cost. He worried about her—he couldn't help it.

He heard a sniff as he went past the cleaner's room, a tiny alcove with a door, and when he stopped outside he heard it again.

She was crying. He'd known it.

He lifted his hand but hesitated. What help would he be? If she hadn't wanted privacy she wouldn't have hidden away. But she was hurting. She wasn't the only one.

He knocked gently and pushed open the door. It was dark. Why on earth hadn't she put on the light?

'Matilda?'

She sniffed and he narrowed his eyes in the dimness, reached out and touched her face. The dampness ran down his fingers and he gently wiped big stripes of tears from her cheeks. She turned her head. 'It's my nose that needs wiping,' she muttered.

'Sorry, but I'm not using my fingers for that.'

He bit back a smile, just glad she had a bit of fight in her and wasn't totally destroyed. 'Take the handkerchief, please.' He pushed it into her hand.

'Thank you.' Muffled but sincere.

'You okay?'

She glared at him through the dimness. 'Why are you in my cupboard?'

He held back another urge to smile. 'It's my cupboard, too.'

She shook her head. 'Typical.'

He ignored her comment and went on. 'I'm here because my friend is in this cupboard. I thought you might need company.'

Even she smiled, albeit a little miserably, but he was glad to see it.

'It's a very small cupboard.'

He said, 'I just wanted to say you were amazing with Stella and Rob.' She sniffed again and unscrunched his handkerchief to use again.

She blew her nose loudly and he couldn't help the glance he cast over his shoulder at the door.

He realised just how damning this could look if they were caught in here, though what people could say if they found them was a long way from Tilly's mind. 'If she'd had the Caesarean, the baby might still be alive.'

He didn't want to think about that. He couldn't because—he just couldn't. 'We don't know that. If we're very lucky the post-mortem will tell us, but you know how often the reason for stillbirth is never found.'

There was a silence he had to fill. 'The birth was very special.'

She lifted her head. 'Even though it was a water birth?'

'In this case I can see the absolute benefits.' He needed to get out of here, in any direction, but he couldn't seem to move.

He reached out and brushed the damp hair off her face. This was ridiculous. Two tall people cramped in a cupboard with cleaning materials, mops, vases, and dead flowers.

He leant forward and brushed her forehead in a kiss. 'I just wanted you to know I thought the birth was beautiful.' He was repeating himself.

So he left.

Tilly knew Marcus blamed her. How could he not? But that was okay because she hadn't stopped beating herself up. She didn't think she could face him, or anyone else, at the minute. Thank goodness it was almost eleven and she could go home.

She was meeting Ruby to share a taxi and hopefully she could get home without bursting into tears. This job could give the most joy and, at moments like this, the most pain. But she wouldn't change being there for Stella and Rob. Not in a million years, but she couldn't help but wonder if Marcus felt the same.

'Poor Tilly.' They were in the kitchen at Hill Street and Ruby put her arms around Tilly and gave her a big hug. Sympathetic tears glinted in her eyes, too. 'Poor you. You do an awesome job. I'd want you there if I was them, and of course it's not your fault.'

'I know, but I feel so guilty. I don't even want to go into work tomorrow.'

Ruby nodded. 'I know. I felt the same last month when that six-year-old came into Emergency after that house fire. It breaks your heart watching other people's pain. You listen and try to support them and somewhere inside it rips your heart a little and even though we're not directly involved it does take a little time to heal. God knows how the ambulance officers do it time after time. No wonder they burn out.' They both shuddered.

Ruby sat the chocolate biscuits in front of Tilly. 'Here. Have the lot.'

'Not the emergency chocolate ration?' Tilly laughed through her tears. 'I get to have the whole box?'

'I'm thinking about it.' Ruby pretended to hover her hand indecisively over the box. 'Better hurry before I change my mind.'

Tilly pushed the chocolate away. 'Actually, I feel sick.' She stood up and hugged Ruby. 'Thanks for being here. And I'm so sorry I didn't know about last month. You didn't tell me about your six-year-old.'

Ruby hugged her back and she put the biscuits back up on top of the cupboard. If they weren't going to help then they didn't need the calories. 'Cort was there. We did our grieving together.'

'You're so lucky.' Tilly chewed her lip. 'I'm thinking I might ask Gina for a week off to go and see my mum.'

Ruby nodded. 'Things not working out with Marcus?'

Tilly shook her head. 'I don't want to talk about that either.'

Ruby patted her arm. 'I think going to your mum's is a great idea.'

After four days, Marcus decided he needed help to find Tilly. She wasn't at work, not around the house, repairing or painting something, and the girls next door avoided him so he couldn't catch them to ask, and his aunt didn't know.

He'd watched vigilantly for her each morning but he hadn't seen her slip out for her swim or stroke her way across the bay.

He'd kept up the swimming lessons with Duggie

and the old man had begun to teach him butterfly and backstroke and he'd had his first surf. He'd have liked to tell Tilly about it.

That morning he'd cracked and asked Gina where she was when he'd done his morning round.

'She's gone to her mother's for a week. Stella's loss upset her.' Gina looked at him. 'Her mother's a friend of mine. She's a home-birth midwife, you know.'

Marcus felt the usual kick from that statement but it wasn't as bad. Not right through his gut anyway. 'I know.' Such a twist of fate but not as important today. Maybe it wasn't the final nail in the coffin of a relationship with Tilly he'd thought it was, because at the moment he was more interested in catching up with her again and seeing that she was all right. He needed to make sure she wasn't blaming herself.

Three days later Marcus was in his office. 'Mr and Mrs Trainer are here to see you, Doctor.' Marcus stood up and greeted Stella and Rob. She carried a small silver folder and to his surprise she kissed his cheek.

She looked subdued but remarkably composed. 'How are you, Stella? Rob?'

Rob answered for her. 'We're both well, Doctor. And you?'

'Fine.' He gestured to the two chairs facing his desk and pulled the one out from behind so he could sit next to them.

Rob gestured to his wife. 'Stella was worried about you.'

'Thank you, Stella.' How could she have a skerrick of emotion left for him? 'I felt your loss very much.' He looked at the pathologist's summary in his hands with mixed feelings and decided to get on with it.

'I have the report back from Katia's examination.' He waited while they absorbed that and seemed ready for him to go on.

Rob reached over and took Stella's hand then indicated they were ready. Marcus didn't doubt he wasn't the only one who found it hard to speak at the moment.

He cleared his throat. 'Katia had a brain haemorrhage, an uncommon and untreatable aneurism, or extreme weakness in the wall of the blood vessel that surrounded her brain.' The parents looked at each other and Stella wiped a lone tear away impatiently.

Marcus went on. 'The examining doctor...' they all tried not to think about that '...seemed to think that even a Caesarean birth would not have prevented the rupture and he was surprised she'd grown so well and for so long inside your uterus.'

Rob swallowed. 'So not compatible with life?'

Marcus nodded. 'The blood-vessel wall seemed to have whole areas of extreme congenital weakness so I'm afraid not.'

Stella sat forward. 'So, in fact, if she'd been born by Caesarean we may not have had that time with her, the tranquillity of her arrival, the calmness to savour that precious time with her.'

Marcus thought about that. There was no doubt that could be true. 'I hadn't thought about that but you're probably right. Of course, there would have been extreme measures used to try and save Katia if the aneurysm had ruptured at birth because we wouldn't have known what was wrong with her.' He nodded. 'Yes, it could have been very traumatic.'

Stella sat back and glanced at her husband. 'That's very comforting.'

Marcus nodded again. It was. A gentle waft of peace crept over him as if a cloud had drifted away and allowed warmth from the sun to suddenly stream in the window. 'I think so, too.' He looked at Stella. 'Do you have any questions?'

Stella smiled sadly. 'We'll always have questions but that's not why we're here.' She glanced at her husband. 'Perhaps we could ring you if we have more?' Rob nodded.

'Of course.' Marcus included them both in his agreement. 'Any time. If I'm not here, I'll phone you back as soon as I can.'

Stella took a deep breath and let it out slowly. 'Thank you for that.'

She tightened her hands around the little book on her lap. 'I wanted to show you the beautiful memories we have of Katia.

'There were parts of that two days we spent in hospital that were a blur and parts that will remain treasured memories. Thanks to Tilly and the other midwives and to you for being so generous with all the time you spent with us.'

Marcus swallowed the lump in his throat. 'To borrow

Matilda's words, it was a privilege to be there with you both for Katia's birth.'

Stella glanced down at the folder. 'Thank you. I hope you don't mind but I've brought our daughter's things to show you.'

She opened the first page and lifted several black-and-white photographs in baby frames, photos of Stella in the birth pool with Katia snuggled against her mother moments after her birth. Rob's arms encircled them all and the picture could have been of any birth.

The tenderness on both parents' faces pulled hard on Marcus's composure.

'And this is Katia's hand-and footprints. Tilly did a good job, don't you think?' The little outlines were clean and stark against the thick white paper and incredibly touching.

Next she handed him a frame with a little white plaster cast of a clenched baby fist and a tiny foot, and then Stella lifted a smaller album with pink rabbits gambolling on the front. He didn't know how much more of this he could take. She passed it to him.

Photographs of Katia, photos of each parent holding their daughter. His throat caught and when he turned the page and saw one of Tilly, tears glistening at the corners of her beautiful eyes and the precious bundle of Katia wrapped in a hand-sewn rug in her arms, he could feel the thickness in his throat.

Someone had even taken one of him, an intense expression on his face as he looked towards the bath, and it brought back the poignancy and the tragedy of that day. And another of his back as he hugged Tilly and the parents in front of them both with their baby.

He couldn't imagine how many times this little baby's mother must have already looked at these and how many more there were to come over the next years. Over the rest of her life, probably.

He carefully handed back the album. 'Katia's photos are incredibly beautiful. Thank you for showing me.'

'Thank you for being there.'

All Marcus could think about was that he wanted to see Tilly. He wanted to tell her about the pathology results. Tell her about Stella's folder. Tell her and see the same comfort in her eyes as there was in Stella and Rob's and his own, after understanding the report.

CHAPTER TEN

TILLY came back to work on Friday and she didn't see Marcus because he'd gone to a meeting in the city. That was a good thing because she wasn't sure she wouldn't cry when she did.

Her mum had been wonderful, had had sage advice for dealing with grieving parents and cautioned Tilly about losing her heart to a man who blamed her for something that wasn't her fault. She wasn't a hundred per cent sure her mother understood how she felt about Marcus but, then again, neither did she. But the solution to the problem was the same. Stay away from him.

It was midnight and Tilly and Ruby had just arrived home from work. Tilly was making cocoa and they were both on the early shift the next morning.

Ruby put her hand on Tilly's shoulder. 'You look worried, Till.'

Tilly smiled ruefully. 'I'm a real life of the party. Sorry to mope around. I haven't seen Marcus yet. Not since Stella lost her baby.'

'You said he was good in the cupboard.'

Tilly had to smile at how strange that sounded. 'Yes, he was good in the cupboard. But I've decided I don't want to see Marcus out of work. Now Mary's asked me to speak to Marcus about being the back-up consultant for a home-birth client and I don't know what to do.'

Ruby brought down the secret hoard of chocolate biscuits again and put two in front of Tilly. 'Why did she ask you?'

Absently Tilly nibbled the edge of one. 'Because I work with him, I guess. Mary's agreed to take the mum on if she'll see a consultant as well.'

Ruby sat down. 'So what's the problem? Ask him.'

Tilly ticked the evils off on her fingers. 'Number one, I haven't spoken to him since I left. Number two, apparently his mother nearly died in a bungled home birth, which I'm not supposed to know, and he hates anything to do with them. And, three, I don't want to get shut down. It hurts.'

Ruby put her arm around Tilly and hugged her. 'Poor you.' She scrutinised her. 'You're having a tough couple of weeks. Plus you still really like him, don't you?'

'Too much. Which is dumb because I don't trust him not to hurt me. And I promised myself I wasn't going to fall into the same old trap with another guy. Especially one older then me. Friends only.'

'Easier said than done. Men are risky. And I can understand your reluctance. Though he's not technically old. He's the same age as Cort.' Her face softened and she smiled a small secret smile. 'But sometimes the risk is worth it.'

Tilly had to laugh. 'You're just saying that because it's worked out for you and Cort.'

Ruby grinned. 'Probably true. I'm happy. The happiest I've ever been and I know it's going to get even better. But it's not about me.' Ruby put down her cup. 'Can you trust him a little bit, Till?'

She sighed. 'Every time I do he comes up with another reason why it won't work. So I've decided to stay out of his way. Plus he's out of my league.'

'Excuse me.' Ruby looked down her nose at Tilly's preposterous statement. 'I'm not out of Cort's league any more than Marcus is out of yours. He'd be darned lucky to have someone as gorgeous and genuine as you are in his life.'

Tilly brushed that away. 'It's all right for you—your brother's work with plastic surgery is famous and your father was a top surgeon, too. My mum's a second-generation home-birth midwife.'

She shrugged that problem away. 'Anyway, the trouble is if I don't ask him for Mary and something goes wrong, it'll be a hundred times worse, and not just for the client. Plus it leaves Mary in the lurch.'

Ruby nodded. 'I say ask him. Make it short and he can ask questions if he decides to think about it. He might be different since Stella's baby.'

Tilly sighed heavily. 'I can't imagine why.'

The next day Tilly watched him from the corner of the ward. Unobtrusively. Nervously. Marcus talking to Gina. He'd finished the ward round, his registrar and resident had departed for the antenatal clinics, and Tilly knew he'd leave for his rooms soon. She wanted to pass on Mary's request, get it off her chest, and she wanted to do it at work.

Marcus left the nurses' station with his eyes on his phone, checking his diary. He'd been thinking about Tilly and he'd had a dozen light-bulb moments about the way she made him feel.

A tiny smile twitched—like lighter and calmer and more philosophical instead of totally relying on control to run his life, which was lucky because when he was with Tilly things seemed to get out of control pretty darned fast.

He'd never be a thrill seeker or a big risk taker and he never wanted to change that his work would always be methodical and thorough.

But he was coming to realise that Tilly, and by association the other midwives, had his patients' best interests at heart and he could be more open to new ideas.

Perhaps even learn to surrender a little of the control he'd felt he needed to apply over his private life, too. He'd always gone for women who were happy for a man to arrange everything and that had suited his tendency to make all the decisions.

He didn't feel like that at the moment. He felt like he wanted to step onto the whirligig with Tilly. Sit in a room and sing impromptu songs. Seize the moment and kiss her until they were both senseless. Maybe jump in his car and just drive for the pleasure of having her next to him, no matter where they ended up.

A month ago that wouldn't have seemed even possible let alone the ridiculous attraction that idea held for him now. He'd have to arrange a meeting with her. Try and find out how she felt before he made a fool of himself.

'Dr Bennett?' He had his finger on the elevator button and it hovered without pressure as she spoke.

Marcus turned. Ah, there she was. He hadn't expected her on this shift. Finally. And gorgeous. It was good to see her, though she looked a little careworn for such a young woman. Like she needed a hug. Lucky he was at work then.

'Hello, there, Matilda. Long time no see. I've been trying to catch up with you.'

Before she could distract him he went on. 'Actually, I've wanted to sit down and talk to you but the time's flown since I found out. I think you need to know as soon as possible.'

He saw her frown, as if she wondered what else she'd done wrong now. It was surprising how unhappy that made him feel. 'Don't look like that. Am I such an ogre?' She didn't answer and he sighed and thought maybe he was. Nothing he could do about it at this minute. He needed to say this. 'Stella and Rob came to see me.'

Tilly brushed a strand of escaping hair off her face. 'I haven't had a chance to ring her since I got back. How are they?'

Typical, Marcus thought, worried about others when the cost on her was so evident. Hopefully this would help.

'The pathology came back and Katia had a congenital aneurism incompatible with life. It's unlikely she would have survived a Caesarean and the resuscitation would have been much more traumatic than the beautiful birth she had.'

He felt again a little of the relief he'd felt the first time he'd read that and he saw Tilly soak in the concept. Tears glistened in her eyes and he wished now he'd taken her up to his rooms, but he wasn't sure he would have been able to stop himself hugging her if he had. Not good to do that at work, even in the privacy of his office. Self-protection.

'So it wasn't because Stella decided to have the normal birth. It wasn't my fault Katia died.'

'It never was, Matilda,' Marcus said quietly. 'I wasn't as supportive as I should have been but it was never your fault. It was all beyond our control. Yours, mine, Stella's.'

She drew a deep breath and he had that urge to hug her again. Instead, he just tightened his hold on his mobile.

She nodded and looked away. 'Thank you for telling me.'

'I wish I could have done it somewhere else.' He shouldn't have been such a coward.

She lifted her head. 'No. This is good. And I'll think about it more later.'

It wasn't quite the response he'd thought he'd get. He'd hoped she'd look more relieved or something. 'If you have any questions, you'll ask, won't you?'

She nodded and brushed her eyes. Then she straightened her shoulders. 'I do have something to ask you. Not related to Stella.'

Marcus was still beating himself up over the way he'd handled that. Protecting himself rather than Tilly, a poor effort, and he promised himself he'd never do that again.

Tilly wasn't sure she had his full attention. But she wanted this out of the way so she went on doggedly. 'Do you remember the home-birth midwife, Mary, from your second day?'

'Yes. I have a memory of lots of things.' He smiled at her and she almost lost her train of thought. What was that supposed to mean? He added, 'She seemed a sensible woman.'

Tilly looked at him in surprise. Had they progressed to that? What was going on here? Maybe he had changed.

'Anyway, Mary has a client who's reluctant to see any doctor, isn't risk free, and Mary wanted me to ask if you would see her with the view of shared care.' Out it came in a rush, a little garbled, and as she finished speaking she tried to sense his possible reaction but couldn't.

His brows creased but not badly. She was a basket case, reading nuances when there wasn't any and second-guessing his reactions. What had happened to the woman who'd declared they weren't handmaidens? The one who'd give anyone an earful if they looked sideways at one of her birthing women. Maybe she'd learnt to see both sides a little more. Imagine that.

Marcus nodded but it was pushing reality to think he said it encouragingly. 'So this mother's high risk and wants to birth at home and you think I should agree to that.'

She'd known this would be hard. 'No. Mary wants to discuss the case with you because she's worried if she doesn't care for her, this mum will go for a home birth with just her husband.'

'I see.' Well, she certainly had his attention. Tilly tried not to squirm. 'Then why isn't she asking me?'

Good point. But she'd come this far. 'I'll tell her to ring your secretary then.'

Marcus studied her noncommittally and Tilly waited. 'Very adroitly handled, Sister.'

A tiny smile that warmed her more than it should. 'Fine. Get her to ring my secretary and we can talk about it.' He pushed the button and the doors opened. Just before they closed he said, 'There's something I want to talk to you about. And we need to discuss carpetbag steak at some point, too.'

When the doors had closed Tilly sagged back against the wall. Marcus at work was so much harder to handle. Except she wasn't going to handle him outside the hospital any more. Ever again.

'What was all that about?' Gina looked up as Tilly approached the desk.

Tilly blinked, still relieved he hadn't shut her down and a little bemused about the steak comment. She wasn't going to take him up on that one. She needed some space and that was definitely an outside-work commitment. 'Mary asked me if he'd see a client of hers as shared care.'

Gina's brows rose. 'Good grief. We have progressed. Well done.'

It was almost the end of the shift when a call came in from another home-birth midwife. Again Tilly was the one to ring Marcus, although the afternoon staff would take over from her in that actual OT. 'Dr Bennett?'

'Yes, Matilda.'

Well, he certainly knew her voice. 'We have a mother coming in from home with foetal distress and the midwife is requesting we prepare for an emergency Caesarean on their arrival.' Tilly wasn't the only one who was aware of the irony on top of the emergency situation.

'Put Theatres on standby.' She had the feeling he was smiling into the phone. 'I'll assess the woman but you get Theatre started. Of course I trust you.'

Yee-ha. 'Thank you.' But it was too late for her. She didn't trust him.

Almost a week after Tilly had come back from her mother's they still hadn't seemed to connect for their morning exercise, which was particularly frustrating when he'd decided he wanted to tell Matilda about his sister. Marcus had decided it was time to try to explain his reservations.

He'd stayed with his exercise time in the mornings but he had the feeling that Tilly had adjusted hers to avoid him. He guessed that was tit for tat. And she was avoiding him very successfully.

She had more leeway with working mostly in the afternoons and even at work his schedule was conspiring against him. He'd had a run of evening meetings and no unexpected birth call-backs at night so he'd seen little of her except in the distance, apart from that conversation at the lift.

He couldn't go chasing her all over the ward, especially when he had the feeling she was ducking into rooms to avoid him.

That morning, before his run, he'd decided to find out if she was waiting for him to leave for work before she went. A meeting at eleven o'clock in the city meant no early round this morning. His registrar rang him to say he had it all covered, just as he heard Matilda's gate open, and Marcus had to watch her walk away from his bedroom window.

'Ring me if needed, otherwise I'll be in late this afternoon.' He ended the call and took the stairs two at a time to try to catch her before she hit the water.

It was after eight when Tilly opened the gate to slip down for her swim. Marcus's car was still there but she'd waited long enough. He'd have no time before work now and she wasn't as happy with the later hour when the beach had more people and her peace often became interrupted by other swimmers appearing beside her through a wave when she least expected it.

But it was worth it to avoid the chance of running into him.

She'd decided she was going cold turkey.

No contact. She'd started painting the kitchen in the house and apart from her brief forays into the water after he'd gone to work, she'd mostly avoided him by being aware of where he was at all times when she was on the ward.

She chose to care for patients who were under different doctors, opted for women in earlier labour, and, when she'd asked, Gina helped to keep the two apart.

The whitecaps were blowing off the back of the waves this morning and she could see a small rip across her usual traverse.

Tilly glanced towards the walled ocean pool but she was fed up with being dictated to by events she couldn't control. Stubbornly she headed a little east of her usual trajectory and splashed through the breakers.

It wasn't long before she realised she hadn't swum wide enough and the undertow was stronger than she liked. She drifted a bit farther out to sea to avoid the centre of a wider-than-average rip but soon realised she was caught anyway.

'Bother,' she muttered as she drifted even farther out, the cold logic of experience telling her not to try to swim out of the rip but to let it carry her until the current stream naturally stopped. It was the first thing she taught the Nippers and junior lifesavers.

Of course, the rip could peter out and drop her in the next bay and she'd have to walk back, but there wasn't a lot she could do about it unless she wanted to exhaust herself uselessly trying to fight the strength of the current.

That was when the shark siren went off. Tilly heard the high-pitched wail of the beach siren and it took a moment until she realised what it was.

The accepting calm she'd just been congratulating herself on suddenly faltered and her already accelerated heart rate jumped another twenty beats. Her head swivelled as she peered into the water closest to her with a dread she tried to control.

She couldn't believe that the first rip she'd been caught in this year had to come at the same time as the siren. There was no way she could get to the beach fast, and if she panicked and thrashed her way through it she'd be a more noisy target for whichever shark had decided that Coogee was a great place to visit.

Funny how the skin on her legs seemed suddenly more sensitive. How the sound of her own breathing was rasping more loudly through her throat until it seemed almost raucous in the morning air. With great difficulty she consciously slowed the kicking of her legs to what she hoped was an unobtrusive up and down glide as she floated as passively as she could with the current.

It would be nice to be able to put her hand up and wait for one of the beach-patrol lifesavers to gun the rubber ducky boat and save her, but it was still too early for them to be out and about and she didn't want some novice being a hero and drowning for her.

Maybe with the shark alarm there was hope the real guys would start earlier.

She glanced around fearfully again. Where was a dolphin when she needed one? The siren sounded again and she closed her eyes and only just resisted the urge to kick into the current towards the shore. Her brain knew the rip was much stronger than she was and the only answer was to allow it to carry her where it wanted before it petered out.

She could feel the waves of nervous energy bleating against her common sense and her legs itched to kick like crazy for the shore.

A wave slapped her in the face and a little more of her composure fled. For the first time since she'd begun swimming in the mornings she raised her arm and hoped for rescue.

CHAPTER ELEVEN

MARCUS looked around when the alarm went off but he had no idea what it meant.

Until a young tattooed man in a wheelchair spun to the edge of the path with a loud hailer pointed out to sea. 'Please get out of the water. Return to the shore. This is a shark alarm.'

Marcus felt as if one of those surfboards heading for the beach had sneaked up on him and punched him in the chest. Tilly was out there. He glanced around to see others hurrying for the shore but Tilly seemed to be drifting farther out as he watched. Why wasn't she coming in?

He jogged over to the man with the microphone and pointed out Tilly. 'Can she hear you?'

'She'd hear the siren anyway.' He frowned out to where Tilly drifted. 'Must be caught in a rip.' He shook his head as Marcus's gut clenched at the words. 'At least she's sensible not to fight it and the sharks are on the other side of the bay.'

He pointed and Marcus could see two dark fins

gliding through the water. There was something menacing in the way they sliced the water like a knife as they lazily circled to the left side of the bay.

The man went on. 'I'm a volunteer spotter until the lifesavers come in. Not much I can do. I've rung them and they should be here in about ten minutes.'

A shark could eat Tilly in ten minutes if it decided to investigate her. He glanced at the big emergency Malibu leaning against the pole. 'Can I take the rescue board?'

The man shrugged. 'If you're keen on finding the shark. The boys'll have the rubber ducky up and going in twenty.'

Duggie had told him of the days before rubber duckies. Of bronzed men swimming with floats and paddling like machines out on their boards to rescue people in rips. He could have lived without the experience but he was quietly confident that if he stayed with the board he could be a help, not a hindrance, to Tilly. The shark he didn't want to think about.

He lifted the board and hugged it against his body as he balanced it under his armpit like he had with Duggie. People hurried from the water and glanced at him strangely as he walked past them to push into the waves.

'Didn't you hear the alarm, mate?' A thin, elderly gentleman indicated the man in the wheelchair.

'Yes, thanks.' He didn't want to talk. He wanted to concentrate on the quickest way to Tilly and as he gauged the direction and distance he saw her put her hand up for help just before a wave obscured her from view.

He narrowed his eyes and any doubts he had fled. She was tiring. He couldn't imagine what was going though her mind after hearing the alarm. Or maybe he could because there were some pretty graphic pictures circling in his head.

Tilly was starting to panic. She'd bitten her lip and it was the taste of blood in her mouth that really scared her. Imagine if she'd let some drop into the water. Duggie had once told her a shark could smell blood a quarter of a mile away and she wished like anything she hadn't been able to remember that little fact.

The swell seemed bigger the farther out she drifted because she lost sight of the beach between the waves. Her sense of isolation grew and thoughts of drifting right out to sea were beginning to crowd her mind. Nobody knew she was there. She was alone. With sharks.

She could die. Finished. Eaten by a shark. The first things she'd know would be a jolting drag as it chewed off her leg. Her friends would be devastated. What about Marcus? Would he care? Why the heck had she been fooling herself she hadn't fallen in love with the man? She should have taken what she could while she could. He'd been looking for her for days and now she had plenty of time to regret lost opportunity. A broken heart was nothing to being eaten by a shark.

Tears mixed with seawater. She'd give her last breath to be in his arms. No matter that he didn't love her. She knew he liked her. At least she would've died happy. She was such a fool.

By the time Marcus reached her she would have clutched the Grim Reaper himself. Avoiding Marcus was the last thing she wanted to do. She kicked towards him and finally she could touch the board. His hand came down over hers and squeezed her fingers and the warmth and strength and calmness began to seep into her panicked mind.

'Marcus? Thank God.' Then she shook her head. 'I can't believe it's you. Am I dreaming?'

'If you are, can we do it when we get to shore?'

She squeezed his hand harder to reassure herself he really was there and his bones were solid beneath her fingers. 'You can use the board?'

'Yeah, I can. Great teacher.' He pulled parallel to the beach. 'Put your arm over the board and grab the hand rope and I'll pull your legs in front of me.'

'I can't believe you came out to get me.'

'Why wouldn't I?' He smiled at her wryly. 'You'd come for me, wouldn't you?'

'Not with a shark alarm maybe.' A brave attempt at a joke.

He bit back a laugh. At least she was honest. He slid carefully down the end of the board, trying not to think of his feet dangling in the water, and ended up lying between her legs. It was amazingly easy to paddle with his hands and Tilly was paddling, too.

They both had good reason to get into the beach as fast as they could.

Obviously the board was designed for this because it didn't seem to have any problems carrying the two of them.

'It wasn't as tricky getting you on here as I thought it might be.' He could hear the relief in his voice as he turned the board back towards the beach, away from the side with the sharks.

'It's easier if your victim knows what they're doing. I've done it before and got the idea.' He could hear a quiver in her voice and he didn't blame her. He'd bet he'd have felt like that, too, if he'd been alone at sea and imagining getting washed up in New Zealand, like she must have.

All he wanted to do was gather her up and hug her. But he couldn't. They needed to get to the shore before some curious shark decided to have breakfast. But he would hug her. My word, he would.

A small swell lifted them and helped glide them back towards the shore, and he paddled the board straighter to catch the next one as well. Suddenly they were gliding swiftly through the water towards the crowd on the beach.

The rubber ducky had been pulled out onto the sand and he could see the lifesavers with caps waiting at the beach. They stopped to watch him come in with Tilly on the board and two of them waded out to help as they reached the shallows.

'You okay, Tilly?' The stocky lifesaver took her hand as she slid off and helped her stand. She nodded and he helped her out of the water up to the sand.

The second lifesaver took hold of the hand rope. 'Well done, sir. I'll take the board if you want.'

'Thanks.' Marcus nodded and took two big strides until he'd caught up with Tilly. When he put his hand on her shoulder she turned and looked at him. The lifesaver must have seen something in his face because he dropped Tilly's hand like a hot potato and went back to help his friend.

'Come here.' His voice softened at the paleness in her face. He hadn't realised how pale she was out there, and he just wanted to crush her against him.

She stepped into his arms and he hugged her into his chest. 'You came for me,' she mumbled against his chest, and the vibration made him smile.

'Of course.' She felt cold and shaky and he hugged her tighter. 'You okay, honey?'

She nodded and her hair brushed his chin. 'The rip I could deal with but not a shark.'

'I'd have had hysterics if it was me.' He dropped a kiss on top of her head.

She stepped back and tilted her head to look at him. 'It was you. You risked your own safety and saved me. You didn't have to.'

'Don't talk about it.' Actually, he didn't want to even think about it. 'You might have turned me off water again.'

'Who showed you how to use the board?'

'Duggie's been coaching me while you were playing hide and seek.'

She shot him a look of surprise. 'Sneak.' Then she shuddered. 'I'm very glad.'

He turned her towards home with his arm around her shoulders. 'Come on. You need a hot shower and some food. The girls will look after you.'

She couldn't stop shaking. 'Everyone's working.'

'Good. I'll look after you.' He sounded quite pleased, Tilly thought vaguely as she moved through a wall of vibrating cotton wool that seemed to be wrapping around her legs thicker and thicker so that she moved more clumsily the farther they went.

Each step up the hill she took the more the delayed shock drained her energy until she seemed to barely move. She couldn't get the thought of the shark out of her mind but funnily enough it was the idea of Marcus putting himself in danger that scared her most.

Pictures of Marcus and thrashing water circled like predators in her head and she shuddered.

He must have felt the vibration because he pulled her closer into his side. 'You okay?' He peered into her face and she'd bet she was whiter than a sheet. She stumbled.

'Can you make it? Do you want me to carry you?'

Yes, please, she thought. 'We're almost there.' She glanced ahead and the gate seemed a mile away.

He scooped her up in his arms like he had the day the hammer had hit her toe and it felt just as good the second time. Better. She closed her eyes and sighed into him. He was damp where he'd pulled his shirt on over his wet body but warm already and irresistibly safe and solid, and she pushed her ear against his chest and listened to the sound of his heart against her ear lobe.

It was incredibly reassuring. Now the gate was too close because she didn't want him to put her down when he got there. But he didn't. He juggled her and opened the gate, still with her in his arms. Then he was through the front door, clicked his tongue when the door opened without being unlocked, muttering as he went on about lack of security, and then he was standing in the lounge room, looking at the stairs.

'Your room upstairs?'

She nodded. 'I'll walk.'

'I don't think so. You've done enough exercise this morning. I've always wanted to see if I could carry a woman upstairs. We'll give it a go.'

He accomplished the feat with remarkable ease and Tilly couldn't help being impressed. No one had ever carried her like this before.

He paused on the landing only slightly out of breath. Even that was endearing. 'Which is your room?'

She nodded towards the darkest one, painted a deep purple, with beads and crystals in the window. He sat her down on the bed with a quick glance around. 'Let me guess. Purple is the midwives' colour?'

She nodded and he looked into her face and seemed reassured she wasn't going to faint.

He dropped a kiss on her lips that warmed her more than anything since she'd got out of the water and she turned her face to kiss him back. Life was pretty darned precious and the idea of feeling Marcus's arms around her made the demons go away. He pulled back after a longer kiss.

'I'll run the shower.'

Tilly watched him go. Still dazed by the warmth she hadn't expected from him. Maybe he'd got a fright when she'd been in danger? Maybe he was normally a warm and fuzzy person. Yeah, right. Sometimes. She reminded herself she'd gone to great pains to avoid him but that didn't include being rescued from shark-infested waters by a man who up until a couple of weeks ago had hated the water.

And now here he was, making sure she was all right. Running her shower. He certainly revelled in organising people. It was nice but he must think she was the dottiest idiot out, getting caught in a rip in the middle of a shark alert.

She glanced around her room, glad there were no undies on the floor for once to embarrass her. She doubted he'd be so lucky in a bathroom shared by four girls. The thought made her smile and she stood up to get dry clothes. The room swam and she sat down again just as he returned.

'You really are faint.'

She blushed, horrified he'd considered she was putting it on. 'I wasn't pretending just to get carried.'

'I didn't mind,' he said softly, and she shot a look at him. The expression on his face confused her. He didn't seem to think she was stupid. He looked like he really did care that she'd had a fright and there was tenderness in his face that made tears itch behind her eyes. He shouldn't look at her like that. What was a girl to think?

'Do you want me to go?'

That was the last thing she wanted. 'Maybe?'

He shook his head and his grin grew wider. 'That wasn't very convincing.' He reached out his hand. 'See if you can stand and if you're okay have a quick shower and get some dry clothes on.' He glanced at her bikini and murmured to himself, 'Not that I'm complaining.'

She pretended not to hear but it was heady to know he was aware of her, physically anyway, as she straightened up carefully. This time she didn't go woozy and her head felt clearer. She'd feel even more normal if the sexual awareness that was growing between them wasn't pulsing like the beat of a drum in her ears. But what did she expect, sitting in her bedroom in her bikini with this man?

Goodness knew what she'd have to do to get him back here ever again, especially if he found out she'd fallen in love with him. Life was too precious. Especially after this morning.

The thought must have crossed her face because he smiled teasingly and turned away. 'Maybe I'll check the shower's cold.'

Please, don't go. She didn't say it out loud but she was darned sure it was in her face. 'Marcus?' He turned back to face her. 'Don't suppose you could stay and hold me for a bit?'

'I'd love to.' He smiled. 'But a gentleman shouldn't take advantage of your weakened state.'

She raised her brows and met his eyes. 'My state's not that weak. It's just a cuddle.'

He patted his damp shirt. 'I'm too damp to sit on your bed.' He reached down for her hand. 'But come up here.' He stood her up, gathered her into his chest, and stroked her hair. 'My poor Matilda. It's been a big morning for you.'

She shivered from the coolness of his shirt, from residual fear and from the idea of losing herself just once in his arms. She couldn't make him love her when he didn't but she could just pretend. 'It could have been my last if you hadn't been there.' She knew it wouldn't mean the same for him but she knew she needed to stay in his arms. Tilly deliberately closed her mind to the reasons she shouldn't ask him to stay with her.

He shook his head and hugged her as if he couldn't help himself then dropped a kiss on her hair. 'The guys in the rubber ducky were coming soon.'

Even with his arms around her she couldn't stop the shaking that had started again. 'Did you know I'd bitten my lip and was terrified the shark was going to smell the blood?' She felt a shiver go through him.

Marcus went cold at the thought and pulled her closer. A sudden dousing of fear ran down his chest. He felt cold, in desperate need of the heat of Matilda. 'Baby. No wonder you were white.' He couldn't imagine the horror if the sharks had sensed the blood. He kissed her lips, and they were cold, too, too cold, and her cheek and her jaw and her throat had such softness of skin it reminded him how vulnerable she was. How terrifyingly easy it would be for her to be gone from his life for ever. He shuddered and this time when he kissed her he showed her he couldn't imagine the horror without her in his arms.

She kissed him back with the same hunger and he slid his hands right down her sides and cupped her buttocks. When he lifted her in his arms she was level with his face, and he murmured, 'Bad sharks,' against her lips. 'Bad, bad sharks.'

He slid her down his body until her feet were on the floor again, a long slide of skin and muscle and unusual prominences she couldn't miss when they both had so little on.

'I'm afraid that's what you do to me,' he said.

'I'm not afraid of you,' she said with a smile, and she watched his eyes grow darker. Not ward eyes, clear and determined, not out-of-work eyes, smiling and fun, but bedroom eyes—deepest, darkest blue. Ones she hadn't seen since that kiss in the kitchen. Eyes that ran over her, possessively, and lit smouldering spot fires everywhere they touched. She'd dreamed he'd look at her like that and it couldn't be wrong if it felt so good.

Such heat and promise and delicious danger lived in those eyes. Her hands slid up his chest, lingeringly, savouring the taut muscles and banded strength, whipcord and curvature she remembered from their lessons, memories stamped in her brain. Dreams that slept with her at night. Why shouldn't she ask for what she wanted? 'If you lifted your arms up I could get that nasty damp shirt off and we could lie on my bed.'

'I could do that.' Back went his strong hands to drag up her sides, skimming her hips and her waist and the outside of her breasts so that she sucked her breath in at the possessiveness he allowed himself with a wicked smile. Then his fingers drifted up her neck, cupped her cheeks and finally lifted strands of her hair until he stood, tall and straight with his hands above his head, daring her to undress him.

The edge of his damp T-shirt scrunched and bunched as she hauled it slowly over his wide chest and finally over his head until it was behind them on the floor. With those eyes on her he reached back with one long arm, shut the door of the room and they were locked in together.

His beautiful bare chest was right in front of her nose, tempting her to flatten her body against him. Teasingly, she resisted, enjoying the fact that she would soon be hard against him, knowing he was impatiently waiting for the same.

'I thought you midwives were really into skin to skin,' he said, as deft fingers undid the bow at the back tie of her bikini and he drew the tiny triangles of fabric over her head until her breasts bounced free and tantalisingly in front of him. He sighed.

'You are…' He enunciated slowly and reverently and there was no humour in his face now, just wonder. 'The most beautiful, sexy woman I have ever seen.'

Then he gathered her into him, bare against his skin, and they both sighed at the sensation until his mouth came down and captured her lips in a kiss that flooded her body with heat.

When he finally lifted his head, he whispered, 'Is that warmer?'

'Much,' she mumbled, and reached up to draw his head back to hers until they were lost again in a kiss.

Much later, when Marcus surfaced, he glanced at his watch and groaned. He kissed her again and rolled to the edge of the bed. He had to go but he so didn't want to. He couldn't believe what had just happened. And didn't want to think about the changes this would mean between them, but for once ramifications could worry about themselves.

'Matilda, my love, I'm so sorry, but I have to go, and if I don't get up now I may not get up at all.' He dropped another kiss on her nose with mock ferocity.

'The next time you want to tempt sharks and precipitate fabulous mornings in bed, can you please give me more notice and I'll take the day off?' He kissed her again, because he loved the fact that she seemed to be still drifting around the ceiling in a post-coital daydream.

'Hmm. I'll try.' She purred like a sleepy cat.

He stood up with a smile. 'Call out if you need me. I'll make us some breakfast and meet you downstairs.' As soon as he'd seen she'd eaten he'd hit the road. He was late already.

Tilly heard Marcus go down the stairs and she opened her eyes. Well, so much for keeping a distance.

She buried her nose in the pillow that still held the indent from his head. But she wouldn't regret this. She hoped.

When Tilly reappeared in her sundress Marcus set the table with slow precision, or he'd have pulled her back into his arms and never left. 'You realise that dress makes me want to slip those thin little straps off your edible shoulders, but I can't or I'll never go.'

She blushed and looked away to the table he'd set and hurriedly picked up her juice.

The toast popped up, and he draped a tea towel across his arm as he bowed over her. 'Would madam like some eggs?'

He watched her eyebrows arch and smiled. It seemed madam would. She nodded and said, 'Good grief. Can you cook as well?'

'I'll have you know I was the favourite chef during my uni years. I worked every morning for a breakfast café in the city.'

She'd probably been in junior high school and he'd bet she was cute.

'I can't cook,' Tilly admitted. 'But I'm great at cleaning up the kitchen after someone else has.'

He kissed his fingertips. 'Then we're perfectly matched.'

Tilly looked down at her fruit and he wasn't sure why she did that. Something had changed.

'So how do you like your eggs?'

'Actually, I'll just have the toast,' she said, but she still didn't meet his eyes.

'What did I say?' He dropped into the chair beside her. 'You okay? It's been a big morning.'

Her smile may have been a little forced but he'd give her full marks for trying. 'I'm fine. Thank you. It's been an amazing morning.'

He leaned over and rubbed her shoulder blades. 'We'll talk about that when we have more time. But, seriously, will you be okay here on your own?'

She leaned back into his hands. 'Why? Don't you have somewhere to go?'

He glanced at his watch. 'Soon. But I want to make sure you're okay.'

'I'm okay. And I'll just have the toast, thanks.'

When Marcus had left, Tilly sank down on the chair in the kitchen and put her head in her hands. What if he dropped her now like the others had? She couldn't believe she'd done it. Not the sex, though that had been a decision fraught with danger and hadn't helped her dilemma, but actually done what she'd said she wouldn't. She'd fallen in love with him.

Completely, utterly, besottedly in love with Marcus Bennett, and in such a way that she knew any previous love she'd thought she'd felt was nothing. That puppy infatuation couldn't rip her into pieces like this emotion could. What if he never came to care for her like she cared? She was doomed.

The man she'd promised blithely she didn't want to be anything but friends with now filled her mind.

Marcus drove into the city and as he shifted between the lanes he thought about Tilly and how explosive and amazing the passion between them had been. Crazy and totally unexpected and almost out of control but fed by the danger she'd faced this morning.

He'd never been so scared for another person in his life and he didn't know how he'd come to be so dependent on her wellbeing. Obviously he was infatuated with her. If it was infatuation and not something much more shattering. He'd always promised himself he'd leave his main focus on work and the intrusion of Tilly into his thoughts was becoming a serious distraction.

But it seemed his ability to be focussed and driven to achieve his goals could be split with a portion diverted and directed towards Tilly and the idea of pursuing her had sprouted in his subconscious. Not a lot he could do about it.

He remembered her saying she was not willing to risk her heart for a few years. Well, at least they had time. Maybe a few weeks was a little quick to capture her full attention but after today he had a whole new armoury of weapons.

He pulled up at the traffic lights and glanced in the rear-view mirror. The bloke in the mirror was smiling like a goof. Let's see what he can do then. Maybe he could start with her passions.

Over the next few days, in every spare moment, Marcus read everything he could find on water birth, home-birth statistics, current trends in birthing, and the latest government initiatives for mothers and babies. A lot of it he knew, some of it he'd had no idea about, and some of it, he had to admit, he'd got the wrong impression about.

'So with a water birth, what's your understanding of why a baby doesn't breathe?' They were sitting on the headland, watching the waves, as the light faded behind them and Marcus had his arm around her.

Several blocks of sutured foam were in a little canvas bag beside them. They'd spent half an hour sewing pretend wound repairs and Tilly was feeling quietly confident she could do a good job. But tomorrow they'd try the steak.

Marcus's arm felt warm and solid, and very dear, and she was starting to wonder if the most stupid thing she'd ever done had been to sleep with him. Because it had changed the way she was aware of him, changed the way all her senses stood up and waved when he was near, nudged her whole body into his space so that it was natural that they touch a lot of the time now.

Except when they were at work. Thank goodness she could block him out at work.

Tilly saw a fish skim through a wall of water and thought about his question. 'Are you saying you don't know or you've been reading up and you want to see what my version is?'

'Tilly, you're beginning to understand me too well.' He glanced at her with a knowing smile. 'I may have been reading a little.'

She smiled. 'I have no idea when you'd get the time.'

'Look who's talking. You swim, teach Nippers, renovate houses and do rallies in your spare moments.

There's always a minute to learn something, isn't there?
So what can you teach me about this?'

So he wanted to learn from her? She didn't quite believe she could teach him anything if he'd been reading.
But you never knew. 'I'm quite good at explaining water
birth.' She was, actually. 'I've had enough practice over
the years with my mother's clients.'

He didn't say anything and she went on with a teasing glint in her eye. 'Because it's the most common
reason people choose to birth at home when the hospital
won't allow it?'

She waited.

'I hear you,' he said mildly, and she had to be content with that. They were both happy their unfurling
relationship didn't spill over at work.

'The theory is that before birth babies are surrounded
by fluid so babies seem to find birth in water effort-
less. It must be less traumatic for them to be born into
the warm environment they're used to rather than cold
air and light and other people apart from their parents
touching them.

'Assuming there's not a torch in their eyes and some-
body grabbing at their head,' he added sagely, and she
had to smile.

'That's true. That's one of the reasons an experienced
birth assistant is needed, yes.'

'And they don't breathe because…?' They way he
kept looking at her and smiling made it hard to concentrate.

'At birth babies are stimulated to breathe by exposure

to air when it hits their face. Trigeminal response. The air hitting the triangle of skin around the mouth and nose.'

'And they breathe when we stimulate them,' Marcus added. 'Rubbing them over with a towel?'

She nodded. 'Which is why babies stay completely submerged in a water birth and aren't over-handled until their head breaks the surface.'

'I'd get nervous if a baby was taking a long time to crown.'

'They don't need to breathe for those first moments. The placenta is still giving them the oxygen, like it does in a normal land birth. We take them out before the placenta comes away.'

'And once they do reach air, they don't go under again.'

'Absolutely not. It's why we don't stimulate them with lots of handling while they're birthing under water. Basically that's the only slight risk and a non-stressed baby would not have the stimulation to breathe.'

'So stressed babies may gasp underwater at birth. I read that.'

'In theory. But to balance that risk there's the inherent dive reflex of babies.'

'I needed a dive reflex to make me go in the water.'

'You've got one now. I saw you.'

'Tell me about the dive reflex babies have.'

'I know you know this.'

'Yeah, but I love the way you explain things.'

'Do you?'

'Yes, Miss Fishing-for-a-compliment.'

Well, I love all of you. In fact, I'm in love with you. But she couldn't say that. He'd run a mile. She dragged her thoughts back to the question. At least the topic absorbed her.

He watched her face. The passion, excitement there, absolute certainty that this was a fabulous way for a baby to enter the world and how she wanted him to see that. He wasn't so sure about it being any better than normal but maybe it wasn't rocket science.

'Well, if water reaches the chemo receptors on a baby's tongue, it doesn't breathe like an adult might. Instead, it swallows and slows down its heart rate and goes into a protective state.'

He was watching her with that strange expression on his face again. She wound down. 'So a baby has this warm transition from warm water to head up on mum's chest and lovely skin to skin with nobody getting cold. Even the air is humidified from the steam in the room for its newly breathing lungs, no bright lights for unaccustomed eyes, and just the parents' hands.' She looked at him. 'It must be soothing for everybody.'

'You're soothing for everybody.'

Then as they sat looking out over the ocean he told her about his parents and his sister and the scars he'd carried for so long. Scars she'd helped to heal just by him knowing her.

CHAPTER TWELVE

'KEEP Sunday free for me. At your castle. Eight o'clock,' Marcus reminded her. He hoped she wouldn't forget.

He'd put a lot of thought into how he was going to woo Matilda. His wooing had to prove not just to Matilda but also to himself that he could let go of his compulsive desire for control.

He still had major issues with Tilly swimming in the bay with those sharks able to glide in at any time, but Duggie had given him a stern talking to about sensible ocean etiquette and the fact that Tilly was an experienced swimmer.

He had to deal with that. He'd always prefer to run. That paddle out to Tilly hadn't endeared him to the beach and now that he could swim, she could have it.

Then he saw her. Here she comes, Marcus thought as she appeared at the bottom of Hill Street. She had on that little green sundress that reflected in her eyes. His body stirred with delighted recognition as that determined little walk he loved closed the distance between them.

If he'd been a dog his tail would be wagging like mad. He was a basket case and he'd never thought he'd be a loon like this over a gorgeous little midwife who drove him insane with lust and laughter. It was as if he'd taken off dark glasses he'd worn all his life. Suddenly, when Tilly was around, the world was a sunnier place and he could never thank her enough.

He saw she had his favourite earrings on and they brushed against her neck. Delightful memories. His smile widened. Earrings for breakfast was a good sign she had an inkling this was special.

He'd tried to make it so. He'd called on all his experience from his coffee-shop days, the way the waitresses had tarted up the restaurant for special occasions, added touches that the women patrons had crooned over.

That's what he wanted for Tilly. Crooning. One day he'd really sing to her. Once he'd learnt the words to the right song. He couldn't help his smile becoming a grin.

When Tilly walked down to the rotunda at the park she had a strange feeling of anticipation. Everything was fraught with danger now that she'd admitted to herself she loved Marcus.

Everything had changed since they'd made love. He was so considerate, seemed always to be aware of her, and the attention was intoxicating. But she was definitely scared that it would all end. She'd got it wrong before and wasn't keen to second-guess his intentions in case she made the same mistake. What they had at the moment was pretty darned incredible and she should be satisfied with that.

She drew a deep breath and the salty air grounded her because life was amazing. To her left two kids kicked a ball, the drone of a plane hummed in the background, and the waves pounded on the beach in the way they had for aeons. The air was still and warm and a few seagulls fought over a dropped crust from a child's sandwich as she walked the last few feet across the park.

Would she be happy with the crumbs if that was all Marcus had? She didn't know.

Her heart skittered and then he was in front of her. Marcus. Waiting beside her castle. Her lovely man. Her knight who cared deeply for others, who wanted nothing more than safe mothers and babies in a world that bred fear, who'd learnt to listen to her perception of trust in a woman's natural ability. It hadn't been easy for him. And she'd learnt to listen. Breathe, even a little, before exploding. She smiled to herself. Which was a good thing.

He was smiling at her and she couldn't take her eyes off him. Such a hunk, it wasn't fair, she just wanted to wrap her arms around him and feel safe and cherished in the way only he seemed able to make her feel.

He held out his hand and the sense of homecoming just by placing her fingers in his melted her heart.

'Your castle awaits.' Magic seemed to shimmer in the air between them and she saw two chairs and a table had been shifted from the take-away stall so they could sit down. He'd commandeered the whole thing. Typical, arrogant male. She loved it. And him.

Then she saw that with the ocean as backdrop, each pole of the wrought-iron rotunda had a flower pot with a profusion of white daisies that waved gaily at Tilly in the salty breeze as she walked up the stairs. It looked pretty and romantic, and crazily extravagant.

Even a red-hatted gnome in the middle looked happy. She blushed but it was very cool. 'When did you do this?'

The plane droned and he nodded sagely. 'I have elves who help me.'

'Why are you doing this?'

'Today is our one-month-since-we-met anniversary.'

'One month. It feels like a year.'

He smiled. 'When I first met you, to my shame, I worried that people would talk about us at the hospital.'

She'd known that but it hadn't worried her. Apparently it had worried him. 'I can understand that. You'd just taken over a high-profile position.'

One of the elves, who looked suspiciously like the waiter from the Beachside Bistro, carried a platter of melons and strawberries and a tub of creamy cinnamon yoghurt across to them.

'For your princess,' the waiter said with a flourish, and his face was spit with a romantic's pleasure. '*L'amore,*' he sang cheekily as he went away.

Marcus reached down into an esky she only then realised was beside his chair and he produced a bottle of sparkling non-alcoholic wine in honour of the park's no-alcohol policy, and two really pretty fluted but un-deniably plastic glasses. He poured carefully, topped up with orange juice, placed one flute in front of her and then one in front of himself.

'A toast?'

'To what?' She was bemused. Kept looking at the daisies, and the gnome and the tablecloth, and the sub-dued mischievousness that emanated from Marcus. An-other different Marcus she hadn't met.

'A lack of sea breeze for half an hour at least. Which is why we're here in the morning and not the afternoon.'

She frowned. 'Because?'

'He needs to finish the sentence.' He grimaced. 'There's absolutely nothing I can do if the wind springs up.' He frowned and then smiled. 'You will be pleased to know I have actually given up control of something.'

Even more confusing. 'Who does? What wind?'

Marcus looked at her and smiled and reached out with those beautiful long fingers and gathered her hand in his again. With his other hand he pointed to the sky over the blue ocean.

'I LOVE YOU TILL…' The plane came around for the last letter and already the 'I' was starting to bloom out into a thicker white letter. Then it was done. 'Y.' 'I LOVE YOU TILLY.'

Tilly couldn't believe this was happening, in the park, on a Sunday, with dozens of people watching. Mr Unobtrusive telling the world. Her name in the blue sky. A declaration for the whole of Sydney to see.

People were pointing to the words in the sky from the beach. Some of them were looking at her.

She could feel a tide of delighted pink staining her cheeks and then she forgot the other people. Could only see Marcus. Could only feel his strength and warmth and love as he took her hand and looked into her face.

'I know this is kind of sudden but it came to me in a flash. Matilda McPherson, I need to tell you something. Loudly. Which isn't my style, so I thought you might like this—and maybe even believe me.'

He paused and glanced at the sky as if for inspiration. 'I love you.' He read it out slowly. And grinned sheepishly—looking as if he couldn't believe he'd arranged that himself. 'You bowled me over on the first day. Literally.' They both looked at the gnome and smiled. 'And you've stolen a little more of my heart every time we've met. And now—you have it all.'

He drew a breath. 'When you were out in the water with that shark alarm I'd never been so scared in my life. I can't lose you.'

Tilly stared out from her princess tower to the sky above and the words that were there for all the world to see—even if only briefly. Fluffy white stretched out letters that were already floating out to sea, stretching into elongated wisps of vapour, dissipating into the sky but written on her memory for ever. She hoped he'd arranged one of his elves to photograph that before it was gone. Knowing him, he would have. She stopped worrying about it.

She sniffed back the tears, the thickness in her throat,

the explosion of heat in her heart. 'Marcus, what can I say after that magnificent declaration? I'm thinking I might even believe you.'

They both stood up, and she wasn't sure how it happened but suddenly she was in his arms, and in the distance she could hear people clapping.

He looked down at her quizzically, almost sternly, like the Dr Bennett she knew too well. 'You could say something else.'

She laughed and hugged him fiercely. 'I love you, too, Marcus. Of course I love you.'

Marcus hugged her back. This place would always be special to him because it had given him Tilly. Already he was plotting what he could do to surprise her when he asked her to marry him. No doubt his aunt and her friends would want to sing at their wedding.

Marcus smiled. He was definitely going to learn to sing, too.

* * * * *